"I like to stay busy," she said, her nose in the air. "If you and Griffin are so worried about me cracking under pressure, come on back tonight and hover however you see fit. I'll be submitting the application at seven."

Clearly she didn't want him to accept. She would have to be disappointed in his diligence. "That's pretty specific."

She shrugged a shoulder. "Part of the background they've created for me," she said. Her expression softened as she studied his face. "You really don't need to worry, Detective."

"Emmanuel," he corrected. He wanted her to think of him as a friend, not the detective who'd testified against her client. "I'll see you at seven. Earlier," he said before he could change his mind. "I'll bring dinner."

Her lips parted and he was tempted to silence her protest with a kiss. Instead, he walked out, closing the door before she could utter a word. Before he could make a fool of himself.

Dear Reader,

It's always a delight to fall in love with another wonderful, heroic branch of the Colton family. And there's nothing quite like the sparks that fly when two people are sure they know all there is to know about each other.

Attorney Philippa Colton's siblings only want to keep her safe in the midst of the cases she is juggling, but the friend they call on, Detective Emmanuel Iglesias, is a man she cannot trust.

Emmanuel is convinced Pippa's quest to overturn a conviction on a case he worked is more about connections and favors than real justice, until he recognizes the signs of a dangerous killer taking aim at her.

Pippa and Emmanuel kept me on my toes as they struggled to overcome the odds and work together for justice...and possibly a once-in-a-lifetime love.

Live the adventure,

Regan Black

COLTON 911: DETECTIVE ON CALL

Regan Black

If you purchased this book without a cover you should be aware that this book is stolen property. It was reported as "unsold and destroyed" to the publisher, and neither the author nor the publisher has received any payment for this "stripped book."

Special thanks and acknowledgment are given to Regan Black for her contribution to the Colton 911: Grand Rapids miniseries.

Recycling programs for this product may not exist in your area.

ISBN-13: 978-1-335-62668-4

Colton 911: Detective on Call

This edition published by arrangement with Harlequin Books S.A.

For questions and comments about the quality of this book, please contact us at CustomerService@Harlequin.com.

Harlequin Enterprises ULC
22 Adelaide St. West, 40th Floor
Toronto, Ontario M5H 4E3, Canada
www.Harlequin.com

Printed in U.S.A.

Regan Black, a *USA TODAY* bestselling author, writes award-winning action-packed novels featuring kick-butt heroines and the sexy heroes who fall in love with them. Raised in the Midwest and California, she and her family, along with their adopted greyhound, two arrogant cats and a quirky finch, reside in the South Carolina Lowcountry, where the rich blend of legend, romance and history fuels her imagination.

Books by Regan Black

Harlequin Romantic Suspense

Colton 911: Grand Rapids

Colton 911: Detective on Call

The Coltons of Mustang Valley

Colton Cowboy Jeopardy

The Riley Code

A Soldier's Honor
His Soldier Under Siege

The Coltons of Roaring Springs

Colton Family Showdown

Escape Club Heroes

Safe in His Sight
A Stranger She Can Trust
Protecting Her Secret Son
Braving the Heat

The Coltons of Shadow Creek

Killer Colton Christmas
"Special Agent Cowboy"

The Coltons of Red Ridge

Colton P.I. Protector

Visit the Author Profile page at Harlequin.com for more titles.

For Mark, my personal hero.
I’d be lost without you, my love.

Chapter 1

At the reception desk of the women's prison, Pippa Colton waited, smothering her brewing impatience under a professionally unflappable demeanor. Probably the most important lesson of law school: never let them see you sweat.

Though *she* wasn't sweating in her charcoal slacks and tailored jacket, it was impossible to ignore the ripe smells of the countless bodies that had passed through. Thanks to its overcrowding and pervasive violence, she could not consider the prison system as anything other than inhumane. No matter how clean on the surface, every prison had a distinct odor of fatigue, resignation and stress that never faded. Her client would have likely thrown a fit and demanded air freshener upon arrival.

The guard on the other side of the window frowned at her credentials, shifting his gaze to a computer monitor and back to her. "You're not listed on the visitor log today."

"There must be a mistake." She reached into her briefcase for the confirmation she'd printed out after registering this meeting through the online portal. This wasn't her first trek to a prison. "I have the details right here."

She slid the page through the gap in the protective window, and on the other side, the skinny man's thin upper lip curled. He seemed bent on turning her away, but jumping through hoops was part of the job. Soon she would be heading deeper into this monstrosity of a facility, and the attitudes aimed her way from both inmates and guards were likely to get surlier along the way.

With a put-upon sigh, the guard keyed in the number at the top of the page and waited. Shaking his head, he pushed the paper back to her, along with her credentials. "Nothing here, ma'am."

"But—"

He shrugged. "There's nothing here. You'll have to reschedule."

She reined in her temper. No one in the legal system wanted to befriend the lawyer trying to overturn a conviction. Especially when that conviction meant freeing the woman everyone loved to hate, Anna Wentworth, who had been transferred to the prison two weeks ago after a jury found her guilty of murdering her lover, David Hicks.

Public opinion had been working against Anna from the start. A prominent married socialite in Grand Rapids, Michigan, Anna had been dubbed the Queen of Mean long before being labeled as a killer. Oddly enough, no one cared that she'd been unfaithful to her husband, Ed, only that she'd allegedly offed Hicks when the younger man ended the affair.

"Could you please double-check?" she asked with a polite smile. Her mind was envisioning outrageous methods of getting to her client. But she wasn't an action hero, just the least popular attorney in Michigan today.

The guard walked away without a word, paper in hand. She had no idea if the man would return to the window or how long it would be until someone else stepped up to return her credentials.

She'd never been outright denied a visit. To get Anna released, she had to give the court the real killer and proof to clear her client. Unfortunately, the case file and collected evidence had yet to point her in the right direction. Why was she the only person who could look at the evidence and see it was too neat and tidy to be true? Her hope was that Anna would cooperate today in ways she hadn't done with her original defense team.

At the time of her arrest and trial, Anna had been certain being innocent—and wealthy—would be enough to get the charges dismissed and the case thrown out. No one could convince her of the severity of the evidence against her. As a strategy, being too wealthy to go to prison was terrible. As a lifestyle it was worse. Though Pippa had also been raised in a wealthy family, she detested Anna's elitist and privileged attitudes. But no one deserved to be in prison for a crime they didn't commit.

The skinny guard returned, looking annoyed that she hadn't given up. "Sorry, ma'am. I double-checked." He pushed the paper and her credentials back across the counter for her. "You can't see your client today. In the future you'll need to schedule an appointment with the new form."

"I scheduled today's appointment with the current form," Pippa said. She pulled up her phone and opened her email app. Briskly, she read aloud the dates of her emails and the positive responses from the prison. "Shall I forward these to you?" she queried.

"No, ma'am. I can't accept that as authorization." His gaze fell and he looked a bit sheepish, and she pounced on the first sign of weakness.

"What can you accept? I've driven over two hours to see my client after filing everything properly. You do know she and I have a legal right to confer."

"Yes, ma'am—"

"Great." She cut him off. "In the past, I've been able to fill out visitation paperwork right here. Is that an option today?"

"No, ma'am. New policy is in effect. I can't let you in without the correct paperwork, completed twenty-four hours ahead of the requested time. Sorry. Ma'am."

His diligent use of "ma'am" struck her ears like nails on a chalkboard, and she was sure that's why he kept it up. She pressed her lips together and started over.

"I respect your position and the system," she began, ignoring the guard's sneer. The anti-Anna movement was in full force today. Again, she mentally scolded her client for making this all so much harder than it needed to be. Clearly, the woman's superiority complex wasn't making her any friends in prison either. Only more enemies.

Elizabeth, Anna's daughter and Pippa's good friend, would be terribly disappointed if Pippa couldn't get inside today. *For Elizabeth*, she reminded herself, infusing her voice with steel. "You, *sir*, are hindering the legal process," she snapped. "May I speak with your supervisor?"

"No, ma'am. He's at lunch."

One more snarky "ma'am" and she would come dangerously close to committing a crime herself. She lightly rested her folded hands on the counter. If she had to wear prison orange, it should be for a better reason than losing her temper. She smiled, absolutely certain the expression was less than friendly. "Is Warden Birrell available? Although we haven't spoken in person since my father's funeral, it would make the trip worthwhile just to say hello and catch up for a few minutes."

Name-dropping wasn't her thing, and she typically avoided throwing around Colton family connections and influence this way, but she was growing desperate.

The guard closed the panel so she couldn't push any more papers at him. "The warden and my supervisor are having lunch together."

"How wonderful for everyone," Pippa said. "I'll wait right here for their return." She planted herself in the plastic chair across from the window.

And didn't that plan shine a spotlight on the differences between her and the prison inmates, including her client. She had the luxury and freedom to stay or go as she wished. It shouldn't have surprised her that the speculation in the press had reached the prison. Calling her the Queen of Mean, the general consensus was that she'd taken on the Queen's case for immediate notoriety. While it was true that getting Anna's conviction overturned would allow her to progress her ideal career path, Pippa was here to right a wrong and to help Elizabeth, her friend.

Twenty minutes ticked by, then another twenty. Although it made sense for both the supervisor and the warden to return through this entrance, closest to their offices, it was clear someone had warned them off. She knew when she was defeated.

Using her phone, she drafted an email to the warden, who really was a family friend, and sent a text message update to Elizabeth on the day's failure. Pulling out her portfolio, she opened it to the notepad printed with her firm's formal letterhead. With her best penmanship, she wrote a friendly little letter to Warden Birrell, praising his staff. She folded the note and slid it into an envelope also printed with the firm's logo. There was no sense pretending the note wouldn't be read long before it reached him, if it reached him at all. Thus the reason for the more direct and candid email she would send once she was outside.

She stepped up to the window once more. "I'd like to leave this note for the warden, please."

"Fine. I'll take it," the guard said.

It didn't escape her notice that he didn't say the note would be delivered. "Thank you." She pushed the envelope across the counter, up to the closed slot. At least he'd laid off the "ma'am" routine. "Have a wonderful day." Chin in the air, she turned and marched out, feeling only marginally guilty that she could leave the prison behind.

Prisons were a necessary piece of the justice system. Defense teams were essential too, and not just to stand up for those wrongfully accused. She knew she was on the right side with the Wentworth case, but it was going to be a hard road to help this particular client.

The crisp autumn air and bright sunshine were welcome and she breathed deeply, closing her eyes briefly when she reached the relative security of her vehicle.

After unlocking the car, she opened the back door and set her briefcase on the floor behind the driver's seat. She paused to send the email to the warden, then shrugged out of her suit jacket and draped it over the hanger in the back. Settling behind the wheel for the drive home, she started the engine, then sat back, checking her phone one more time, just in case the warden had seen her email.

Having dawdled as much as she dared, she backed out of her parking space and drove away.

The prison guard kept an eye on the security monitors, waiting until the gates closed behind the snooty attorney. He waited a few minutes more until she pulled out of the parking lot. Then he called someone to cover him so he could go have a smoke. Outside in the employee parking lot, he stared out at the line of trees blocking the prison yard from the rest of the world.

He lit his cigarette and took a long, deep drag. The persistent woman had been almost as annoying as the inmate she wanted to see.

Pulling out his phone, he called the number he'd been given. It rang three times before anyone picked up.

"Go," said the voice on the other end.

"She's gone," he said. "No meeting with her client."

"Got it."

"And the daughter?" the guard asked. It was going to be a whole lot harder stonewalling that one, but he could find a way if it meant extra cash. "Hello?" He checked his signal and saw the Call Ended icon flashing on his screen.

"Whatever," he muttered, tucking his phone back into his pocket. He'd done his part. If the money wasn't in his account when he got home tonight, he'd do things the right way next time.

Detective Emmanuel Iglesias checked his phone as he finished his lunch outside the GRPD headquarters. One of his favorite food trucks had parked nearby today and it was too beautiful outside not to soak up the fall weather. He dealt with the less appealing facets of Grand Rapids most days and last year, on the verge of burnout, he'd promised himself to focus on the nicer elements as often as possible to balance the scales.

Seeing the text message from his friend Griffin Colton, he hesitated. The preview on the app mentioned Griffin's sister, Pippa. Emmanuel tried not to groan out loud. Why had he agreed when Griffin asked him to keep an eye on his sister?

Because friends stepped up.

He opened the full text message. No word from Pippa today. No answer at her office or condo. It happens when she's focused, but I'd feel better if you have time to check.

Apparently Pippa had a reputation within the family for being a little too reckless in the pursuit of justice. As a business, founded by Griffin's older brother Riley, the siblings worked together as Colton Investigations and they had their hands full with the escalating RevitaYou situation.

RevitaYou, a daily "miracle" supplement, promised to make a person look ten years younger after only one week of use. With rave reviews from consumers and falsified medical endorsements, a new business had exploded with investors and distributors. But something in the formula was off and turning into deadly Ricin. One death had already been linked to the supplement and everything indicated there would be more.

The GRPD and Colton Investigations were cooperating to prevent more untimely deaths, though Emmanuel knew a top priority for the Coltons was locating Brody Higgins, a young man they considered part of the family, who had borrowed money to invest in RevitaYou. Unfortunately, he'd borrowed from Capital X, a loan shark operation disguised as a legitimate financial group. The Coltons were determined to find Brody before the Capital X enforcers hurt him—again.

Changing directions, he headed for his car to swing by Pippa's condo and office. He'd keep his word and try to find something to ease Griffin's mind.

Emmanuel knew Griffin worried about Pippa getting caught up in Brody's mess, since his last direct contact had been with her. Now that she was the new lead attorney for a convicted killer, Emmanuel had other concerns. He wouldn't define Pippa's choice to defend Anna Wentworth as a reckless pursuit of justice. In his mind, it was more like career suicide.

Having worked the Wentworth case, he knew it was solid. He'd testified at the trial and walked the jury through every piece of evidence he'd found. Pippa hadn't been on the defense team then, but now resentment was brewing against her in the GRPD. No one liked having good work picked apart in the search for a technicality that would set a criminal free.

Anna Wentworth was guilty, Emmanuel was certain of it, and promise or not, he wouldn't let one idealistic attorney unravel everything so a murderous socialite could get back to her mansion.

Once Pippa was out on the deserted stretch of road that eventually connected with the highway, she finally let out the scream of frustration that had been building for over an hour.

Feeling better with just that simple, primal release, she found a radio station playing heavy metal music and turned up the volume. People usually took in her conservative wardrobe and professional manner and decided she was a prim, entitled lawyer with musical tastes that didn't veer from serene and classical. They couldn't be more wrong. She was more than willing to dress the part and play the game to get a job done, but she wasn't afraid to get her hands dirty. Blame those traits on her mother, a woman who had died before accomplishing all her big goals to help people who struggled in their community. With heavy bass pounding through the speakers, Pippa rewound and reviewed every detail of her interaction with that guard.

Obviously he'd been instructed to block her at all turns. Who on earth had the influence to prevent her from meeting her client? More important, who had a reason to do so?

She'd initially kept up with the Wentworth trial to support her friend, believing from the start Anna wasn't a killer. It was only after Elizabeth had hired her that Pippa had pored over the case page by page. After two weeks, she had the case pretty much memorized from the first emergency call to the reading of the verdict. For the life of her, she couldn't come up with anyone close to the victim who could successfully frame Anna.

Pippa firmly believed in the theory that every crisis held the seeds of opportunity. If she couldn't speak with her client, she was back to square one with the overwhelming evidence that was too perfect. It wasn't enough that Anna wasn't the sort to do her own dirty work. And making it clear she didn't consider the victim a threat had backfired during the trial. What was her next move?

The warden, assuming he'd actually been in his office, wasn't interested in helping her. The guards didn't seem to like Inmate Anna. No shock there. The woman wasn't easy at the best of times. Used to having her own way on her own terms, she was probably raising a stink over having her days controlled by others.

According to the last count, only Elizabeth; Elizabeth's father, Ed; and Pippa truly believed Anna was innocent of the Hicks murder. Unfortunately, Ed was so frustrated and angry over his wife's indiscretions and arrogant behavior during the trial that he was content to let her stew in her own mess, offering little in the way of support.

Anna's unswervingly self-centered choices and her habitual delegation of everything from car pool duty to signing Christmas cards would never win her awards for best wife or mom of the year, but she wasn't foolish enough to kill a man and leave a piece of her stunning bespoke jewelry near the body. Yes, shock and rage affected the mind and impaired critical thinking, but even if Anna had been capable of those extremes and had managed to fire the two bullets that stopped David Hicks's heart, she wouldn't have tossed the gun into her beloved rose bushes less than three feet from the body.

In Pippa's opinion, if Anna had been bothered enough

to want a person dead, she would've hired someone to handle the job. For as long as Pippa had known Elizabeth, that's how Anna Wentworth operated. The vast majority of her volunteer hours were handled by assistants. Anna wrote checks and dressed up in glorious gowns and gems, but she *never* got her hands dirty. Trouble was, she didn't have anything concrete to prove Anna's innocence.

Using the controls on the steering wheel, she muted the radio and called her office, leaving a message for her paralegal about the derailed meeting. When she was back home, she would review her notes on the case one more time to find a way forward. At last, she called her twin sister, Kiely, and let her know she was on the way back to Grand Rapids. That left her with two hours of uninterrupted drive time to figure out how she could effectively circumvent the prison to interview Anna.

Last week, she'd spent an entire day with this case file in the evidence room at the Grand Rapids Police Department. She could arrange for the evidence to be reviewed by an independent lab, but it was a pricey option that was unlikely to be helpful since there were no glaring gaps in the chain of evidence.

It would have been nice if Pippa could back up a theory that Anna had been railroaded, but it just wasn't true. The detectives on the case had been thorough and cautious, refusing to give the press anything that might color the investigation or the trial. They'd also come to the wrong conclusion.

Whoever had framed Anna had done an excellent job.

If the prison system wouldn't allow her to have reasonable meetings with her client, she would just find another way to get any helpful information out of Anna.

As Hicks's lover, she might not even realize what she'd learned about him and any enemies who might have motive to kill him and frame her.

Pippa was still working her way through the transcripts of the interviews and depositions. At some point there must have been a different suspect, yet somehow the GRPD investigation had decided the motive and evidence fit and pinned the murder on the wrong person.

Yes, Anna had been having an affair with Hicks. Yes, Hicks ended it before Anna was ready, and he'd reportedly threatened to tell her husband if she didn't pay him off. But Ed had known about the affair. At some point Ed and Anna had agreed to break their wedding vows. Infidelity was one weird cog in the machine that kept their marriage working. Pippa had heard of stranger things. Her parents' marriage hadn't been nearly the picture of perfection that the public assumed. What worked for the Wentworths shouldn't make any difference to the case or to anyone else, though it fed local gossip columns for weeks.

The sound of a big engine behind her drew her attention back to the roadway. An SUV painted in the blue of Michigan State Police troopers was bearing down on her, lights flashing. Her pulse kicked up a notch as she checked her speed—within the limit—then she eased closer to the shoulder to give him room to pass.

He blew right by her. Relieved, she merged back into the lane. For several seconds she'd thought her botched trip to the prison was going to get worse. She was jumpy. Only ten days on the job and she'd had her fill of the press hounding her for interviews and explanations.

Well, as her dad would have said, the right choice wasn't always the popular choice.

Grand Rapids wanted to enjoy the implosion and downfall of the society Queen of Mean. They weren't interested in the more pertinent facts about David Hicks. The victim was more than a decade younger than Anna, and from what Pippa could see, he'd shown a distinct pattern of risky behavior. He chose to be seen publicly with wealthy and influential married women. There were plenty of pictures and videos of him caught in unmistakable displays of affection and intimacy.

Pippa figured any number of husbands wanted him dead, and probably a few ex-girlfriends too. She was sure Anna wasn't the first woman, single or married, that he'd tried to blackmail in the course of a breakup. She just hadn't been able to prove it yet. The man enjoyed an active dating life, and he thrived on rubbing elbows with society's elite. Sleeping with Anna had provided Hicks with a serious boost of notoriety. And when he'd been ready to move on, he'd probably been shocked Anna didn't care enough about his threats to pay him off.

Shocked, yes, but he hadn't shot himself in the chest.

As Elizabeth's friend and a familiar face, Pippa held out hope that Anna would be more forthright about what she knew of Hicks's habits, instead of dismissing those questions as irrelevant. Pippa needed a kernel of truth to run with, something that would turn that case file upside down.

She sang along with the radio for a time, her mind still sorting out the pieces and players.

The prosecution insisted the insult of being dumped combined with the threat of blackmail pushed Anna to kill and to make mistakes in the process. That might have been enough with anyone else. Although Anna was self-absorbed, she wasn't stupid.

Her defense team had been caught in a sticky web. Everyone in the area had an impression and opinion of high-profile Anna Wentworth. If her defense made her seem too smart or too into Hicks, that only made it easier to believe she could commit murder. The prosecution portrayed their case as a crime of passion and claimed the damning evidence had been left almost in plain sight because she'd been overwhelmed and enraged.

Naturally, Anna's fingerprints were on her jewelry but they hadn't been on the gun. No gunshot residue on her hands, either, but those facts hadn't swayed the jury.

Bottom line, no one wanted to believe Anna's side of the story. It would've helped if she'd had a decent alibi, but she'd been working from home that day and the timing of the messages she'd left her assistant weren't enough to clear her. It didn't help matters that during the trial Anna had referred to Hicks as a dirty rat whose only redeeming quality had been his handsome face.

The defense team recognized they were finished, though they'd fought right up to the closing arguments and sentencing.

What they'd needed—what Pippa still needed—was another valid suspect, another theory about the motive. The threat of blackmail sounded like enough, until you dug into the Wentworth marriage. So far the only chink in the prosecution's armor was the lack of an interview with Ed. Or even Elizabeth. She'd found the notes from the detectives working the case that confirmed those alibis, but shouldn't they have taken a closer look at the cuckolded husband?

That fishy detail wasn't enough to reopen the case, but it was something she wanted answered by Sergeant Joe McRath and Detective Emmanuel Iglesias, who had worked Anna's case.

She muted the radio and dictated more notes into her phone, brainstorming ways to get the GRPD to cooperate with her. Her family had connections in the GRPD from her sister Sadie, a crime scene technician, to Detective Iglesias, a good friend of her brother Griffin. She had to tread lightly because this case was polarizing, and win or lose, she still had to live here when it was done.

Pippa was absolutely certain the real killer was still out there, and she needed to convince the police, but so far no one would speak with her about it. Since taking on the Wentworth case, she'd been dealing with a rash of threats on her office voice mail and one nasty postcard delivered to her home. All par for the course these days when representing an unpopular client. While she logged each incident, she knew a few random threats wouldn't inspire anyone to take a second look at what appeared to be a solid conviction.

Another death would do it. Her stomach cramped at the thought.

She had been tempted to use her siblings as a sounding board or even ask for some hands-on help. All of them supported and lent their professional expertise to Colton Investigations, the family business investigative agency. But the team had its hands full at the moment, and the press ganging up on her was bad enough. No way would she drag that public relations quicksand closer to her siblings.

The music wasn't helping anymore. Restless and

feeling idle, she cued up a recording of the trial provided by Anna's defense team and picked up where she'd left off, listening to the smooth, mellow voice of Detective Iglesias on the stand.

She remembered that day in court. He'd worn a charcoal suit and his wavy hair had been brushed back from his face. Short stubble had defined his jaw and the steady confidence in his warm brown eyes never wavered. Not even under cross-examination.

It was easy to understand why the jury had gravitated to him, taking his every word as unassailable truth. Even though Pippa knew better, it was easy to believe his testimony. He'd been the star witness for the prosecution, all but guaranteeing Anna's conviction.

Her phone suddenly interrupted the flow of his voice, announcing an incoming call. She used the control on her steering wheel to answer. "You've reached Pippa Colton. How may I help you?"

"Hi, Pippa. It's Elizabeth." Her friend sounded miserable. "I'm sorry to bug you. I just couldn't wait to hear how it went. Did Mom cooperate?"

More than anything else with this case, Pippa regretted that a mother-daughter relationship, already under pressure, had been nearly destroyed by the trial. Elizabeth and her father had been in the gallery every day to support Anna, but it hadn't impressed the jury. And Elizabeth's testimony as a character witness during sentencing had hit a sour note, giving the impression that she was fabricating a few good moments with her mom just for the hope of leniency. Her strident belief in her mother's innocence came across as too little, too late.

It broke her heart to say it, but she had to be truthful. "I didn't get to meet with her," Pippa replied.

"Why not?" The worry in Elizabeth's voice was sharp as a blade. "Did something happen?"

"Your mom is fine," Pippa assured her. "They told me it was a system glitch on their end," she hedged. "I'll reschedule."

"So she still doesn't know I believe her."

Elizabeth sounded utterly defeated. Pippa had seen this struggle between Elizabeth and her mom practically since day one of their friendship. The Wentworth mansion was impressive for all of the architecture heirlooms and history, but it would never be called a happy home during Anna's reign.

"She knows it," Pippa insisted. "You go out there every day."

"Not today."

"Well, no." Because they'd thought one visitor per day was enough. Maybe if Elizabeth had been with her, she would've gotten inside. Too late to second-guess things now. "But you'll be there tomorrow."

"And every day after until this is over," Elizabeth agreed.

Pippa swallowed her irritation with the runaround she'd been subjected to. "I'm glad to hear that. You may have to be the go-between right now." The conversations wouldn't be protected legally, but she didn't see another option.

"What do you mean?"

"I think she's annoyed the guards," Pippa explained. "Which means they aren't inclined to do anything that works in her favor. Or mine."

Elizabeth grumbled. "I've warned Mom to cool it."

Pippa laughed, though the situation wasn't funny.

"You really think your mom is going to listen to anyone right now?"

"A daughter can hope."

"Agreed," Pippa said. "I want you to hang on to that hope. I need you to hang on to that hope. Yes, it would be easier if she could find a measure of humility and soon, but I'm not holding my breath. In the meantime, please do what you can to reassure her that the guilty verdict isn't permanent."

"I'll do my best."

"And if possible, get her talking about Hicks. The man had another enemy, and your mom might not realize she knows who it is."

"You think he talked to Mom about someone else he was seeing?"

"Probably not, but we have to ask. Maybe he talked with her about other interests. I can't find any signs that the police looked very closely at anything beyond his relationship with her, but we both know there's more to the story."

"I'll do my best," Elizabeth repeated.

"Same here," Pippa vowed, more motivated than ever to speak with Anna. The woman needed to understand how committed Elizabeth was to her mother's cause. Most likely Anna had never been an easy person. Somewhere along the way she decided that being the wealthy Mrs. Wentworth meant avoiding everything she found uncomfortable or distasteful. She prioritized her idea of perfection over personal relationships, preferring to nurture power and influence rather than people. Having watched all of the heartache and strife through the years, Pippa worried that no one would ever convince Anna how much her daughter loved her.

"You sound so sure of yourself."

"This is one small setback, that's all," Pippa said. Far bigger challenges awaited them.

Overall, Pippa preferred the challenges. *An easy sea never made a good sailor.* So she had embraced every speed bump and roadblock on the way to her goals. She didn't mind when people underestimated her focusing on appearances and ignoring her grit and steel spine until it was too late. She considered that her secret advantage.

"I'll be back in town soon," Pippa said. "Let me know how it goes with your visit tomorrow."

"I will. Thanks for everything you're doing, Pippa."

The call ended, but Pippa was still unsettled. Since she'd agreed to tackle the task of proving Anna's innocence, talking with Elizabeth was no longer easy. There was too much weight loading down every conversation. She didn't regret helping a friend; she just hadn't expected the burden would be so heavy.

Chapter 2

Emmanuel hadn't had any luck during his brief search for Pippa. She wasn't at the office. The place had been locked up tight and all the lights were out. Though he'd been told she worked from home, she hadn't answered the door when he stopped at her condo. He'd cruised around her neighborhood but didn't see the woman or her car.

He wasn't eager to tell Griffin he'd failed, but he had to give his friend something. Once he'd returned to the GRPD, he sent a text that he would keep looking.

His phone rang before he could get out of his car. He expected Griffin and instead, the Caller ID showed his mom's number.

Smiling, he picked up the call. "Hi, Mom."

"Emmanuel. I'm sorry to bother you."

"Never." She was always a bright spot. He and his

siblings knew how lucky they were to have warm, involved parents. No matter where their careers took them, they all knew the door was always open at home. "What's up?"

"I had lunch with Sofia today."

His mother, Lucia, and her younger sister were both retired and had lunch at least once a week. "How is she doing?"

"Amazing." Lucia didn't sound happy about it. "She went on and on about how great she felt."

His stomach dropped. *Please don't let this be about RevitaYou.* "And that's a problem?"

"She's taking that new pill."

"RevitaYou."

"That's the one," Lucia said. "You told me it wasn't such a miracle, but she looks good and says she feels better."

"Stay away from it, Mom. Please. It doesn't work so well for everyone," he added. "They haven't figured out what makes it effective for some people." And deadly for others, but he wouldn't say that to his mom.

The scientist who developed the formula had disappeared, but what Emmanuel had learned from Griffin's fiancée, Abigail, was enough to convince him he didn't want anyone he cared about taking a chance. "If you can, try to get Aunt Sofia to give it up too."

"I see."

And he knew she did. Lucia understood there were limits to what Emmanuel could share and when. "Thanks, Mom."

"I'll make sure she throws away her supply and doesn't buy any more. You'd best get back to work," she said. "Come for dinner soon."

"I promise. Love you."

"Love you, too."

As he walked into the station, he was more determined than ever to put an end to this RevitaYou case. Whatever it took.

Finally home, Pippa parked in her assigned space behind her building. She couldn't wait to get upstairs to her condo and pour a glass of red wine. After a hot, steamy shower she might even think about food as well as other things before she sat down with the case again.

And she'd had plenty going on in her personal life recently. Her foster brother, Brody Higgins, had gone missing. But he'd recently gotten in over his head with a health supplement company that carried a single product: RevitaYou. The product supposedly reversed the signs of aging by at least a decade. Unfortunately his no-fail investment didn't pay out as soon as promised, and now he was hiding from Capital X, a loan shark operation posing as a legitimate finance company.

Brody had agreed to a loan with impossible terms, and after he was unable to meet the repayment timeline, enforcers had been sent out to motivate him. He had the information that would put an end to Capital X, but only if CI could find him first. Pippa had been texting with Brody, relieved they were about to get him into a safe house, when he stopped responding. At least they had a new plan to help him. After much debate and discussion, she would be putting in a loan application tomorrow night with Capital X in an effort to draw out the enforcers. That would enable the Coltons to track them back to the bosses behind the operation.

She gathered up her phone, jacket and briefcase and

hurried into the building. Autumn put a bite in the air tonight. Turning, she aimed for the mailroom and fished out her key, hesitating before she opened her box.

Threats had been trickling in since that first press conference following the verdict, when Elizabeth announced Pippa's addition to the legal team. Calls to the office were typical when an attorney took a stand on a polarizing public issue. But the postcard a few days ago had thrown her off, made her nervous.

DON'T BE A FOOL. SHE IS WHERE SHE BELONGS.

The note had been written in all caps, with a blood-red marker. The picture on the front was an iconic shot of the Wentworth mansion at Christmastime. It hadn't been stamped or postmarked, either, which indicated the sender had delivered it personally.

Although unsettling, it happened with prominent cases. The general sentiment matched the tone of the phone calls the office staff had screened on her behalf. Although she'd worked on other wrongful conviction cases involving women, the timing of the note and the photo of the mansion tied it clearly to Anna. No one wanted to see this particular murder conviction overturned, because everyone was so damn sure the woman was guilty.

Why couldn't anyone understand the potential trouble of having the *wrong* person behind bars?

The postcard wouldn't have bothered her nearly as much if it had come to the office. Her home address wasn't exactly well-known, but it was public record. She'd bought the condo in her own name, never imagining a time when someone would turn against her.

Standing here wringing her hands wasn't her style. She was being silly, letting herself be bullied by one piece of disturbing mail. She hadn't reported it to the police, only her twin. Kiely understood she didn't want to cause an upset when little could be done at this point. She had placed the card in a plastic bag labeled with the date and time it had arrived and locked it away in her safe with the other materials she was gathering on the case.

Working against public opinion wasn't fun, but it was the job. An attorney who took only popular clients would eventually get burned. There had been a few cases in her father's career as district attorney when he'd made decisions that resulted in public backlash. No one appreciated lawyers, but at some point every person—even if only as part of a community—needed legal expertise or advice.

She opened her mailbox and stuffed the correspondence into the side pocket of her briefcase without looking at it. Better to wrestle with anything unpleasant in the privacy of her condo than get upset here, where a neighbor might walk up and ask too many questions.

Assuming, of course, her neighbors weren't the ones sending nasty cards.

She'd never taken much time to socialize. As one of six kids in the Colton family, Pippa had grown up with plenty of company on any given day and enjoyed her solitude now. She knew the other residents on her floor and wouldn't be at all surprised if they'd sided with the rest of Grand Rapids against her decision to help Anna Wentworth. And with her current caseload she didn't have much time to meet anyone.

Her shoulder strap slipped as she climbed the stairs to the third floor, and she slowed to adjust the load. Although the elevator would have been easier, she wanted movement after the hours in the car. One of the perks of her building was the fitness center. She was considering a quick workout before the shower and wine as she tapped the code into her electronic door lock.

The gears gave a soft whir and the dead bolt slid back.

Home at last. The day's frustrations started to dissolve as she crossed the threshold. She halted when the strange smell hit her. Bitter and powerful, the scent stung her nose. Wondering if she'd missed a message from maintenance about a repair, she set her briefcase and jacket down just inside the door.

The lamp she'd left on low this morning was turned off. Uneasy, she reached for the light switch near the door. The overhead lamp in the entry came on, and the glow spilled out into the front room.

"What in the world..."

The strange odor was spray paint. She took a step closer to the vicious message scrawled across her wall in red: *DO-GOODERS END UP DEAD.*

She couldn't comprehend this. Who would have done this? Why? How? Her door had been secure. How had the vandal found a way inside?

She turned in a circle, her temper rising. The threat and stench were bad enough. Her home had been searched. Ransacked. For a specific purpose or just to hurt her?

At the other end of the hall, she heard a door open. Concerned, she shut her own front door quickly. She leaned back against the door, one hand still on the door handle, knowing better than to go forward and contaminate the scene.

Now, when it was too late, it occurred to her she

should have stopped on the other side of the door. What if the intruder was still here? She thought she was alone, but it was hard to hear anything over her pounding heart and the blood rushing through her ears.

She nearly dropped her cell phone as she scrambled to pull it from her pocket. After two failed attempts to unlock it, she tapped in the nine and one before she stopped herself. Was this a true emergency? She wasn't actually in immediate danger. Maybe better to just call her brother Riley. But that would wreck his evening. She started to dial the primary police line when she heard another sound in the service hallway.

Anger and fear bounced through her system and jumbled her thoughts. Wishing she could avoid the inevitable chaos and questions, she pressed the three numbers into her phone and waited for the emergency operator to answer.

Every second seemed to last forever until a woman with a firm voice was taking her information. Relaying her address and the situation, Pippa followed instructions, staying on the line as instructed while she exited the condo to meet the police downstairs.

With each step away from her front door, her anger ratcheted higher. Someone had invaded her home, her private sanctuary, and caused havoc. Scrawled a threat across her wall. Had they just gotten lucky that she wasn't home, or was someone keeping tabs on her? Would they have done worse if she'd been there?

The note in her mailbox suddenly felt far more sinister.

Assuring the operator she'd reached the front door and would not go back upstairs without police, she ended the call and quickly dialed her twin sister. If anyone could help her unravel this mess without any extra fuss, it was Kiely. She was one of the best freelance private investigators in the region. Highly sought after, she frequently worked with police, FBI and Colton Investigations, going wherever she was needed.

Pippa needed her now, but once more she had to leave a message. She took a deep breath. Kiely was probably caught up with an urgent case elsewhere. Trying to calm herself, Pippa turned to watch the sunset. Days were getting shorter and cooler. Autumn was usually her favorite time of year, with the trees changing color and the college football season underway, but she was struggling to find anything restful in recent days.

Her phone rang in her hand and she jumped. Irritated at being so flighty, she spoke sharply when she answered.

"Easy, sis. You called me."

Kiely. Their connection steadied her, took some of the sting out of the lousy day.

"Pippa? What's wrong?"

"Nothing. Well, a little bit of everything," Pippa admitted before she got control of herself. "I was hoping you could come by. Just for a few minutes."

"This is a bad time." Kiely said with regret. "I'm sorry. I'm following a lead on Brody. Can you call Riley or Griffin?"

"No worries," Pippa replied brightly. She didn't want to face either of her brothers tonight. Not while she was so rattled. "This can totally wait." The case involving Brody was a much bigger priority. "Stay on that lead and track him down."

"Pippa? Are you there?"

"Yes."

"I swear I'll come as soon as I can."

Flashing lights appeared at the end of her street. "Don't worry, Kiely. It was just a bad day."

"All right," her sister sounded less than convinced. "You can unload tomorrow afternoon when we deliver the materials for that seven o'clock appointment."

"Great." She forced cheer that she didn't feel into that single word. That didn't give her a lot of time to get her house back in order. Tomorrow evening it was her turn to do her part for Brody and the investigation. It was the last thing on her mind right now, but she couldn't admit that to her twin without raising more concerns. "Keep me posted."

Detective Emmanuel Iglesias and his partner, Daniel Gomez, were heading back to the police station with burgers for a working dinner when they heard dispatch send officers to a possible home invasion. Recognizing the address, he felt a prickle of unease between his shoulder blades.

"You mind if we drive over and check it out?" Emmanuel asked.

Daniel shook his head. "Works for me. Saves the patrol a call if it's serious."

"Right." Emmanuel hoped it was a coincidence rather than something serious. He turned on the emergency lights and headed away from the station.

"Want to tell me why it's an issue?" Daniel asked.

Emmanuel shrugged, shifting in his seat. "No issue." Not definitely, at any rate. "A friend of mine has a sister living at that address."

"I'm in." Daniel swiped a french fry out of the bag and then tipped it so Emmanuel could do the same.

"Thanks." He appreciated working with a man who wasn't afraid of long hours and unexpected detours.

They were only a few minutes away from the neighborhood, giving Emmanuel time to consider his approach. He might not approve of her newest client or agree with the hopes to overturn the conviction, but she had a reputation for being good at her job. All of the Colton siblings had a keen understanding of the law, thanks in part to being raised one of the best DAs to ever serve in Michigan.

"So what's her name?" Daniel queried in a voice that promised relentless teasing.

"Philippa Colton," Emmanuel replied.

"Oh." Daniel gave a low whistle. "Safe to assume she's not your biggest fan. I guess you want me to do the talking?"

"We'll see."

Daniel made a snorting sound that might have been a laugh. "That we will."

Based on her serious demeanor in press conferences, he doubted she'd lay into him when she heard his name. Not with witnesses, at any rate. He had no intention of hassling her about her lousy taste in clients. He was only driving out to help at the request of her brother, but if she had an obvious problem with him, he'd leave.

The responding patrol officers, Jeffries and Simmons, were already there when Emmanuel parked on the street in front of Pippa's building and notified the station of their arrival.

"Nice place," Daniel said. "I've always liked this one."

Emmanuel agreed. The developers had restored the brickwork and kept the arched windows that made this building a favorite subject of photographers. The neighborhood had a low crime rate, despite its proximity to the city center, and this particular repurposing of an old factory had been met with full support from the community.

The detectives joined the two officers speaking with Pippa on the sidewalk near the stately front entrance. She stood with perfect posture. Her briefcase strap crossed her trim body shoulder to hip, and a coat was draped over one arm. It was chilly enough tonight that she should be wearing that coat properly.

Their paths hadn't crossed often, but he'd always found her pretty and tonight was no exception. Her silky brown hair was down, skimming her shoulders and framing her face. Her big blue eyes were somber and there was no sign of the usual smile on her soft pink lips.

The urge to step in and usher her away from the crisis hit him like a punch to the gut. He was supposed to keep an eye on her for Griffin, not get drawn in like a moth to flame.

He caught the nervous gesture as her hands clutched her cell phone while she explained the situation. "I walked in and found my home trashed. Vandalized. That's when I called you."

Her voice was flat, each word precise. Either she was processing things quickly or this was the first sign of shock. Her expression didn't give anything away; that serious, sweet face could've owned a poker table in Vegas.

Officer Jeffries, a slender woman with several years of police experience, seemed to be taking the lead. "You didn't see anyone inside?" she asked.

"No," Pippa replied.

Emmanuel watched as her gaze skimmed over his partner and locked onto him. Her eyebrows flexed into a frown, but in an instant, her face was a neutral, emotionless mask. Emmanuel wasn't fooled. He'd been recognized.

"Did you notice any problems at your door? Scratches on the lock or door jamb? Maybe your key didn't work as well," Jeffries continued.

"No problems," Pippa said. "Everything appeared to be fine when I walked up."

"If you could lead the way," Simmons suggested, opening the front door. He'd been on the force for as long as Emmanuel could recall. They were both good officers.

Emmanuel and Daniel were likely overkill here, but he'd stick it out. The four of them followed her to the elevator in the lobby, and she pressed the button.

"Did you take the elevator earlier?" he asked.

Her gaze snapped to him and the scowl returned. "No."

"If you don't mind," Daniel said, drawing her attention. "We'd prefer you followed your earlier footsteps."

Pippa checked with Jeffries and waited for her agreement before turning to the wide stairs and marching up the three flights. She stopped in front of her door. "I entered my code—" she pointed to the keypad "—and the lock opened without any trouble."

"Go ahead and unlock it again," Jeffries suggested.

Emmanuel couldn't see anything out of place on or around the door and lock. "Miss Colton, you can change that code at any time, correct?"

"Yes, of course." Instead of a frown, she wrinkled her nose. "It was the smell that tipped me off first," she said.

The smell?

The door swung open, and they all caught the unpleasant odor of fresh paint. Emmanuel expected her to step aside, but instead she walked in before Jeffries or Simmons could insist on taking the lead.

"What did you do when you smelled the paint?" Officer Simmons asked.

"I stopped right here and set down my briefcase and coat. My first thought was that maintenance had entered to make some repair. But then I turned on the light."

Daniel pushed a hand through his hair. "And you saw that."

"Yes."

All of them were staring at the threat scrawled across her wall. *DO-GOODERS END UP DEAD.*

Pippa's attitude was too cool for Emmanuel's comfort. Granted, everyone dealt with shock in different ways, but victims of home invasion usually exhibited more fear or outrage or bafflement. Griffin warned him she was tough as nails, but smothering intense reactions could backfire. One more thing to watch for as he fulfilled his promise to her brother. "Pardon me if you've already answered this, but how long ago did you come home?"

She ignored him, addressing Officer Jeffries. "I didn't touch anything other than the light switch and my door."

"Good." Jeffries used her radio to request a team to process the scene for evidence.

"Is there a neighbor you can stay with while we clear the home?" Simmons asked Pippa.

She shook her head, her lips a firm line. "I'll wait right here."

At Jeffries's pained expression, Emmanuel insisted they step out into the hallway.

Daniel pulled his gun and followed Simmons and Jeffries. It was unlikely the intruder was lingering even if they had been in the condo when Pippa walked in. Still, they needed to find the point of entry. Normally, he'd knock on doors, but he didn't want to leave her alone. And he sure didn't want her to join him in that endeavor.

"I know Griffin sent you," she said in icy tones. "He overstepped."

"He's just—"

She cut him off with a sharp look from those green eyes. "It might be best if I work with the other officers."

Before he could comment, the officers called an all clear, and she darted inside. He never expected everyone to like him, but her clear distaste was grating on his nerves. If this was about Wentworth, he'd only been doing his job. Like it or not, the case had been straightforward, and they'd left no stone unturned.

"Over here," Daniel called out. "We have a print."

They followed his voice to the back door of the condo.

"Whoever it was came in right here." He pointed to a boot print far too big for Pippa. "A man, most likely. Used a key. Judging by the scratches, I'm guessing it gave them some trouble. Or they were nervous. Simmons is looking for a trail or anything that might identify the perp," Daniel continued. He returned his gun to the holster on his hip and pulled out his phone. "I'll try to get ahold of any surveillance in the area."

Emmanuel's mind wandered, and he was distracted by her small foot tucked into a stylish black shoe with a low heel. In the charcoal slacks and soft blouse, she dressed like a lawyer with a superb sense of style. He supposed it was a type of armor, like his badge, but the shadows deepening under her eyes concerned him that she couldn't hang on to the facade much longer.

"All right," Pippa prompted. "What next?"

"Is anything obvious missing?"

Pippa scanned the room. "Nothing obvious, no."

"I'm going to speak with your neighbors," Jeffries stated. "Detective Iglesias will take over and stay while the technicians do their thing. When they're done, you can take a closer look. We'll be as efficient as possible," she promised.

Although he appreciated having an official reason to stick around, he could tell Pippa wasn't happy about it.

Emmanuel cleared his throat. She shot him a look that could have melted concrete block, confirming her low opinion of how things were working out. Crouching for a closer look at the lock, he asked, "Who has access here?"

"It's the service hallway." She spoke with deliberate emphasis on each syllable. "Anyone with trash going out or large deliveries coming in would be back here. If a concern is outside of building maintenance, most service men and women use this access too."

"Who has keys to your door?"

She closed her eyes for a moment, clearly struggling to hold on to that rigid composure. "There are only two keys. The maintenance staff has one, and I have the other. They send me text messages in the building app to schedule appointments or to let me know when they need to come inside."

Standing, he scowled at the footprint and took a picture. "After you." He gestured for her to lead the way back into the condo.

"Will the CSI team need to go through my entire place?"

"Wouldn't hurt," he said. "Is there somewhere you can wait or even stay over tonight?"

She set her coat and briefcase on the peninsula countertop in the kitchen. "I'm not leaving."

Emmanuel recognized that arguing was futile at the moment. He walked away from her to gather his thoughts and take pictures of the scene with his cell phone. The candid shots gave him perspective to use as they worked a case.

She trailed after him this time, documenting the damages herself until Jeffries and Simmons returned to finalize their report. Emmanuel just listened, considering what he would ask about when they were alone.

And they would be alone, because he wasn't going anywhere tonight. Griffin would kill him if he left her here by herself. Frankly, as he walked through the scene, Emmanuel's concerns multiplied.

The crime scene unit arrived and went straight to work. While they gathered any available evidence, Emmanuel called one of his cousins to change the lock on the back door. He wasn't sure if Pippa was relieved or frustrated that her sister Sadie, a CSI with the department, wasn't on duty. It would have been a conflict of interest, anyway. For that matter, where were the rest of her siblings? He'd been told time and again the family was close.

If this had happened to one of his sisters, he'd be here in the thick of it, officially or not.

He was about to call Griffin with an update when Daniel returned. He could tell by his partner's face they hadn't had any luck finding tracks or a witness.

"Whoever did this didn't leave a trail," Daniel said.

"Ready to call it a night? We have two cold burgers waiting for us downstairs."

Emmanuel ignored his rumbling stomach. "Can you catch a ride with Simmons and Jeffries?" he asked quietly.

Daniel's eyebrows shot up toward his hairline. "Seriously? That's fast work. I got the impression she didn't like you much."

"She doesn't like me at all," Emmanuel said. As Wentworth's new attorney, she probably thought she had good reason. "Regardless, I'm sticking around until the place is secure."

"She's staying here?" At Emmanuel's nod, Daniel whistled softly. "Stubborn and cute is a bad combination."

Just as he'd thought, the teasing had begun. "Shut up, Gomez. It's not like that." Besides, cute didn't fit Pippa at all. Sophisticated. Smart. Lovely. And a tendency to make cutting remarks, at least when she interacted with him.

Daniel grinned, unrepentant. "Good luck. I'll get the paperwork rolling."

"Great. See you in the morning."

He closed the front door behind his partner and prepared for a series of awkward conversations. Griffin would be hot about the trouble here but grateful Emmanuel planned to stay over and keep things under control. Pippa would likely be equally furious that he'd called her brother without discussing it with her. And he was pretty sure she'd post a strong argument against his plan to sleep on her couch.

He looked at the couch, with its torn-up cushions, and decided he'd sleep better on her floor. Smiling to himself, he thought she might agree with that idea.

Chapter 3

Progress, the man thought as he continued his disposal of anything that could tie him to Philippa Colton's sleek condo. No wonder the Wentworth bitch hired her to try to flip the unanimous decision of a good jury. They were two of a kind.

How did the daughter of a top DA wind up defending arrogant killers? Good thing Graham Colton hadn't lived long enough to see this. Her father would've been heartbroken.

He hadn't meant to do more than search for her case notes and leave her that message to scare her off. But he'd unloaded a few frustrations in the midst of his search.

The call from the guard out at the prison had come at the perfect time, helping him focus on the first priority: sidelining the misguided lawyer.

Unless there'd been trouble on the highway, she should've found the mess he'd made by now, but he kept the radio off. That way he wouldn't have to worry about being surprised when they talked about this at the station.

And they'd talk. There was always plenty of gossip when the upper crust of society was involved.

Overall, he was pleased with how today's effort would shake out. By the time the cops got to looking, all of the evidence of his visit would be destroyed or disposed of in areas no one would connect to him or her.

The gloves he'd worn to keep from staining his hands with paint were stuffed in his pocket, inside out, until he could drop them in a public restroom well away from the scene. He'd wiped down the can of spray paint, too, tossing that into a big garbage can behind a community theater several miles from her fancy address. The service coveralls were generic enough and already deep in the collection box for a local charity group. Although he was in his own car, he wasn't worried about being spotted or identified. He had friends all over Grand Rapids, in law enforcement and in various communities. He had the friends that came along with years of public service.

He'd worked his butt off to build his stellar reputation. Sure, there had been a misstep here and there, but no serious blemishes on his record. Nothing actionable. He'd keep it that way. No lawyer with uppity artwork and impossible idealism would trash his reputation.

After nearly three decades of solving crimes, he knew how to commit most of them. More important, he knew how to avoid getting caught.

When he'd heard that Wentworth had some eager

new lawyer trying to overturn her conviction, he'd experienced a blinding panic. But that had been a clean case from start to finish. Anna Wentworth wasn't 100 percent guilty of killing Hicks, but she sure as hell wasn't innocent. Behind bars was the best place for her. Everyone involved knew it. Hell, everyone who'd ever met her knew it.

He hadn't expected anyone to raise much of a ruckus. Standard appeals, nothing more. Wentworth had money, but few friends. Throughout the case, it felt like everyone in Grand Rapids wanted to share their story of the woman's rude behavior. No one had any doubt she'd been hiding murderous tendencies behind her charitable fundraising and flashy jewelry.

If only the woman's daughter had shut her trap, things might've blown over after the verdict. If only. Unfortunately, the daughter had hired Philippa Colton, vowing that the real killer would be found, true justice served.

What the hell did she think he and the rest of the cops in this city did all day, eat doughnuts?

He and his fellow GRPD officers weren't bumbling hacks. He wore a sergeant's stripes and had received commendations for various actions in the line of duty. Neither he nor anyone in the department deserved the glare of media scrutiny they were under now.

Hiding an annoyance that edged toward anger, he'd been cautious, careful not to overreact and draw unwanted attention. No one was happy with the wrongful conviction rhetoric, and he kept his trap shut, letting the chatter flow around him.

Waiting, watching, he mentally lined up his moves to prepare for the worst if the new lawyer convinced a judge to reopen the case. An appeal was one thing, with all the legal posturing and arguments. What the new lawyer proposed was entirely different.

The Wentworth conviction was rock-solid from the detectives arriving on the scene to the testimony given in court. He smiled now, just thinking back to Detective Iglesias on the stand. That man had the kind of face people trusted, along with a steady gaze and pleasant voice. The jury had been hooked, leaning forward in their seats, hanging on his every word.

It had been perfect. Done. It should've stayed that way too.

A niggle of resentment crept over his skin, raising goose bumps the length of his arms. Thanks to a daughter's refusal to accept her mother's true nature, it wasn't done.

That fresh-faced lawyer had come for the evidence box. Par for the course and nothing too worrisome. He knew what was in there. She'd spent a few hours poring over a case they'd worked by the numbers for weeks. They hadn't taken any shortcuts, hadn't skipped a single step. Hell, they'd been working to convict one of the most notorious people in the city.

Still, the lawyer made her notes, took pictures of what they'd found and gathered at the scene. Hindsight was always perfect, an impossible standard. He'd seen eager, bleeding hearts who believed a convict's sob story turn a case inside out on the basis of a misplaced comma in a report. The second-guessing from people who didn't have a clue how real police work was done was one of the worst aspects of his career.

As if all that time in a classroom and libraries full of court rulings was somehow better than real-life, on-the-street experience. No way would the world improve by legally manipulating the system to get one snobby socialite out of prison.

Colton certainly wasn't winning any friends in the GRPD, or the city at large, but she wouldn't quit. A couple of witnesses attached to the original case had told him she'd reached out, asked questions.

She'd forced his hand. If Pippa Colton wouldn't stop, he wouldn't either.

Damn idealists.

He had to move with care. The media was all over her. He'd thought the negative press would be enough, yet she persisted as if she was the key to righting some tragic wrong.

With a little planning and a couple of phone calls, he'd set things in motion. Having so many friends in and around law enforcement came in handy, giving him a heads-up about Colton visiting her client in prison. They'd happily agreed to make that visit problematic.

His next stop was to pick up a case of beer for the pal who'd kept Colton out there, stringing her along that she might actually get into the conference room. After making the purchase, chatting up the clerk behind the counter, he loaded the beer into his trunk, sliding it between two plain cardboard boxes.

The entire Wentworth case was right there. Stealing the paperwork from the cage without getting caught had been a stressful nightmare, despite the rush of making sure Colton would be out of luck if she came back for another look. He'd taken the case files out of her reach, but now he was stuck. He needed the right disposal solution for the contents of those boxes. He considered planting the entire mess in her office, but that was too obvious, and everyone coming and going made the timing complicated.

Getting rid of a can of spray paint was easy. Hell, breaking into her condo had been a cake walk. Wearing a ball cap, keeping his head down, and walking with a group made it easy to avoid the security cameras that were mostly useless. Would've been nice to find something though. He'd searched as long as he dared and hadn't found the first page of all those notes she'd taken on the case. He hadn't expected her to haul it all to the meeting.

For tonight, the nasty message and damage would have to suffice. He could take things up another notch if the home invasion didn't make her reconsider her attempt to set Wentworth free.

With one last look at the boxes, he closed the trunk and headed out to deliver the beer and shoot the breeze with an old friend. He'd figure out something; he always did.

Pippa was hungry and well beyond weary. She hadn't had the wine or the shower she'd been counting on, but she still had plenty of unwanted company. And plenty of cleanup to tackle as soon as everyone cleared out.

Detective Iglesias wandered back to the kitchen after another chat with the technicians processing her home. "You'd probably be happier elsewhere. Can I drive you someplace?"

"No, thank you." It took all her willpower to keep her gaze away from her wine rack. But that left her looking at either the mess or the detective. Both views rattled her for different reasons. The mess reminded her someone harbored enough hatred for her—or her work—to invade her home. Iglesias…well, with that confident swagger and trim beard, he was far too sexy for her comfort. She saw through his friendly, supportive demeanor. He was *not* her friend.

She supposed hiding in her bedroom until this was over was unacceptable behavior, especially in front of him.

Bedroom. Detective Iglesias. Her pulse kicked. Best to never think about those two topics at the same time again.

"Can you tell me a little bit about your active cases?" he asked.

As if he didn't know what this had to be about.

He tapped his pen to the small notebook in his hand, waiting. It was such an old-school motion, and yet somehow it captivated her. He intrigued her on a level that had nothing to do with crime scene procedure. She had to get him out of here, quickly.

"I'd rather give a statement to your partner," she said.

"He isn't here. He went back to the station to start on the reports."

Would nothing go right today? "You should probably join him," she said. "There's no need to stay. If you have more questions, just call."

"But I'm here now." He aimed that pen at her office. "Looks to me like whoever did this searched your office. So again, tell me about your cases. Please."

The man was insufferable. She'd had a dreadful day, spent hours on the road, made zero progress on her most important case, and now she had to deal with the man who had almost singlehandedly put Anna behind bars.

Her gaze cycled from wine rack to ransacked home to detective. "I'm sure you feel some obligation or whatever to my brother," she stated. "It isn't necessary." She'd told Griffin she didn't need a babysitter. And yet here he was.

"Even if I agreed with you, I'm not leaving just yet." He smiled.

On another man, that smile would warm her right up, maybe tempt her to kiss the deep creases bracketing his lips. "I think we both know that this incident has everything to do with my representing Anna Wentworth," she said at last. "That message doesn't fit my other cases." She turned her back on all of it, on him, too, going to the refrigerator to pour water from the pitcher she kept chilled.

Being rude, even to him, made her feel small and petty. "Would you like a glass of water?"

"Yes, please."

She filled a second glass and carried both back to the counter. For several minutes he was quiet, sipping his water and watching the crew finish. When her doorbell rang, she groaned. "That's probably my twin."

"Let me get it," he offered, striding away.

Why argue? At least his absence, however brief, gave her a reprieve from more questions. And from this vantage point, she could enjoy the view without getting caught ogling the enemy. The man was tall and well built, and his dark jeans fitted his long legs and firm backside perfectly.

Detective Iglesias walked back into view with another man at his side, slightly older, a few inches shorter and thicker through the middle. But the twinkle in the older man's eyes and the wavy brown hair gave her the impression they were related.

"Pippa, this is my uncle, Carlos. He's here to replace the lock on your back door."

Carlos held out his hand. "A pleasure," he said, beaming as she shook his hand. "A few minutes and I'll be out of your way."

"Um," she stared at the locksmith, then at his nephew. "I thought maintenance handled this kind of thing."

Carlos glanced at his nephew, and getting a go-ahead nod, scooted down the hall.

"Detective Iglesias," she snapped. "You can't just do that."

"What?" he asked, the picture of innocence.

She wasn't buying it. "Take over." Griffin had put him in her way and her brother would hear about it. "This is *my* home."

His dark brown eyes swept over the kitchen behind her. "I'm aware. Do you still plan to stay the night?"

"Yes." She pressed her lips together, seeing the trap as it snapped shut.

"Then let Carlos handle the lock. If the building requires something different, you can deal with it in time, but I can't allow you to stay if your home isn't secure."

"Because of Griffin."

He shook his head and motioned for her to sit down at the counter. "Because when everyone clears out, you need to be able to rest with confidence."

Her mouth fell open. She only knew because he tapped her chin to close it. Of all the reasons he might have provided, that was the only one that guaranteed her cooperation. "Thank you," she managed. That point where his finger had touched her chin tingled pleasantly. It took significant effort not to rub the sensation away. Definitely overtired.

"Were you at the office all day?" he asked.

This question didn't feel like an interrogation, especially not with the warmth in his gaze. "No. I…" She looked up and her gaze collided with his, the words getting lost between her brain and her mouth. He seemed genuinely interested in her responses. In her.

What was her problem? Of course he was interested. Anything she said would reveal too much about her attempt to overturn Anna's conviction.

"I drove to the women's prison to see Anna Wentworth."

"How did that go?"

She studied him. Was he playing dumb? "Seriously? I'm not about to discuss anything about that with *you*."

Whatever he might have said was cut short by the CSI team packing up to leave. They assured her she could clean up the house and that the detectives would get the reports as soon as possible.

While Detective Iglesias walked them to the front door, Pippa refilled her water glass and pulled up the app for her insurance company. She could get started on the claim right now and have her agent come by first thing in the morning.

"Pippa," he called out. "Have you reset the code?"

She wanted to snipe at him for making himself too much at home, but his uncle was still in earshot, and that would just make her look bad and confirm the rumors that Anna was rubbing off on her.

Joining the detective at *her* door, stubbornly ignoring the state of her home, she stared at the electronic panel, trying to choose another code she and her twin could recall with ease. Making a decision to use her mom's birthday, in reverse order, she tested the new code a couple of times.

"That feels better, right?"

"A little," she admitted. Her gaze drifted back to the message, and she did her best to view it as a compliment. She was a do-gooder, and she wouldn't apologize to anyone for living out her values.

"I feel obligated to tell you not to give that code to anyone," he said.

"Someone has to have it. What if my plants need water?" All of her plants were silk and would stay that way until she was ready to make more time for her personal life. Only the aloe vera in the kitchen managed to thrive, despite her neglect.

"You can program multiple codes. We recommend you only hand out one spare key and only when necessary."

"The whole safety lesson is great, but the intruder didn't come in this way."

"We'll sort out how he got into the building as we review the video from the security cameras," he promised. "Now can you talk me through this, please?"

"Detective—"

"Call me Emmanuel."

She would *not*. That was too familiar, too normal. As much as she might appreciate the potential of him on a personal level, he was a threat to her case. To her career goals. If she thought the media attention was difficult now, it would be impossible if it came out that she was on a first-name basis with the detective who put her client in jail.

"Pippa—" He raised his hands in surrender when she

glared at him. "Miss Colton. I'd like to pin down more details while things are fresh in your mind."

She feared the wrong details were crystallizing while the important things were becoming a blur. All the urgency to find the intruder that flooded her system an hour ago was gone now that the adrenaline rush was over. "Let's finish this in the morning. I'll come to the station." She looked around at the mess and somehow managed not to swear or cry. "I have too much cleaning left tonight."

"Emmanuel will help." Carlos had a sparkle in his eye when he volunteered his nephew. "My sister raised you right," he said to Emmanuel. "You can ask your questions while you are helping." With a broad smile, he handed Pippa two keys. "One for you and one for the building staff. Assuming you trust them."

"I do." Or she had. Still did. Maybe. Good grief, her brain felt like oatmeal. "Thank you. Do you take checks?" She started for her office, picking her way through the debris to the drawer where she kept her checkbook. Pulling it open, she was relieved to see everything still there, if not as neat as she'd left it, confirming the motive for someone making this mess wasn't fraud or theft.

"You okay?" the detective asked.

"Yes," she lied through the fatigue. "How much do I owe you?" She looked up when Carlos didn't answer. The older man was gone, leaving her alone with his nephew. "I didn't pay him."

"He said he'll send an invoice."

"I didn't hear that."

"You zoned out for a minute." He approached her as if he thought she might fly apart at any second. He might be right. "When was the last time you had something more than water?"

She shook her head. "I have no idea." Where was the grit that had carried her through the death of her parents, long nights of law school and that nasty breakup just before she sat for the bar exam?

Her siblings were an invaluable source of support, and she loved them for it, but she couldn't rely solely on them. Not when they were all consumed with Brody, RevitaYou and the Capital X investigation.

"You don't want me here, but I'm not leaving you alone."

She had the absurd urge to thank him. "I'll be fine."

"Of course you will. But my uncle will flay me if I leave you to handle this by yourself." He shrugged out of his jacket and draped it over a stool at the counter. His button-down was open at the collar, and she was mesmerized as he rolled back the cuffs, revealing strong, tanned forearms dusted with dark hair. "Go change clothes or whatever. I'll figure out food."

What was happening? "Your family is big on service?"

He shot her a look. "You could say that."

She'd touched a nerve, but she was just too tired to understand which one.

Chapter 4

Emmanuel put his focus on feeding Pippa, hoping she'd wander off while he rummaged through her kitchen for something fast and hearty. She needed fuel. The woman was running on fumes. But still running, which was impressive.

He found cereal in the cabinet and milk in the fridge along with some fresh fruit and orange juice. As if a stranger hadn't done enough invading tonight, he kept digging and came up with a better meal plan when he found frozen vegetables, eggs and some precooked sausage patties.

He didn't want to like her. She sure didn't like him. He was fine with her as just Griffin's sister. And he understood her work was important to the legal system overall, even when that meant second-guessing good police work. When he heard the water in the pipes between the walls, he had to force his mind away from the images of her stripping away her professional clothes and stepping into the shower.

All woman, no pretense. And completely off-limits.

Not just because he valued his friendship with her brother and wanted to keep the peace with her sister in the crime scene unit. Pippa was also several years younger and a whole lot less jaded.

The sausage was sizzling in one skillet, and he had another pan heating while he whisked up eggs in a bowl, adding ground pepper and the vegetables. When she walked in, her hair was down, the light brown waves brushing her shoulders, and she'd changed into faded jeans and a soft blue T-shirt. His pulse tripped over itself, his fingers itching to discover if her hair was as soft as it looked. He caught himself and pointed to a glass of orange juice. "That's for you."

She stared at him, her lips tight and her brow furrowed. "You're cooking?"

Was that bristling reaction her default with everyone or just him? "As I said." He poured the egg mixture into the pan.

"You said you'd figure it out."

"I did. This is faster than delivery."

"If you say so." She picked up the juice glass and drank it down. "This smells good."

His shoulders relaxed with the compliment, and he hid his smile. Hopefully the meal would fortify her for the many questions as well as the cleanup ahead of them.

Loading up two plates, he brought them to the countertop. She set out the napkins and forks while he refilled their water glasses. "Did you want coffee?"

"No, thanks," she replied. "I had more than enough caffeine during the drive today."

The drive to the prison. He had questions about that, but he didn't want to ruin the meal for her.

At her first bite of the omelet, she sat back and closed her eyes. "This is amazing. Thank you."

It beat the cold burger and fries waiting for him in the car. With so much going on with the RevitaYou crisis, he hadn't taken much time with friends and even less trying to date. He'd almost forgotten how nice it was to share a meal with a pretty woman.

When her plate was clean, there was more color in her cheeks and the spark was back in those big green eyes. Turning to face the office, she crossed her legs, and he noticed her feet were bare. They were slender, like the rest of her, and her toenails were painted with a deep rosy pink. What a contrast to her sleek professional image. The simple awareness took on the weight of a privileged secret.

"What a mess," she muttered.

"Definitely a focused effort there," Emmanuel agreed. He started to clear the dishes, but she stopped him.

"You cooked. Let me do this." She cleaned the dishes with an efficiency his mother would appreciate.

"Where are the cleaning supplies?" he asked.

"Hall closet." He found what passed as her laundry room with a stacked washer and dryer, a pull-down drying rack and a shelving unit. "You'll want to put shoes on before you go in there again."

"Hey, Detective?" She was behind him, paused at her bedroom doorway. "I don't need another big brother."

Right. He wasn't feeling brotherly. Uneasy with his

not-at-all-fraternal reaction to her, he gave her a nod and then pulled out the broom and dustpan along with a couple of trash bags. He started in the living room so she wouldn't think he was trying to interfere with her work.

He was carefully sweeping up broken picture frames when she joined him. For a second he thought the scowl was for him, but her gaze was on the wall.

"I can't believe you walked into this," he said quietly.

"Me neither." She tiptoed over to the wall and swore. "I thought so."

"What is it?" He helped her lift up a large framed painting of a sunset over a lake.

"The jerk tagged this too," she said, clearly disgusted. "Can you put it near the door? I'll take it for repair and reframing tomorrow."

He did as she asked, taking a closer look at the piece. It was definitely a statement by size as well as subject. The soft-focus blur of trees, vibrant with autumn color, tucked up close to the edge of the lake was calming. In fact, her home must have had a comfortable vibe before the vandal blew through. The colors and fabrics she'd decorated with were gentle and soothing, and nothing he would've expected from the stern and stressed woman from a few hours ago.

"It's not quite as bad as I thought," she said.

"Is that a joke?" he wondered.

She gave him a genuine smile and the unexpected rush left him momentarily speechless. "I thought the cushions were destroyed, but the upholstery is only unzipped," she said, wrestling foam back into the fabric. "You have no idea how long it took me to find this couch."

"It's a big decision," he agreed. "When I bought

mine, I could've skipped squats for a week with all the ups and downs."

"Exactly!"

She brought out the vacuum and cleared away any small bits of glass, and they soon had the couch back to normal.

"I can work in here if you'd rather get started on your office," he offered. Maybe she'd have an easier time with his questions if there was a bit of distance and distraction. "You need to be sure nothing's missing."

"You mean like my files?"

"Yes." The glass clinked as he swept it into the dustpan. "I assume you took your computer with you."

"I didn't," she replied. "But my laptop and all of my case notes are secure."

He glanced across the room. "At the office?"

"No, in the floor safe."

"Seriously?" He was impressed by her security measures. Maybe he shouldn't have given her a hard time about the lock.

"Yes." She was distracted by a stuck drawer in her desk. "This piece was my grandmother's," she muttered. "This drawer is a bear to reopen when it gets closed all the way."

He walked over, about to offer an assist, when the drawer gave and she stumbled back, right into him. His hands spanned the sweet dip of her trim waist, and he breathed in the faint citrus fragrance of her hair.

"Thanks," she said, an adorable rosy color rising in her cheeks.

"Anything missing?"

"Not so far, but the vandal was definitely searching."

He retreated to the other room, unable to hold back

the flood of questions any longer. "Did you call the police immediately?"

"Sort of. At first I tried to talk myself out of dialing the emergency line due to the lack of imminent danger. Then I called Kiely. She's a private investigator. But she was tied up with another case tonight."

"I've met her," he said. "Never had the pleasure of working with her."

"Your loss. Should've called her in on the Wentworth case when you needed a hand."

He bit his tongue rather than wreck a few positive steps by snapping at her. They hadn't needed any help on that case. The evidence had been clear, all of it leading to one specific guilty party. "Who knew you were headed to the prison today?"

"Kiely, my clients and my paralegal at the office." She'd cleared her desktop and was wiping it down.

He dragged his gaze away from the little flash of skin that showed between her shirt and jeans when she stretched. "By client, you mean Anna Wentworth?"

"Yes. Along with her daughter, who is overseeing this effort and footing the bill."

He had all the big pieces of glass picked up and was now vacuuming the smaller bits.

"You don't have to do that," she called out over the sound. "I'll call a professional cleaning crew tomorrow."

He ignored her, determined to make the space around the couch safe for her bare feet. "Why did you take Anna Wentworth's case?" he asked when he finished.

"Aside from the retainer?"

"It's okay to be financially motivated," he said, unfazed by her sarcasm. "You're not the only lawyer making more money by taking on a wealthy lost cause."

The bristling and scowling returned in force. "She is *not* a lost cause, and I *will* prove it."

He spread his arms, as frustrated as she was with all of this. "Do enlighten me."

"Fine." She leaned back on her clean desk. "First of all, Elizabeth is a good friend from school and I've known the family for years. Anna might be an awful snob who is happier writing a check than investing any real energy, but she isn't capable of murder. Plus, I don't take on loser cases. Not even for a friend."

"At least tell me Wentworth is grateful you're on board."

"I wish I could." Her gaze dropped to the floor. "I'm sure Elizabeth told her about hiring me, but today was supposed to be our first meeting about the case."

"Supposed to be?" he echoed.

She looked him dead in the eye. "We didn't get to speak at all."

"Was there trouble? It wasn't your first time meeting a client at the prison?"

"No and no." She sighed. "I had all my ducks in a row, even printed the confirmation of the scheduled appointment. They should've walked me right back to the conference room." She chewed her lip, lost in thoughts she wasn't sharing.

He wanted to know everything and not just because of the home invasion. "But?" he prompted.

She snapped out of it. "When I arrived, they claimed the paperwork was missing, that there was no record of my appointment in the system. I tried the waiting game, then name-dropping. The warden is an old friend of Dad's. That didn't work either. The guard claimed Mr.

Birrell was away at lunch and couldn't spare a minute to help me straighten things out."

"That's weird." Normally Birrell was very helpful and professional. Then again, Emmanuel came in as a cop, not a defense attorney seeking to overturn a conviction. He bent down to pick up a pencil that had fallen near the baseboard. Turning, he studied the message on her wall. She'd clam up or get mad if he pressed on the Wentworth issue. "What else have you been working on lately? Any chance this is related to another case?"

"I don't see how. Aside from the RevitaYou investigation I'm working with my siblings, Anna Wentworth is my only open case."

"All right." He handed her the pencil, and she dropped it into the cup on her desk. Then he strolled back toward the kitchen.

"That's it? You're leaving?"

"You don't have to sound so excited about the prospect." He refilled his water glass, watching the disappointment come into her eyes.

"I like my space," she said.

He filled her glass too. "You'll have plenty of it. After a few more questions."

Her jaw clenched, but she drank down half of her water. "Go on and ask," she said.

She was defensive again, and he needed to change tactics. "Griffin and I go back, like you and Elizabeth. He's a good friend." Based on the deepening scowl, he'd made things worse. "He gave me a heads-up about the loan shark operation Colton Investigations is trying to take down and your part in it."

"That," she flung her hand toward the wall, "has nothing to do with the Capital X case."

"You sound sure." He admired her confidence.

"It's too soon. I haven't done anything significant with that case yet."

Yet. That one syllable seized his full attention. Griffin had said she'd play a key role in bringing down the loan shark operation. Colton Investigations and the GRPD were quietly working together on cases involving Capital X and the RevitaYou vitamins. Several people in the city had become sick, and one death was already attributed to the product. According to the research Abigail had conducted, more deaths seemed likely. On top of that, Capital X enforcers were the prime suspects in a recent murder in Heritage Park, since the victim had suffered eight recently broken bones in addition to the fatal gunshot.

"I don't believe this has anything to do with Capital X," she continued. "When they go after someone, they hit direct and hard and leave behind broken bones, not graffiti."

She wasn't making him feel any better. "Your sister is in the thick of that investigation already," he reminded her. "And the two of you share a strong resemblance."

"You're implying someone from Capital X followed me by mistake or even followed Kiely when she stopped by."

"It's possible, right?" He could almost see the wheels turning in her head. "Just don't want to leave any stone unturned."

"Because you're trying to impress me with your thoroughness." She wrinkled her nose. "Being thorough now doesn't mean you didn't overlook something on Anna's case."

Insulted, he had to agree with Daniel. Cute and stubborn was a bad combination. When his jaw unclenched enough to speak, he said, "Did Elizabeth mention she also was a questioned as we worked the case?"

"At the time, she told me you spoke, that's all. I assumed it was to clear suspects or verify an alibi. She's no more a killer than Anna."

"She was a concern," he reiterated. "And far too vocal about her mother's innocence."

"Because she knew Anna didn't kill anyone."

"The point is, I turn over every stone and I work my cases with integrity. Her alibi was solid and she had no interaction with Hicks before or during the time he was seeing her mother." He leaned close, noting the way her eyes widened at the apparent revelation. "And I'm good enough at my job that your friend didn't realize what I was doing."

Her gaze narrowed. "If she was a person of interest, why isn't that noted anywhere in the case file?"

"It is."

"Not." She shook her head.

He nearly repeated himself, but that sounded too much like a sibling argument and he had no desire to lump Pippa in with his sisters. "I filed everything. We looked at Elizabeth as well as her father, Ed."

"Anyone else?"

"Of course. We worked the case, Pippa. Followed the evidence and motives."

She was quiet a long time. Then she walked around him to pour herself a glass of wine. "It would've been nice to see some indication of that in the case file."

What was she talking about? His notes and reports had to be in there. He didn't appreciate the insinuation that he'd been inept or even slack about that particular case. Everything had gone to the prosecutor's office for the trial preparation. Maybe something got mishandled, but it had all been there.

She settled back on the stool, watching him. "Tell me something before you go."

He wasn't going any farther than her couch or floor tonight, but that argument would come soon enough. "What's that?"

"Why are you so sure Anna is capable of murder?"

It was a fair question, one he had asked himself often since catching that case. And one he was thankful he'd never had to answer in court.

While Pippa waited for his reply, she had to give Emmanuel points for being helpful this evening. And she couldn't criticize his manners or his cooking, though she did *not* want to like him. He was patient and neutral. Professional. Even Elizabeth had commented on how warm and kind he'd been during their conversation about the relationship between her mother and Hicks and when it had soured.

She wondered if he'd taken that warm and friendly approach while interrogating Anna or if he'd been cold and tough when facing off with a suspected killer. It was hard to sort out tone in the dry written transcript, and she hadn't yet listened to that recording provided by Anna's defense team. She'd been focusing her time and energy on the peripheral interviews and witnesses, looking for anyone else who had a real motive to kill Hicks.

"I'm surprised anyone believes that self-centered socialite is innocent," he said quietly. "In court I only spoke the truth."

"That's not much of an answer."

His head fell back for a moment. "Can I have another glass of water?"

"Help yourself." She watched him refill his glass from the pitcher in the fridge and ran out of patience after the long day as the silence stretched on. "Stop stalling, Detective."

His lips twisted to the side, his eyes on the water in his glass. "Anna was her own worst enemy long before the trial. It didn't require any extra help from the GRPD to put her behind bars where she belongs. She killed a man."

Pippa tensed at the certainty in his tone. Too bad for him she was equally certain the police and the jury were wrong. "She did not kill David Hicks. From what I've seen and heard, your mind was made up before you asked her the first question."

"Not true. Every case deserves good police work. Due to her standing in the community, we were even more thorough on the Hicks case."

She bit back another protest. He couldn't have been too thorough or an innocent woman wouldn't be in jail right now. They were clearly entrenched on opposite sides of this issue. "You've met killers. Caught them and seen justice served."

"I have," he verified.

"What does Anna have in common with those criminals?" She was pleased to see that question put a dent in his pervasive confidence.

What if the person who had trashed her home was the real murderer? She rubbed the sudden chill from her arms. Dwelling on that with someone as observant as Emmanuel nearby was a one-way ticket out of here.

No way would she run from such an obnoxious and cowardly act.

"Not much on the surface," he admitted after a moment. "There are exceptions to every rule."

She waved that off. "Don't try to sell me the 'crime of passion' line. Anna isn't capable of extreme emotions with people."

"We found her jewelry near the body," Emmanuel said. "Maybe she killed Hicks because he tried to steal it."

She motioned for the wine bottle, pouring just a bit more into her glass. They shouldn't be talking about this. "I'm asking about you, personally," she stated. "Forget the evidence. Why were you so convinced she could take a man's life?"

"First of all, everyone is capable of doing terrible things."

He wasn't wrong. "This is murder we're talking about, though."

"I know. A big crime with big players and big stakes. I'm not going to lie—there was pressure to solve the case quickly. From the Hicks family as well as the Wentworth family. There was also pressure to do it right, coming from the mayor and the GRPD brass."

She folded her arms across her chest, refusing to let him off the hook. It was impossible to reconcile the considerate professional he'd been tonight when he'd had such negative tunnel vision about Anna Wentworth.

"She was mean," he finally said. "A mean and cruel woman. I'm aware that sounds childish."

"It is childish."

"At the heart it's the truth," he said. "You can't sit there and tell me Anna Wentworth is a nice person."

She opened her mouth, but he cut her off. "Charitable contributions do not make someone a nice person. She's rude to her staff, aloof with her family, and she can hardly make eye contact with anyone with a smaller net worth than her husband."

He had a point. "Go on." There was more to this, more he clearly didn't want to talk about. Pushing at his hair, he muttered something under his breath, possibly in Spanish. All that did was make her want to ruffle his hair too. The untimely and inappropriate distraction irritated her.

"This is irrelevant," he said with a patently false smile. "But you win." He planted his hands on his lean hips. "We worked the case properly. Whatever I thought of Anna, I worked the evidence that was there."

"The evidence was compelling," she admitted. That was part of her problem. It was *too* compelling. Seasoned detectives like Emmanuel and Sergeant Joe McRath should've recognized that.

"If you believe the evidence, why are you convinced she *didn't* do it?"

"You first." More muttering in Spanish. "Detective Iglesias, would it help to consider this an exercise in my due diligence?" she asked. "I needed to speak with you, officially, anyway."

"Not much."

"But some?" She slid her wine glass aside and rested her elbows on the countertop. "Nearly every day you ask others, witnesses and suspects alike, to talk about uncomfortable and potentially embarrassing situations."

"Fair point."

"I'm not going away. You told Griffin you'd keep tabs on me anyway. Might as well get some work done too."

"You're impossible," he said. "My mother was a maid in the Wentworth mansion when I was little. Mrs. Wentworth didn't have children then. Maybe things would've been different if she had."

This wasn't the bias she'd been expecting at all. "Different how?" An image flashed through her mind of him as a little boy with tousled brown curls and big brown eyes sliding down the polished oak banister of the central stairway while his mother worked. Assuming that kind of thing would have been allowed.

"I never talk about this." His voice was a deep, unhappy rumble that heated her skin. "Mom had to take me to work one day. I guess the babysitter was sick and Dad was working. Who knows? I can remember her making calls, frantic to find someone to take me. I was too young to stay alone, and my brothers and sisters were in school."

"You're the youngest in your family?" she asked.

"I was then." He paused, his dark eyes knitting together over his straight nose. "Mom must've been pregnant, though it was probably too early for anyone but Dad to know." He stalked back and forth, as if he couldn't settle.

"It wouldn't have made a difference to Anna," Pippa admitted.

He raised an eyebrow and then continued. "So, yeah. I was the youngest. Mom was pregnant. She must've been sure Anna would fire her if she called in sick, so she took me with her." A faint smile hovered at one corner of his mouth. "That house."

"I know." Pippa had been equally awed when she'd seen it for the first time as a ten-year-old. Truth be told, the mansion was still an impressive and intimidating museum of a house.

"Whatever." He paced away and back again. "Mom let me bring along a toy truck and a small teddy bear. The same quiet toys she let me take to church on Sundays. The three of us trailed after her, room to room, as she did her work." He shoved his hands into his pockets and refused to look at her. "I was quiet," he said, grumpy again.

Her heart ached for that little boy he'd been, and she was sure he'd behaved perfectly. "Just like in church?" she asked.

His lips curled up into an all-out grin. There was a fresh tingle to go with her heated skin. What was wrong with her? She couldn't indulge any of this curiosity or interest, not with him.

"Just like Sundays," he said. "We learned early and were reminded often of the penalties of outbursts or tantrums in church."

"I assume your mom issued the same reminder before you entered the Wentworth mansion?"

"She did." He met her gaze, and the earnestness in his eyes floored her. "I swear to you I wasn't making a sound when Mrs. Wentworth noticed me. She fired my mother on the spot."

He'd been a child, though she didn't doubt the whole thing must've been an ordeal. "In the interest of playing devil's advocate, are you sure she didn't give your mom a chance to explain?"

"I'm sure. I remember Mom pleading to be allowed to gather her things." His eyes locked on her once more. "Did you hear me? She didn't plead to keep the job—she begged for access to *her own belongings*."

Pippa groaned. "That sounds like Anna."

"So how can you sit there and *not* believe that a woman so cruel and selfish is capable of murder?"

Because she knew Anna better than most people. "Being a terrible human being doesn't necessarily make her a killer."

It was like striking a match to paper. Emmanuel erupted. "My mom barely got out with her own purse and her car keys. She didn't get a reference or severance or even that day's pay. She drove halfway home and then pulled over. I sat in the back seat and watched her *cry*. Totally helpless."

She wanted to cry for him, for them, all these years later. She wanted to drive right back to the prison and yank the woman out of her cell and shake her until she apologized.

"The woman was heartless. *Is* heartless. Was I doing anything to harm her? No. Was I keeping my mother from her work? Again, no. Anna Wentworth forgot my mother's name the moment we were gone." He paused to gulp in air. "But Mom getting fired sent *my* family into a tailspin. Mom had to scramble for a new job without a reference. Very few positions paid as well as the Wentworths."

It was all Pippa could do to keep her voice even, calm. When she finally spoke with Anna again, she'd… well, she didn't know what she'd do, yet. "So you've been angry all this time."

"Yes," he admitted. "Yes, it's been years. My mom got another job and my family survived and I'm *still* angry. That doesn't mean I didn't do my job." He drilled his finger into the granite countertop. "Everything I said in court was true. I didn't embellish any of it. I didn't have to. The dead body, the murder weapon, that outrageous brooch in the grass, splattered with the victim's blood. Add in all of her rude, unkind and outright mean antics through the years and it's not a big leap from Queen of Mean to murderer."

"I know it looks that way from—"

"Looks that way?" he echoed. "Pick up a tabloid, grab a newspaper, scroll through the gossip blogs. It *is* that way."

"You're helping my case if you're admitting online gossip influenced your investigation," she warned.

"Go ahead, try to pick my work apart. It'll hold up."

It couldn't. Pippa knew deep in her gut that Anna had not killed David Hicks. A grave mistake had been made, some detail had been overlooked or purposely suppressed and a murderer was still roaming around free. In her mind, the proof was scrawled across her wall. She needed Emmanuel to understand.

"You might be her daughter's friend, but you'll never convince me that Wentworth values you for anything more than your last name."

"I wouldn't try," Pippa said. She was suddenly exhausted again, her second wind gone. "I'm fairly sure she doesn't value me at all. But as Elizabeth's friend I have seen a different side of the woman everyone loves to hate."

He raised an eyebrow and rocked back on his heels. "Give me one instance where she exhibited compassion."

Well, that was a tough one.

"With more than a checkbook," he clarified.

Now she was stuck. "I've never seen an instance of hatred or anger hot enough to be deadly," she countered. "Taking a life requires effort. Hicks was shot in the heart. I'm not sure Anna has even held a gun."

"The lab decided she'd worn gloves and wiped the gun down."

Pippa waved that off. "Whoever killed Hicks wore gloves and wiped down the gun," she insisted. "You know Anna Wentworth doesn't lift a finger if she doesn't want to."

"So she hired someone to have it done."

"And asked the killer to drop the gun in her prized roses to frame herself?" She snorted. "Give me a break." Restless now, she stretched her arms overhead and then walked over to her desk. "More important, she would've had to care about the man enough to want him dead. He was convenient, but she didn't need him."

"She needed him to keep quiet about their affair," Emmanuel said.

"The prosecution was wrong about that," Pippa said. "I'm telling you blackmail wasn't a problem. Ed knew about the affair. He knew about all of her affairs before Hicks. No one would've paid him off."

"You're serious?"

She nodded. Emmanuel's disbelief was no surprise. "The Wentworths' marriage wasn't typical." Or maybe the happy-ever-after sort of relationship was the exception. She and Elizabeth had grown up in wealthy families with unconventional dynamics, and they had adapted differently. They'd both chosen personal accountability over convenience, one of the hallmarks of their friendship. Pippa understood that wasn't always the case. Money might open doors, but unlike Anna, Pippa and Elizabeth valued the hard work and kindness that built lasting connections.

Pippa understood she'd grown up with opportunities many kids didn't get, but she'd taken on Anna's case as a matter of righting a wrong. Much the same way her father had taken an unpopular stand to see that Brody wasn't wrongly convicted.

Life had crazy rippling effects on people. Elizabeth still believed in love and true devotion and all of that, despite the poor example set by her parents. And Pippa struggled to trust anyone outside of her siblings.

Clearly she and her siblings had adapted differently even under the same roof. It was still odd to think of her brothers partnered up with women who made them wildly happy. Riley and Charlize would soon be parents, and Griffin and Abigail, with their foster daughter Maya, already were. New examples of family dynamics rooted in love and hope.

But life had taught her that what worked for others wouldn't necessarily work for her. Dating was pointless when she was too busy to feed herself, much less find a few minutes to have coffee with a stranger from an app. She was happiest when she was up to her neck in a challenging case.

"Pippa?"

She blinked, rearing back as he waved a hand near her face. "What?"

"You checked out," he said. "It's been a long day. Let's pick this up again in the morning."

"Right." She pressed her hands to her eyes. "I do understand." She dropped her hands and caught the flare of concern in his gaze. The urge to step into the warmth and strength of him was nearly irresistible. "At least you have a valid reason to hate Anna, beyond the tabloid antics."

"I handled her case objectively," he said quietly.

She really wanted to believe him.

"Mom got a better job eventually," he continued. "A better boss. I should be over it."

"It was a defining moment." She forced her lips into a smile. "It's also late." Scooting past him, she aimed for the front door, but he didn't follow. "As you said, we can pick this up in the morning."

"I'm staying."

"No." She couldn't have the detective who'd testified against Anna stay here. "Locks are all new and I'm safe, so thanks again." She motioned for him to head out. He didn't budge. "I don't care what my brother asked you to do. I'm thirty years old and I can take care of myself."

"Normally, I'd agree." He tipped his head toward the nasty message on her wall. "That implies you need backup."

She swore under her breath and pushed a hand through her hair. Pointing at the screaming red paint, she said, "That mess is on my wall because the GRPD made a mistake." No more warmth in his eyes now. He was cold, his entire body braced against her. "In your opinion."

At the moment, the home invasion was the closest thing she had to hard evidence. "It's more than that. I'm getting threats and stonewalled at every turn because I understand there's a killer loose in Grand Rapids."

"Threats?" He took a step closer. "This isn't the first trouble you've had."

She wanted to bite off her own tongue. "Why won't anyone try to see this my way?"

"Because everyone else believes the evidence."

"I know how it must have looked," she allowed. "If

you want to solve this home invasion, then you might have to rethink that. People in general might not like what I'm doing on the Wentworth case, but only the real killer has motive to drive me off of it."

Her heart thudded against her ribs as they stared at each other.

"There are other explanations, other cases past and present," he said. "I'm only being objective and doing my job."

"That's true. So am I. I will see you tomorrow." She opened the front door. "I'll discuss this with you and your partner then."

His expression stony, he grabbed his jacket and walked out. Almost. He paused in the doorway. "Be careful, Pippa." Something resembling doubt flashed in his eyes. "If we need anything more, we'll come to you." He cleared his throat and bent his head close to her ear, his breath fanning her cheek. "Tomorrow I'll review the Hicks murder case one more time. With fresh eyes."

Then he was gone, pulling the door closed behind him. She locked it, and for several long minutes she simply marveled over the fact that she had finally gotten through to someone...especially that infuriatingly handsome detective.

Maybe the day wasn't a total loss after all.

Chapter 5

Emmanuel took the stairs down to the street two at a time, his mind spinning as he exited the building. Pippa truly believed in Anna Wentworth's innocence. Based on her brother's descriptions and anecdotes, he'd thought she was levelheaded. He'd assumed she was just helping a friend exhaust every legal option.

But she really believed it. Worse, her dogged determination had him rethinking everything. What if she was right and there was a killer on the loose, ready to stop her before she exposed the truth?

As a detective he'd seen more than his fair share of homicide victims through the years. Picturing Pippa snuffed out and lifeless gave him a chill he couldn't shake. Even without the promise he'd made to Griffin, he wouldn't have left her alone tonight.

Antsy, he wasn't ready to settle into his car yet. He

walked around the block while he called Daniel to check in. "How are things there?" he asked when his partner answered.

"Slow tonight, thankfully," Daniel replied. "Are you on your way in?"

"Not until morning." He'd reached the back of her building. The parking lot, drive and a walkway leading to the main sidewalk were all paved, but there was grass on either side of the walkway and landscaping around the residential rear doors. Daniel had already searched the area for any prints or other evidence, but another glance never hurt anything.

Fresh eyes.

"Did you get our prickly victim delivered to her brother?" Daniel asked, distracting him.

"No." He sighed. "She's staying the night."

Daniel chuckled. "She didn't strike me as the runaway-from-trouble type."

"No," Emmanuel allowed. "I wouldn't classify her as cooperative either," he added.

"Stubborn and cute."

"Don't start that," he said. "She's a victim." That status alone should nix any personal interest. Having sisters of his own, he could just imagine Griffin's reaction if he voiced any of the observations swirling in his head.

"But what if she wasn't?"

Without any caveats, Pippa would be a woman he'd want to know better. Intelligent and witty and independent was a heady combination, even before he factored in her beautiful eyes and figure. His palms warmed, recalling that moment when she'd lost her balance.

"A shame she's leading an investigation that could cause the department big trouble," Daniel said.

"Stop." Daniel had just made everyone on the GRPD a potential suspect for the home invasion.

"Have you even had a date in the last six months?" his partner challenged.

"Of course I have." He must have gone out with someone lately. It just hadn't been memorable. "Have you found any security cameras that might help us find the perp?"

"The church nearby has a few cameras covering the doors and the street, but no one answered when I called. I left a message and will follow up in the morning."

"Good." Emmanuel moved toward the street until he spotted one of the church's cameras. It was placed high enough it might help them. "What about the building?"

"I spoke with the head of maintenance for the building. He confirmed there were service teams in and out all day and we'll get the footage. More to the point, everyone coming in is supposed to use those paper shoe covers."

"That explains one partial," Emmanuel said. Maybe the paper cover had torn or slipped and the perp hadn't noticed. "All right. If you need me, I'm keeping an eye on things from the car tonight."

"For your friend?"

"Yes," Emmanuel replied. He managed to catch himself before offering more excuses that Daniel would only use to tease him later. "I'll be in first thing in the morning," he said. "Call if you need me before that."

He ended the call and walked back toward the building, right up to the service entrance. The motion-sensor floodlight came on and he stopped, searching for any kind of clue. Red spray paint had been used, by a man, based on the size of that partial boot print in the hallway. Whatever the man had walked through, Daniel hadn't seen any evidence of it in the building, and he hadn't picked up any trace of prints out here.

No surprise. Everything at the service entrance was paved.

Emmanuel kept thinking about that lone partial print, just inside Pippa's back door. How long would the sole of a boot stay damp enough to leave a mark? He searched the landscaped areas around the residential door, then followed the walkway to the parking lot. Coming up empty, he returned to the door and started over, this time examining the opposite end of the wide paved steps.

His light caught on a bit of crushed ornamental grass and displaced mulch. Jackpot. Well, *maybe* a jackpot. He took a couple of pictures, using his hand as a reference for scale. The depression wasn't really clear enough to warrant making a mold, but someone had stepped off the path recently. It was a big leap to assume this mark was made by the same boot heel they'd found upstairs, though he was happy to have a target, something to watch for when they reviewed the videos from the security cameras on both buildings.

If the intruder had come in or left through the residential exit, did that mean they were looking for one of Pippa's neighbors in disguise?

It was plenty to think about. He could run a preliminary background on the other residents from the computer in his car. Rounding the building, he unlocked his car and settled in for a long night.

Pippa stood back, pleased with cleaning efforts. The office was back to its normal, organized state. She'd even pulled her laptop and the Wentworth file from the floor safe so she could dive right in first thing in the morning.

She went to the hall closet and found a reusable grocery bag. Carefully, she loaded up the pieces in need of new glass. Hopefully the framing shop could help with that too. Some of them had been purchased during her travels and weren't easily replaced.

The mess on the wall gave her a fresh rash of goose bumps every time she walked by, as if the person who'd put it there was still watching her, challenging her resolve.

"Not for long," she decided.

Opening the app on her phone, she reviewed the list of service providers recommended by her insurance company. She would definitely complete her claim, but whether or not they paid didn't matter. She couldn't leave things like this. Having done volunteer work around the city scrubbing graffiti off public buildings, she knew that red spray paint wasn't going to be covered with a simple coat of paint. Or ten.

The cleaning and restoration company at the top of the list had a five-star rating and offered a twenty-four-hour answering service, so she called to schedule an appointment for tomorrow afternoon. Within minutes arrangements were made, and she'd uploaded the pictures she'd taken of the damage through the link at their site.

It wasn't until she was out of things to do that it all hit her. Someone had been in her house. She stared at that message. Someone had entered her home intent on intimidation, threats and destruction.

The trembling started in earnest, and no amount of

calm breathing eased the pressure. Her knees shaking, she double-checked the locks at the front and back doors. Everything was secure.

She was safe.

She clasped her hands together to stop the shaking. How long would it take for her to believe it? Her fingers itched to pick up her phone and call her twin. But Kiely was working and her other siblings were likely settled in for the night. She could handle this and discuss it calmly tomorrow.

Frozen in the hallway, she wrapped her arms around herself as a dozen worst-case scenarios ran through her head. What if she'd been home when the man who'd left the boot print came through the back door? She often worked with her earbuds in and the music volume cranked up high. Would she have heard anything in time to protect herself? With surprise on his side, he might have done far worse than trash a room and ruin a wall.

"Stop!" Her intended shout emerged a hoarse whisper.

Nothing dreadful had happened. This type of vandalism was the work of someone who didn't want to face her. The person had come when she had been away, intent on scaring her off the case. She'd been inconvenienced by the property damage, that's all.

It was over. She was alone and safe. No one could get in without her knowledge. Not her sister, not even maintenance until she gave them the key.

Still, her hands shook as she walked into the kitchen to wash the glassware.

She didn't have to stay here tonight. There was plenty of room in the house where they'd all grown up, the house where Riley still lived and where they conducted Colton Investigations business.

And if she ran away to Riley's house, which was how she thought of it now, she'd be interrupting his new life with Charlize. Once she told them about this her siblings would circle the wagons and try to protect her. Griffin would raise more concerns about her involvement with the Capital X case.

She couldn't let them down. They were all worried enough about Brody. She would tell them in the morning, when she felt strong enough to overcome any discussion.

The fact was she was safe. She was just overtired and frustrated because her home had been trashed. But that would be set right again soon. Topping off her water glass, she retreated to her bedroom with her laptop.

There was absolutely no indication the intruder had bothered with anything in here, though everyone from Officer Jeffries to Detective Iglesias had taken a look around.

Before she'd left, Officer Jeffries explained the prevailing theory was an intruder had slipped in with a work crew, gained entry with a master key stolen from the maintenance office and slipped out again with no one the wiser. With a little luck the police would find something helpful from the security cameras around the area.

If she kept dwelling on the trouble, she'd never get to sleep. Changing into her softest nightshirt, she added some extra moisturizer under her eyes and then settled into the bed to watch a movie on her laptop.

As the streaming site loaded, showing her what was trending and what she'd been watching, she smiled a little. The intruder had most likely been searching for information on the Wentworth case, but having her search history on this site exposed would've been really embarrassing. Her reputation as a tough, serious and cerebral lawyer would take a hit if anyone discovered she was a sucker for sweet romance movies and shows.

She treated herself to these light, pleasant hours because it was the only time a happy ending was guaranteed. Although one of the reasons she worked so hard for her clients was to reach a happy conclusion, sometimes making things right didn't make things whole.

Too tired to focus on something new, she turned out the light and chose an old favorite with plenty of humor to scrub the worst of the bad day from her mind. The hero reminded her a bit of Emmanuel. Confident and smart, he took charge unapologetically, yet kindly. While she didn't always appreciate it when her brothers forgot she was an adult and tried to step in and protect her, she did appreciate Emmanuel's efforts tonight.

He stirred her up inside, despite all the reasons she shouldn't let herself be distracted. It was more than his sharp good looks. She didn't have any regrets about prioritizing a case over a man when it was all superficial, but add in the intelligence and the life experience that gave interest and depth to his face and she felt like a bee in a field of blooming flowers. She dozed off, her mind on Emmanuel, her imagination spinning movie-caliber scenes of quiet walks in the park and deep, drugging kisses.

Hours later, her alarm clock sounded, and Pippa discovered she'd spent another night with her laptop on the pillow next to hers. Another secret no one needed to know.

Except today, as she rolled to her back and stretched her arms overhead, her muscles were as soft as pulled taffy and she was warm all over. Oh, no. She'd dreamed of Emmanuel—Detective Iglesias—all night long. Even in bed alone, the ridiculous dreams of romance and tender intimacy mortified her. She covered her face with her pillow. This was *not* good. The man was a trained observer. How would she face him today? Ever?

She leaped out of bed and headed for the bathroom, avoiding her reflection. A cold shower and a cup of coffee would clear her head and body. People had sex dreams all the time with inappropriate partners. It wasn't as if she had to discuss it with anyone. Clearly it was a fragment in her subconscious linking her biggest stressors.

The dream was an outlet. No need to make herself crazy about it. As soon as she saw him today, she'd remember the man was the opposition. He was the biggest enemy to her making the case, even if he had gone above and beyond to help her last night.

The bracing shower helped, and drying off, she caught the scent of fresh-brewed coffee. Today was going to be so much better. Pausing at her closet, she quickly decided on dark cropped jeans and a more casual white tunic blouse since she'd be working from home between meetings with the adjuster and cleaning crew. And if she had to go to the police station?

Emmanuel said he and his partner would come here.

Dressed, her hair pinned up in a loose knot, she took her laptop into the kitchen, setting it on the counter. Once she filled a mug with fresh coffee, she added a spoonful of sugar and carried it back to the bathroom to apply her makeup.

Feeling almost normal again, she went to work. The threat staining her living room startled her. It shouldn't have. Though it would've been nice, she'd known it wouldn't miraculously disappear. Determined not to let herself fall into another fearful paralysis, she deliberately turned her gaze to the desk and her thoughts to Emmanuel.

She hadn't expected him to help her clean up or see that her locks were changed. Was that all out of some obligation to Griffin or was that just his way?

Watching her parents' marriage fade into too much silence, diverging interests, and separate bedrooms had eroded Pippa's faith in the institution of lifelong partnerships. She could count on her siblings, but she didn't want to rely on anyone else. Didn't want to need anyone else. Her insistence on handling life's challenges on her own created some friction with her siblings, who only wanted to protect her. Between her stubborn streak and her tunnel vision when it came to a case, relationships didn't stand a chance.

The system had worked for her. Right up until tonight. Something about Emmanuel made her want to rest, to share theories on a case or the burdens of a bad day. He made her want to lower her guard.

He couldn't possibly take care of all the victims he met the way he'd cared for her. She had assessed his recent caseload. He worked like a man with no hobbies.

Not unlike herself.

She wanted to admire that despite his testimony sending the wrong person to prison. And now she knew beyond any doubt he held a grudge against her client.

This obsession with him wasn't healthy or practical; it was dangerous territory. She had to get the man out of her mind.

Would he really look at the case with fresh eyes today? Was it even possible for him to remain truly objective?

With her second cup of coffee in hand, she opened the curtains, just enough to let in some light without giving anyone outside a view of the nastiness on her wall. That just couldn't come down fast enough.

On the street she noticed an unfamiliar car. Nerves struck immediately, and she was reaching for her cell phone when the person in the driver's seat moved. She recognized the jacket and the curl of hair around the man's ear. Both belonged to Detective Iglesias.

Had he spent the night out there? That was ridiculous. He'd left his business card; she could just call him. Concerned there had been more trouble, she decided to go down and talk to him. She wouldn't know if she should be charmed or irritated by his presence until she had some answers. Whatever his reasons for being here at this hour, she would get further if she was nice.

Filling a travel mug with hot coffee, she walked downstairs. Stepping out of the building, the first thing she noticed was the frown on his mouth as he spoke into his cell phone. Cautiously, she looked around for more law enforcement. If there was an immediate crisis, she couldn't imagine he'd be here without backup.

She crossed the street and tapped on his window, regretting the bold move when his head jerked up and around in surprise. She hadn't meant to startle him. His brown eyes darted from her condo and back to her, as if he couldn't make sense of her being in the wrong place.

He rolled down the window, and she saw his eyes

were red rimmed. She could almost feel the distress pouring out of the car.

"What's wrong, Detective?"

"Just tired." He smiled, but she wasn't fooled. "Long night."

"Were you out here all night?"

"It was the right place to be," he replied.

Everything about him was strung tight, from his smile to his white-knuckled fingers curled around the steering wheel. Something was terribly wrong. "You're upset," she said, stating the obvious.

"No. Just tired."

That time she heard his voice crack. "I brought you a coffee, but maybe you should come upstairs and talk it out. This time I'll fix breakfast."

"That's…generous, Pippa," he said. "I couldn't possibly eat, but thanks all the same."

Why couldn't men just share rather than waste time in denial? "Come upstairs anyway."

"I'm fine. Really."

She hung on to the coffee she'd brought for him. "Maybe I'm out here because someone else is up there."

His gaze narrowed, and he reset his grip on the steering wheel. "That isn't funny."

Probably not, but she wouldn't let him sit out here alone with whatever was troubling him. She could analyze her reasons later, but seeing him so unhappy troubled her. "Ask anyone who knows me, I won't give up."

Grumbling, he rolled up his window and got out of the car.

She handed him the coffee she'd brought downstairs. "It's black," she warned. "I wasn't sure how you take it, but—"

"Caffeine is caffeine at this hour."

That's exactly what she would've said. "Right." She crossed the street, and he got the door half a step before she could, holding it open for her. "Thanks."

Upstairs at her condo, she did a double take when her lock wouldn't open. Her palms went damp and her pulse skittered.

"You changed the code," he said, his voice rough.

She paused, drying her palms on her jeans before she tried again. More than forgetting the new code, the flash of fear rattled her. This was her home, and until yesterday walking inside had been a comfort. She'd been gone only a few minutes, and she was afraid that she'd catch someone in the act when the door opened. What would happen when she came home again after being gone all day?

"It's just us," Emmanuel said, as if he could read her mind.

His certainty soothed her as much as it embarrassed her. She'd invited him up to talk about his troubles, not to rehash hers. The door opened and she stepped inside, studiously ignoring the damaged wall as she went straight to the kitchen.

Behind her, Emmanuel closed and locked the door.

Striving for a breezy hospitality, she said, "If you want to clean up or anything, go ahead. The guest bath is fully stocked." He knew her place as well as she did after last night.

"Seriously?" He took a drink of the coffee. "I'll just be a minute. Thanks," he said, excusing himself.

He wasn't the only one who knew how to be thoughtful. When he returned a few minutes later, she had bacon in the oven and water simmering for poached eggs.

"What's all this?" he asked.

"Breakfast." She grinned. It was basically the same thing he'd prepared for them last night. "Most important meal of the day."

"I've heard studies that contradict that," he said. "And I really need to get going."

She wasn't sure how to read his expression. His gaze was haunted, but since leaving his car, he seemed intent on being cheerful. She'd earned her reputation for being pushy, and right now she thought he needed a push to open up. Maybe even a shove. "You have time for coffee."

His expression turned mulish. She'd seen it plenty when her brothers were trying to avoid an uncomfortable topic.

"I don't give up," she reminded him for the second time in five minutes. "Did something happen at home or with your family?" She dropped the eggs into the water, stirred gently and covered the pan.

"Please don't do this," he said.

"You don't like eggs?"

"Pippa. I don't want to talk."

"You helped me last night," she pointed out.

"So pestering me today is how you say thanks?"

She didn't reply, just checked the bacon and dropped slices of bread into the toaster.

With a sigh, he sat down on a counter stool and laced his fingers together, thumbs pressing back and forth. "I got some really bad news. An email landed in my inbox a few minutes ago."

"I'm sorry."

She set down plates and silverware, napkins and condiments.

He fiddled with the utensils. "Two more deaths have been linked to RevitaYou."

It took all of her self-control to hold back a tidal wave of questions. News had spread that the miracle vitamin was making some people ill, and one death had already been attributed to a toxic element in the proprietary formula. Yet people were still taking it, choosing to roll the dice for the sake of feeling and looking younger.

"Do you know the victims?" she asked, plating the bacon, toast and eggs.

He stared at the food for a long moment, then pinched his eyes closed before he looked up again. "Thanks."

"You're welcome." Taking a seat at the end of the peninsula, she started to eat, but Emmanuel kept staring at his plate. She knew he wasn't seeing the food, but rather someone who had been important to him.

"I only know one victim directly. Ingrid Glucksburg." His lips canted to one side and he sniffed. "She was a GRPD informant. The report listed her as fifty years old."

That sounded far too young to Pippa for someone to be buying antiaging supplements, but that was exactly why the market was huge. The sadness in his voice made her heart ache. Tempted her to reach out and soothe him. She kept her hands busy with her breakfast.

"Before she became an informant, she was a petty thief." A smile flitted across his lips. "I can't tell you how many times she joked that all she needed was a good facial and a day at the spa to erase the years. She swore if she could look young enough to turn my head, she'd ask me out."

"She sounds like a real character," Pippa said.

"You have no idea." Emmanuel sighed. "She was

ornery and spry and smart as a whip, despite the bad choices she once made."

Nothing she'd read or heard in the trial transcripts prepared her for these facets of Emmanuel's character. Last night's generosity and his compassion today were a surprising counterpoint to the yawning grief that seemed to be threatening to swallow him whole.

"I'm really going to miss her," he said, pushing his eggs around his plate.

Pippa wished he would eat his breakfast. He needed to keep up his strength. "How did you become friends?" she asked.

"Catching Ingrid in the act was kind of a rite of passage in a way." He tore his toast in two, and buttered one piece. "She would give new patrol officers a run for their money on the street. There were times when her interactions with officers gave us better insight than any formal training or evaluation."

"What do you mean?" she queried.

"You know the *Star Wars* movies?"

Not the question she was expecting. "I'm offended you have to ask." When he only stared at her, she took a bite of her bacon, hoping to trigger a mimic effect. It worked. He took a bite of his bacon, as well. Hooray for those psychology classes she'd aced in college.

He chewed and swallowed and his smile seemed a little stronger. "Remember when Yoda pesters Luke after he crashes in that swamp?"

"Of course. It was an attitude test." She ate a bit more, and he did the same.

"The first of many," Emmanuel agreed, chasing a bite of eggs with more coffee.

"Ingrid was like Yoda," he continued. "She often

knew right away who would turn into a good cop and who would be problematic or quit at the first sign of adversity."

Fighting the strangest urge to pull him into a comforting hug, Pippa cradled her coffee cup in both hands. A dozen more questions zipped through her mind, but he was eating well now and she didn't want to interrupt him.

When he finished, he stared at the empty plate as if he wasn't sure what had happened.

"More coffee?" she offered. "There's more bacon too."

"I'd better not." He checked his watch. "Daniel's expecting me any minute. Thanks for breakfast. And for listening."

"My pleasure." And it had been. Most of the time when she remembered to eat, food was only functional. Feeding Emmanuel had felt far more personal and filled her with a new and delightful satisfaction. She enjoyed sharing meals with her siblings, even pitching in with the cooking or clean up. And she often found helping others energized her. This was different; it created a fluttering sensation around her heart. She couldn't quite put a label on it. Wasn't sure she wanted to. She hadn't enjoyed the topic, but she had enjoyed his stories and insights about his friend. The man was dangerous territory, indeed.

"I am sorry for your loss," she said, walking him to the front door. "It's all the more reason to put an end to this RevitaYou nonsense and the Capital X enablers issuing those impossible loans. I'm glad I'll be part of the solution when I apply for a loan tonight."

She pulled the door open, but he shoved it closed, his face clouding over. But this wasn't sorrow, it was anger.

Chapter 6

He couldn't have heard her correctly. Taking her by the shoulders, he turned her away from the door, held her firmly. "What did you say?"

"Let me go."

Her green eyes blazed. She was angry. He understood that. "Answer me first." She could *not* be entertaining the idea of deliberately putting herself in harm's way. Griffin hadn't mentioned how she would work on the Capital X case, only that she was determined to make a difference.

He stepped back and rubbed at his gritty eyes. He hadn't slept well. It wasn't possible to truly rest in the car with his body braced for trouble and his mind preoccupied with the woman in front of him. And now Ingrid. He was overwhelmed, that's all.

Her death would take some time to get over. He pressed his fist to the ache deep in his chest.

"Are you okay?" she asked.

"Yeah. Fine." The coffee would kick in soon and all of this would make sense. "Repeat that last thing, please."

Her brow flexed, then cleared. "Oh. I'm going to apply for a Capital X loan tonight. Colton Investigations is putting the final touches on things today." She bounced on her toes, and he noticed her feet were bare. "We're all set to go at seven o'clock tonight."

"That's crazy." Couldn't she hear how crazy that sounded? "Those people are dangerous. Why would you set yourself up?"

"The loan isn't for me," she said. "They've been working on an alias, complete with identification, a background, the works. I'm just the one filling in the details online."

"No." He couldn't let her do that. He turned away from her, his gaze slamming into the threat on the wall. What if that hadn't been about Wentworth? And she'd implied there had been other threats too. "You can't."

He'd shown up to help a friend, but something about her made him want to do more. A lot more. The idea of her in danger scraped at his frazzled nerves like a burr in a sock. "I'll talk to Griffin. You'll make a new plan."

Her gaze grew hard. "That's not your place."

"It should be," he shouted. "It's too easy to trace IP addresses," he said, forcing his voice to behave. "Capital X will come after you—"

"That's what we're counting on. But not me, not here," she added in a rush. "Relax, Detective." She reached out, rested her hand on his arm. "We're professionals at Colton Investigations. They did some masking thing to make it harder to find this laptop."

He did know CI's good reputation. At the moment all of his attention had zeroed in on the place where her hand touched him. He could feel the heat of her through the layers of his shirt and jacket. He wanted to take that hand in both of his and—

"Maybe you should go home and get some rest."

Great, now she thought he was inept. Or too grief stricken to work. But work was what got him through. "I'm not doubting the expertise. I'm pointing out that you're planning to apply for a loan from a bank that doesn't only charge late fees. This company," he used air quotes, "is vicious. They break bones."

"I'm aware." Stepping back, she folded her arms over her chest, taking away the sweet-hot contact. "We have a foster brother out there hiding from Capital X enforcers while his broken bones heal. We can end this. I'm not walking away because it's risky."

Damn it. There was plenty of room between walking away and walking right into the line of fire. "I'm not asking you to walk away. Can you tell me what precautions you're taking?"

"I'm afraid that's confidential."

This was the worst morning he could remember in a long time. He'd promised Griffin to watch out for her, and he intended to do so despite his caseload and that she wouldn't want him underfoot. One threat was already painted on her wall. He understood the desire to help; he'd go the distance for his siblings too. But he didn't want her setting herself up for more trouble.

"I'm sure you have a busy day ahead, Detective Iglesias. I do, as well." She reached for the door again. "Take care."

"Pippa, come on. Aren't you dealing with enough right now?"

"I like to stay busy," she said. "If you and Griffin are so worried about me cracking under pressure, come on back tonight and hover however you see fit. I'll be submitting the application at seven."

Clearly she didn't want him to accept. She would have to be disappointed in his diligence. "That's pretty specific."

She shrugged a shoulder. "Part of the background they've created for me," she said. Her expression softened as she studied his face. "You really don't need to worry, Detective."

"Emmanuel," he corrected. He wanted her to think of him as a friend, not the detective who'd testified against her client. "I'll see you at seven. Earlier," he said before he could change his mind. "I'll bring dinner."

Her lips parted, and he was tempted to silence her protest with a kiss. Instead, he walked out, closing the door before she could utter a word. Before he could make a fool of himself.

He wasn't buying that lie about her limited involvement in the Capital X investigation. If Griffin had believed she was only going to tap a few keys anonymously, he wouldn't have mentioned it to Emmanuel at all.

In his car, he called Griffin. "What are you thinking?" he demanded as soon as his friend answered.

"And good morning to you too. Did Pippa shoot you or something?"

"Sorry." Emmanuel pulled himself together. "And

of course not. It's been a long day, and I'm not even to the station yet."

"Pippa can do that," Griffin said with a chuckle. "She's a junkyard dog when she sets her mind on a task."

Emmanuel bristled at the unflattering description. He didn't mind her feisty side. Grit and determination were positive traits in his book, especially in the pursuit of justice. On that they were agreed, even if they had different approaches and opinions on how that should be accomplished. He was far more troubled by the way her green eyes flashed when she was mad and she nibbled her lip when she was lost in thought.

"Iglesias?"

"What?" He'd lost track of the conversation.

"I asked if she demanded you recant your testimony."

"No." Though, like her brother, he expected her to suggest it at some point. "She did convince me to take another look at the evidence."

"Seriously?"

"You heard me," Emmanuel said, resigned. "I'm almost to the station. Need to double-check the report from her break-in last night and then—"

"Is she doing all right?"

"Seems to be. Is she always so stubborn?" Emmanuel asked.

"She prefers the term *independent*, and yes. Pippa and Kiely have both been that way since the day I met them. That's why I asked you to step in."

He remembered the story about Griffin, a couple of years older than Pippa and her twin sister, being adopted into the family when he was eight.

Emmanuel drove past the station, deciding he wanted

a shower and a change of clothes before dealing with anything else this morning. "Independent or not, she's taking a hell of a risk with this plan to get a loan."

"I'm sorry you disapprove," Griffin said, his voice cool. "Again, that's why I asked for your help. She's mad at me because I insisted we take the time to work up a solid alias. She was willing to handle it under her own name."

Stubborn and cute. It was a fascinating combination. Was the fierce independence rooted in the awareness that her siblings always had her back? But that kind of stunt could've wrecked her credit, put her at risk with the Michigan bar, not to mention practically a guarantee of physical harm. Her blatant disregard for her own welfare was shocking. "Anything for family?"

"Pretty much the Colton motto."

Despite the awkwardness and inevitable pitfalls ahead, he was weirdly grateful that Griffin had involved him. "I'll keep you posted," Emmanuel said.

"One second. You can't leave me hanging," Griffin said. "How did she convince *you* to take another look at the Wentworth case?"

He couldn't tell her brother the whole truth, that he was worried for Pippa's safety. Neither could he voice his concern that the man who'd trashed her apartment would try again if she made any progress on overturning the conviction. He sure wasn't ready to admit that Pippa's fierce faith in a woman no one else liked had made him question himself.

"It's the only way to prove I'm right about Wentworth," he replied.

"Good luck, then."

"Thanks, Griffin."

Emmanuel ended the call as he pulled in to the driveway. He dashed inside, cleaned up and changed clothes in record time and, feeling like he'd hit the restart button, headed to work. Through it all, he thought about how she challenged his view of Anna Wentworth. Maybe he had been too quick to dismiss alternate suspects.

The mood was somber as word spread about Ingrid's death. All of them thought the world of her and no one could believe she was gone. It was almost a relief when he sat down at his desk and found a stack of paperwork that needed his attention.

"You okay?" Daniel asked, peering over his computer monitor. "Tough night, tough news this morning."

"I'm fine," Emmanuel lied. "Rather not talk."

Instead of cooperating, Daniel came over and dropped into the chair next to Emmanuel's desk. "I was hoping you'd have more of a glow after spending the night with the cute attorney."

If only. "Not the time," Emmanuel said, keeping his head and voice down. And not the right woman, since Pippa considered him a roadblock to her goal of freeing Anna.

He flipped open the first file on the stack. "This is the report from the break-in at the Colton condo?"

"Thought you'd want one more look before I filed it."

"Definitely. Thanks." Emmanuel read it, taking his time because he knew he was tired. "The paperwork looks good." He sat back. "Does it bother you that everything was so clean?" Other than the partial boot print, they didn't have anything to go on. "Did you get anything from the security video?"

"I haven't been through it all yet, but so far I haven't spotted him." Daniel leaned an elbow on the corner of the desk. "Do you really expect us to solve this one?" he asked. "She's trying to free a woman the city loves to hate. If she gets Wentworth released, all of your cases and all of McRath's cases will come under review. We'll need a whole new department just to deal with the attorneys and their dreams of legal glory."

So Daniel did realize that anyone on the GRPD with the right shoe size was a potential suspect. And that was in addition to everyone in town who viewed Wentworth as the wicked witch and Hicks as an "innocent" victim of her wrath.

"I'm aware."

"So how much effort are we putting in?"

"As much as it takes," Emmanuel replied. "I can't believe you'd even ask. We're the good guys, remember?"

"Does she remember?"

Emmanuel tipped his head back and stared at the ceiling. "Yes," he said, though he wasn't sure Pippa wasn't bearing her own grudge against the department at the moment. "Let's focus on the break-in." He righted himself and drummed his fingertips on the report. "That's our job."

"All right. Setting motive aside, the method doesn't match any open cases or recent complaints."

"Any other pesky trouble in the building?"

"Not so much as a stolen package," Daniel answered.

Zero crime news should be cause for a victory dance, but Emmanuel felt defeated. "That's one bored building security team."

"It's all remotely monitored off-site. They have one guy on the desk for packages and stuff, but that's it. When he's off duty, the maintenance supervisor is expected to step up."

"Have you talked to him yet?" Emmanuel asked.

"Meeting him in an hour."

"Good. Do you need help getting through the video files?"

Daniel snorted. "I've gone through everything from the building. Twice. I focused on the hours after I saw Miss Colton head out to her car. At this point, I'm wondering if it's someone in the building. Maybe Wentworth or Colton pissed off a neighbor or the condo association."

Emmanuel tried to laugh it off, but it sounded false to his own ears. "Did CSI go back to that boot print I found in the grass?"

"Sent it to them this morning. Not enough to make a mold," Daniel said.

He'd been afraid of that. "What about the message itself? I'll look for a similar MO in the files of other vandalism cases. Maybe something will match up."

"I'll see what I can find from the church cameras. Unless the man was inside, he didn't just fly away."

Emmanuel stood and walked to the break room for more coffee, Daniel right behind him. "Take a closer look at her neighbors," he suggested. "I don't trust myself to talk to anybody for a couple of hours yet, and we need to find a lead."

"All right."

"I'll review the security footage too." Tired as he was, watching the modern-day equivalent of silent movies was about the safest use of his time. "Maybe I'll catch the intruder coming in earlier in the day with one of the service crews."

"Good luck. I saw a few strays, but nothing helpful.

Most of the deliverymen came and went within minutes. What happened in her condo took some time."

Fresh eyes. On a new case and a closed one.

"Divide and conquer it is," Daniel said.

By midday Emmanuel caught his second wind, though he had yet to pinpoint which of the people entering Pippa's building could possibly be the vandal.

It was beyond frustrating. Most people weren't this good at hiding in plain sight. Especially not people angry enough to deface a wall and ransack a home. He'd almost convinced himself it must have been someone on the building maintenance staff who had gone in, done the damage and returned to work. He texted the list of names to Daniel so his partner could follow up after visiting with her neighbors. They would have to look into the backgrounds for everyone on staff in her building.

Daniel texted back immediately, confirming they were on the same page. He reported that the maintenance staff spoke well of Pippa and none showed much more than a passing curiosity about Anna Wentworth.

Though he didn't want to label the break-in unsolvable, it was lining up that way. Worse, he knew if it had been reported by anyone else, they would've filed the report and put it aside after a day's cursory investigation. With no injuries and no missing items, it wasn't a GRPD priority. Under typical circumstances, they would watch and wait for the perp to strike again and a pattern to emerge.

He couldn't set this aside and wait. Not just because he'd promised Griffin, but because his gut was telling him Pippa was in danger. When he gave his word, he kept it. That integrity was vital to him, ingrained into him and his siblings practically from birth. His parents raised them all with a strong work ethic. His mother had given her word to show up when she was scheduled to work, even when it wasn't easy. Even when her employer had no compassion.

Although Pippa wasn't as well-known as her newest client, she did have a good reputation in the area: generally viewed as a chip off her father's block in terms of the types of cases she took on…except for this one. Attorneys made enemies, just like cops did. It was part of choosing a specific side of an issue. He would definitely ask her again about her other recent cases, but he agreed that this was likely tied to Wentworth. The timing, the high profile, all of it tracked.

Who would have known she was headed to the prison?

People in her office, probably an assistant, and if she did her job properly, she would have notified the prison of her intent to visit. After only a few hours in her company, he had no doubt Pippa had done things correctly. He believed her when she'd said the forms were received and approved.

Yet they'd denied her upon arrival. That was skirting the line, especially when it came to attorney and client meetings. He didn't care for the doubt creeping in, bringing him right back to the conclusion that the best way to protect her was to remove any question of Wentworth's guilt.

If he had made an error during the case, it wouldn't be the first time a legal professional was swayed by belief more than facts. Same for her. She might claim to know Anna Wentworth better than anyone outside of the family, but he'd caught a peek of her heart on her sleeve when she'd talked about Elizabeth.

Pippa had been genuinely startled when he told her they'd looked at Elizabeth for the crime. But while working background on the victim, it had become apparent that Hicks dated a lot of women. Jealousy was a powerful motivator. Emmanuel and Joe needed to confirm Hicks hadn't been the center of a love-triangle between mother and daughter. He accessed the case file on his computer and started reading. The details came flooding back. Hicks had been found by one of the landscapers in a rose garden behind the house. Detective Joe McRath and Emmanuel had caught the case. Joe took the lead when they arrived, questioning the landscaper while Emmanuel assessed the scene.

Hicks had taken two bullets in his chest, and Emmanuel found the two casings a few yards away. No stray bullets were found. Closing his eyes, Emmanuel could see it all perfectly. The man's clothes had been mussed and his shirt wrinkled, as if someone had grabbed him during some mild altercation. No powder burns had been found on the clothing, so the killer must have fired from several yards away. They'd noticed a bruise on his face as if he'd been slapped hard. During the trial, the prosecution provided witnesses to several instances of Anna slapping people who'd offended or angered her.

A gun had been located immediately under a rose bush next to the body and later confirmed to be the murder weapon. The most incriminating evidence, one of Anna's unique sapphire brooches, had been discovered under the body by the coroner.

The photos were there organized as an attachment to

the file, but Emmanuel didn't particularly need them. He read through Joe's raw notes and his own. No one remembered hearing gunshots around the time of death. The GRPD had found the car Hicks had driven to the scene and the blackmail note addressed to Anna's husband in the glove box, but no witnesses who could put the two of them together that day.

While the grounds surrounding the Wentworth mansion were monitored, there were plenty of ways to get in and out without being too obvious, and Hicks, her lover of at least four months, would've known the gaps in the security coverage.

Wentworth had verified that Hicks had visited her more than once in that rose garden. She denied seeing him on that day, though she admitted to escorting him into the mansion through the sunroom to a guest suite where they could be alone and undisturbed on prior occasions.

He and Joe had spoken with everyone who worked at the Wentworth mansion and everyone who'd been near the mansion on the day of the murder. No one had seen Hicks or had contact with him. No one with easy access to where the body had been found had a motive to kill him. Emmanuel skimmed the original interviews with the family. Ed Wentworth had been out of town and Elizabeth had been away from the house. Neither of them had even heard a whisper about any blackmail threats.

Hicks's new girlfriend, Jenny Dawson, gave a statement that he'd gone over that day to break up with Wentworth. Again. Because Anna hadn't accepted the fact her ex-lover had broken up with her, that it was over.

Emmanuel stopped and read through that interview

transcript again. Joe had spoken with the distraught new girlfriend initially, and they'd gone back later, together. Jenny's theory was Hicks had broken up with Wentworth and she'd then shot him when he threatened to tell her husband if Anna didn't leave him alone. The girlfriend hadn't provided any evidence or tangible examples to back up her claim that Wentworth had been harassing Hicks to come back. And she claimed no knowledge of Hicks trying to blackmail Anna.

Naturally Wentworth denied all claims that she'd wanted Hicks back. She'd said he was a grifter and had dumped her when she refused to invest in some new business venture. She swore she'd never touched a gun, much less purchased the one used against Hicks. Fortunately, the prosecutor hadn't needed the new girlfriend as a witness or gun receipts during the trial. The evidence at the scene combined with other witnesses and Wentworth's snobbish outbursts had zipped the case up tight.

He couldn't see a mistake. Couldn't identify a place where he'd allowed his bias to color his decisions or his testimony. Would it have been nice to have found gunpowder residue on Wentworth's hands or her prints on the gun? Sure. But they'd found gloves similar to those the staff used in the trash in her private bathroom, and the crime lab analysis backed up everything found at the scene. It was Wentworth against the state of Michigan.

Neither public nor private opinion had come into play in any significant manner.

And still, Pippa was adamant the wrong person was doing time for the crime. If she was any other defense attorney, he might think she was posturing to sway the media, but not Griffin's sister. She'd insisted the GRPD hadn't looked for anyone else. Obviously they had, since the records were right there in the system database. He was half tempted to invite her in to look for herself, but a detective cooperating with the attorney trying to undo his work would stir up too much trouble.

It bothered him that she hadn't noticed how thorough they'd been when she'd studied the case file in the evidence room.

Pushing back from his desk, he headed downstairs. The case was recent enough that all the documentation would still be here. He'd feel better when he could confidently tell her that Wentworth was the only person with motive and access to commit the crime. Then she could drop that case and he would only have to shelter her from the less direct threat of Capital X.

Considering how that "bank" operated, it would be more than enough to keep him busy.

He signed in with the officer on duty at the evidence desk and was allowed into the cage. When he reached the shelf where the Wentworth box should have been, it wasn't there. He double-checked the case number. "Must be misfiled," he muttered to himself.

He verified that the cases boxed up before and after were in place, but there was no sign of the box he needed. A chill skated over his skin. This didn't have to mean anything suspicious. Someone had probably checked out the box, or shoved it out of place when they were looking for another case. Happened more often than anyone in the department wanted to admit. Sometimes people were just in a rush.

Like he was today. This was supposed to be quick. Over and done.

The lack of sleep made him grumpy, and he started

dragging boxes off shelves to check the contents. The Wentworth case had to be here. Feeling frantic, he stifled curse after curse when he kept finding cases unrelated to the Hicks murder. Where was it?

All the noise he was making brought young Officer Swanson from the front desk. “Detective Iglesias, do you need a hand?”

“Please,” he replied. “Bring over that ladder.”

“Sure.” Swanson complied in a hurry.

“Who’s at the desk?” he asked over the obnoxious metallic rattle as the young officer dragged the rolling staircase closer.

“No one right now,” Swanson said. “I locked the window to come check on you.”

Emmanuel stomped up the ladder to the top shelf, a sick feeling in his stomach. He could hope forever, but the Wentworth case file wasn’t up here.

“Which case are you after?” Swanson asked. “I can help.”

Ignoring him, Emmanuel moved every box on the top shelf, checking inside each one, careful with odd shaped objects and paperwork so he didn’t compound his current problems. “No, thanks.” He would not say the case name aloud. “There’s nothing matching the case number I need. It’s not here.”

From the floor, Swanson gazed up at him earnestly, like a puppy eager to please the big dogs. “Let me run it and see who checked it out,” he offered.

Emmanuel bought himself a minute to think while he descended the rolling stairs and pushed them back out of the way. “I guess that’s the smartest next step.” Though he did *not* want anyone knowing he was looking at this. The rumors alone would be problematic, especially after he responded to the call at Pippa's condo last night. He took his time, making sure every box was in the right place. Little comfort when the effort only made the absence of the Wentworth case more obvious.

"Wow, thanks," Swanson said. "I really appreciate that, Detective. You must have worked down here."

Emmanuel had never had this job, but he believed keeping things organized helped everyone. "Are you calling the GRPD a bunch of slobs?" he joked.

Swanson cleared his throat. "Well, coming back and straightening up is part of the routine."

He clapped the kid on the shoulder. "I'll try to remind everyone to do better," Emmanuel said as they walked back to the front of the secure area. He slid the paper with the case number on it across the counter. "Can you let me know who checked out this file?"

Swanson entered the case number into his computer, and they waited for the system to respond. With a little luck, the kid didn't follow gossip columns or the upper echelon of Grand Rapids society.

Luck was not on Emmanuel's side today. The kid gave a low whistle and shot Emmanuel a look. "Wentworth?"

"That's the one." He was paging through the log of recent visitors. Any officer or visitor had to sign in with their name and badge number, and the visit was entered into the computer system, as well.

Swanson studied his computer screen, a frown tugging the corners of his mouth. He typed something else and then used the mouse, scrolling up and down. What Emmanuel wouldn't have given to see what had upset him.

"What's the matter, Swanson?"

"No one has checked out the box, Detective. It should be there." His fingers pounded the keys again. The poor kid looked like he might burst into tears. "I don't have any record of it being signed out."

"Do you recall anyone asking about Wentworth besides me?"

"No, sir."

Pippa implied she'd been here. "I thought I heard something about her new attorney stopping by." Had she lied to him?

"Well, yes," Swanson said. "Her new attorney called and set up an appointment. She came in ten days ago."

The sign-in log in front of Emmanuel went back only seven days. He pulled out his phone and opened the app he used to take notes. "What day?" he asked. "Were you here?"

"Yes, sir," Swanson confirmed. "She was very polite."

No doubt. He suspected Pippa could turn on the charm when it suited her purposes. Not that he blamed her. He did the same thing at times.

"I carried the case file to the back table for her," Swanson said. "She was here for hours."

"Do you have the sign-out time?" Emmanuel made another note of the kid's answer. "Did you put the box back or did she take it?"

"I don't know. She was still here when the shift changed and Officer Mitchell replaced me." Swanson tapped a pen rapidly on the counter. "He would've put the box back for her."

"Anything else?"

"No." That pen kept tapping. "I don't have any requisitions for the file or notes. This is bizarre."

"Agreed." Emmanuel sighed heavily, thinking of Pippa's floor safe. She'd never opened it in front of him. Because she didn't want him to know she'd taken the evidence box without permission? Would she have pushed the line that way? If someone believed she had the documentation on the Wentworth case that would explain the break-in and search.

But not the message. It was a rare burglar who came armed with spray paint, just in case he needed to leave a threatening message.

He jerked his thumb toward the security camera over the door. "How far back do we keep surveillance footage?"

Swanson shrugged. "I'm sorry, Detective. I don't know."

The feed was monitored by someone. If his lieutenant didn't know, the captain would. Or one of their administrative assistants. "Thanks for your help," Emmanuel said. "I'll take it from here. I'm sure there's a logical explanation."

"Any suggestions on how I should write this up?" Swanson asked.

"I'm guessing there's a form." The kid nodded. "Just fill it in to the best of your ability," Emmanuel continued. "It'll work out. Most likely we're dealing with a clerical error. No one likes to admit it, but we all know those happen."

"Am I in trouble?" Swanson wondered.

"Not from where I'm standing. Just fill out the form."

Fired up, Emmanuel went straight to Lieutenant Tripp McKellar's office to get a look at the security footage. If Pippa had walked out of this station with the Wentworth case file, he was going to lose his mind. His thoughts ticked back and forth like a metronome, sure she hadn't been so foolish and certain she'd taken the risk to save her client.

Then again, if she *had* taken that risk and the box had since been removed from her possession, he couldn't imagine her waiting it out in her condo last night. She would've leaped into action of some kind. Unless she'd had the box in the car—the one place no one had checked.

At the lieutenant's open office door, Emmanuel knocked. "A minute, sir?"

McKellar waved him in. The lieutenant was a rising star in the department who'd earned the trust of the officers he supervised. When Ingrid had met him, she'd told Emmanuel that McKellar had promise and a good character.

"What's on your mind, Iglesias?"

"I was doing some research and just found out an evidence box is missing from storage."

The lieutenant's eyebrows lifted. "Not misfiled?"

"No, sir. We've searched top to bottom," Emmanuel said. "It's possible the box was removed by the last person who accessed it. Any chance you have access to the footage from that camera over the door?"

McKellar scowled. "Can you narrow that down with a date?"

"Yes, sir." He gave the date of Pippa's visit and the time Swanson's shift ended.

"Let's take a look." McKellar invited him to watch the monitor over his shoulder.

When the footage for the right day came up, Emmanuel caught a high-speed view of Pippa signing in. Just as the young officer had said, she stayed for hours and the shift changed. When she exited the room, she had only the briefcase she'd brought in.

Emmanuel hadn't realized he'd been holding his breath until it all came out in a whoosh of relief. Why did he care so damn much if she was guilty or innocent?

"See something helpful?" the lieutenant asked, pausing the video with Pippa frozen at the door.

"Yes and no," Emmanuel replied. If Pippa hadn't taken the file, then who? And when?

"That's Sadie Colton's older sister, right?" McKellar asked.

"One of them, yes."

"Right. Graham Colton had four daughters." He didn't sound entirely thrilled by the fact. "Hope she found whatever she was looking for. I'm not entirely comfortable with having Colton Investigations so involved with the Capital X and RevitaYou situations."

Emmanuel agreed wholeheartedly. "I would've thought you'd have a bigger problem with her trying to find something to reverse the Wentworth verdict."

McKellar laughed. "Let her dig. We all know that case is airtight."

It helped to hear it from his lieutenant. "Thanks for the assist," Emmanuel said on his way out of the door.

Relieved in one aspect, he was still twisted up over too many other unknowns. If Pippa hadn't taken that file to support her efforts to overturn Wentworth's conviction, who had?

He kept running into the same dead-end conclusion. With the evidence box missing, the break-in and search at Pippa's condo, and her inexplicable trouble at the prison, the culprit was likely tied to the GRPD.

He would need to find a way to keep reviewing the video footage.

His stomach cramped, and the discomfort had nothing to do with being overtired, grief stricken or hungry. Someone in this building—or at least someone with access to it—was determined to keep the truth under wraps. He checked his phone for any word from Daniel that might be better news.

Nothing.

Did he dare tell Pippa and fuel a hunch she was surely entertaining? The woman was too smart not to think her client had been set up by someone on the force. Might be better to do more digging first. Notions wouldn't free her client, only facts. He smothered an oath, thinking about her reaction if she ever learned he'd kept this to himself.

"Trouble, Iglesias?" Joe McRath asked, pausing as he walked through the bullpen. "You look like hell."

"Ingrid," he said. He couldn't tell Joe what had him really upset. Emmanuel wasn't in the mood for a lecture on career longevity right now. The sergeant believed that working a case, solving it and moving on was the best way to avoid burnout. Only the cold cases were worth dwelling on in Joe's opinion.

"We're all gonna miss her." Joe swiped a hand over his eyes. "Heard anything about the service or final arrangements?"

"Not yet." Thanks to the RevitaYou connection, he wasn't even sure when the body would be released for burial.

"Go on home, Iglesias. Get some rest."

Not a bad idea. "Is that an official order, Sergeant?"

Joe smiled. "It is."

"Thanks."

Emmanuel grabbed his cell phone and headed out, but his mind kept stewing over the real problem. If someone on the force was interfering with Pippa's review of the Wentworth case now, it was a short hop to assume that same someone framed Wentworth at the time and he and Joe had overlooked someone who hated Hicks that much.

Furious that he might have been duped then and was being sent on a merry chase now, he sat in his car and sent Pippa a text message. He didn't dare talk about any details over the phone. Not this close to the station.

In a few hours, he'd be face to face with her and they could talk candidly. Or argue. He smiled despite the hellish day. The simmer in his veins whenever he thought of Pippa was an unexpected bright spot in this twisted mess. While he wasn't looking forward to explaining what he'd found, he was definitely eager to see her.

Chapter 7

After Pippa met with her insurance adjuster, assured the claim would be paid in a timely manner, she'd deliberately turned her back on the violent message scrawled across her living room wall. The morning hours ticked by as she resumed her work on Anna's case.

Around noon, when her suspect list was as weak as it had been yesterday, she reached for her coffee cup and found it empty. She stood up to stretch a bit and give her eyes a rest, debating whether or not to have one more cup of coffee. Probably better to switch to water and a healthy snack.

With an apple in hand, she walked out to stare down that message on her wall. "We all end up dead," she said aloud. "Personally I'd rather go out knowing I did something right."

In the meantime, it might be better to stop talking to walls.

It still annoyed her that one of her favorite framed prints would have to be redone. She returned to her desk and flipped to her calendar, reviewing her schedule for the rest of the week. After tonight's appointment with the Capital X loan application, she didn't have any set appointments. As some point she needed to get back to the prison and have a face-to-face with her newest client.

Excitement simmered through her system whenever she thought about what she was going to do tonight. Her part in helping Brody—and who knew how many others—might be small, but it was crucial. Griffin and Riley had wanted to shut down the unscrupulous loan operation for a long time.

Though she tried, she couldn't suppress a thrill of anticipation that she would see Emmanuel again tonight too. But that was hours away.

She answered several emails and dictated a few more notes about how to approach the witnesses tied to Anna's case before the cleaning crew arrived at the back door. Just like this morning, opening the door took more effort than it ever had in the past. She couldn't stand being afraid. Though it hadn't even been a full day, she wondered how when she would feel like herself again.

Craig and Rachel Norris were a brother-and-sister team and equal partners in their small business that specialized in cleaning and restoration. "When we saw the pictures, we thought we'd better handle this one ourselves," Craig said when introductions were made.

"This is a great building," Rachel added.

The pair put Pippa at ease immediately, and she caught herself smiling as she led them into the living room.

"Wow," Craig said. The siblings exchanged a long look.

"This is going to look worse before it gets better," Rachel warned Pippa.

"I understand it's a process," Pippa said.

"All right." Craig cocked his head as he studied the wall. "Might be faster to cut out the drywall and start over."

"He's kidding," Rachel assured her with a confident smile. "We'll take care of it and make it as good as new."

"Thanks." She wondered if even with a clean slate she'd ever *not* see those words.

Her phone rang as they started unpacking their supplies. Seeing Elizabeth's number, she picked it up right away. "Good morning," Pippa said brightly. "I'm sorry I couldn't get back with you last night. Things got a little hectic once I got home."

"What's that noise?" Elizabeth asked.

Pippa moved away from the cleaning efforts, but regardless of their friendly, bonded and insured status, she wasn't willing to leave them unattended. At the moment she didn't trust anyone outside of family. And Griffin was on thin ice for planting Emmanuel in her life.

"Nothing to worry about. I'm just having some professional cleaning done."

"Really? Your place is always so perfect. Well, I just wanted to let you know I'm going out to see Mom this afternoon."

"Good," Pippa said. "Be careful, Elizabeth." She hoped they wouldn't change the routine and give Elizabeth trouble now too.

"Is there anything you want me to tell her?"

"Officially, no." Elizabeth's conversations with Anna wouldn't be legally protected. "Just let her know I'm sorting things out. If she's had an epiphany about who might have wanted to kill Hicks, that would be great, but otherwise, just enjoy your visit."

"All right. I was going to let her know you had trouble getting through yesterday, if that won't cause any problems."

"Please tell her about that," Pippa said. "I'm hoping to have an explanation before the next time I go out." That task had topped her to-do list today, but so far her calls to the warden and the prosecutor's office asking for clarification had not been returned.

None of that would comfort Elizabeth, and any extra burden on her mind would make her visit with her mother more of a challenge. "You can also tell her I'm requesting another look at all the physical evidence in the case."

"I thought you'd done that," Elizabeth said.

"I've been through the reports and transcripts and I've taken pictures of the evidence, but I want to see it firsthand again." She wasn't ready to share her concern that she'd overlooked something. Last night Emmanuel had been surprised that she hadn't seen any record of the interviews he'd conducted with persons of interest, and that bothered her.

"Drive safe," she said. "And please let me know how your mom's doing." With just over two weeks in prison, Anna would either be adjusting or melting down.

"I promise," Elizabeth said, ending the call with another thank you.

Pippa wished she'd done something to earn her friend's gratitude. So far this case seemed to be one high brick wall she kept slamming up against. There had to be a way over, around or through because Anna was innocent.

Curious, Pippa made the mistake of peeking into the front room. She couldn't stifle her subsequent groan of dismay. The wall was definitely worse. An ugly, wet mess of grayish-red. She snapped a picture with her phone, not even sure why it mattered to have documentation of the cleanup process. This wasn't something she planned to share on social media.

She returned to her work, doing her best to stay focused, but the smell of solvents soon got the best of her. Craig and Rachel had set up a big fan and an air purifier, but she cracked the window to bring in some fresh and crisp autumn air. Maybe she should just go to the office, but it made her ridiculously uncomfortable to have strangers alone in her house after last night. She grabbed her favorite sweatshirt and was pulling it over her head when her phone chimed with an incoming text.

It took her a second to realize the number was Emmanuel's. He was reaching out already? Maybe he'd come to his senses and was canceling his plans to join her tonight. She was an adult and she didn't need supervision to fill out an online form, no matter what her brother believed.

Just because Griffin trusted Emmanuel didn't mean she had to. Although…no, that was her sexy dreams talking. He'd been nice last night, but one good deed didn't change the role he'd played in Anna's conviction.

She scolded herself for demonstrating the same kind of bias she'd accused him of applying to the Wentworth investigation. So the man rubbed her the wrong way; that wasn't the end of the world. She'd learned that it was impractical and impossible to get along well with everyone. There were days she didn't even get along with her twin sister. And none of them thought much of Sadie's fiancé.

While she didn't appreciate that it was primarily his testimony that sent Anna to jail, she'd found no indication that he'd done anything inappropriate or incorrect as he worked the case. Plus, Griffin had excellent instincts about people. Whether or not she liked the detective, she would find a way to deal with him politely. The first step was probably not to think the worst or turn surly at the sight of his name.

Bracing herself to be a mature professional rather than a snarky little sister, she opened the app and read his text.

Digging on this end.

Suggest you look for connections to top players within the GRPD.

She stared at the message, reading the brief lines over and over. Was he kidding? He hadn't struck her as the type of man to have much sense of humor about Anna Wentworth. Which left her with the obvious conclusion that he was serious. What had he found?

She deleted the text message. He hadn't recommended it, but it seemed like the practical move in light of the crap she'd dealt with yesterday. Anyone in the GRPD would likely have ties within the prison system. But ties high enough to prevent an attorney-client meeting? That was a serious problem.

Phone in hand, she paced the hallway, thinking. Yesterday he was thoroughly convinced of Anna's guilt and the department's faithful execution of the investigation.

Today he was telling her to take a look with an eye for new suspects in his own police force?

She couldn't ignore it, and honestly it had occurred to her. Going in guns blazing without any proof would only backfire, hurting her, her client and her family. Colton Investigations currently enjoyed a strong partnership and mutual respect with the police department, so she'd been tiptoeing around that research. And at first glance, the case was so cut-and-dried that the number of people who could affect the outcome was limited.

With a clear direction in mind, she sat down and opened the file, printing out a list by hand of every name connected to the case, from the 911 operator who took the call to the responding officers, Detectives Iglesias and McRath, and everyone who touched the scene in some way or another.

Sitting back, she smiled. Detective Iglesias was now on her official interview list. Maybe it was immature, but it amused her greatly to think of the roles being reversed on Anna's behalf. It also forced her to consider how he and McRath would have built their own list in search of witnesses and suspects in the case.

They'd interviewed Ed, which made sense. The husband was always a top suspect in such a case. And they'd interviewed Elizabeth, covering every angle. Pippa was determined to be even more thorough. Anna was in jail, in part, because the real killer had not had an obvious motive or connection to Hicks.

Next, she segmented the list based on duration of the person's involvement. That would make it easier to clear people. And she repeated the process based on their possible connection or opinion of Anna Wentworth. As she'd learned from her siblings, working a case properly meant considering everyone as suspect, even the most unlikely.

Craig called her over before she could start eliminating anyone. "How does this look to you?" he asked. Beside him his sister smiled as she turned on an industrial fan to help dry things out.

It looked like the most beautiful blank wall she'd ever seen. The wall needed primer and paint, but the ugly message was completely gone. "That's a vast improvement," she said. "Thank you."

"Are we painting this for you?" He reached for his clipboard with her service order. "Once it's dry, that is."

"I elected to handle the repainting once it was clean," she said. "I'm considering changing things up with a feature wall rather than just a coat of paint."

Rachel studied the wall, turning a little to take in the entire space. "Can I make a suggestion?" At Pippa's nod, she continued. "You wouldn't want to go too rustic, but you could do something natural that still marries modern and homey. Bamboo would work well, and beadboard could be interesting too."

Pippa tried to envision her suggestions. "I always think of beadboard in country kitchens or revamped attics converted to bedrooms or sweet nurseries."

"Him too," Rachel replied, elbowing her brother. "It has more uses, I promise." She handed Pippa a business card, pointing out the link to her design pages on a social media platform. "I have several idea boards that might spark things for you."

"She wants paint," Craig said. He tilted his head at his sister. "She wants to be a designer," he explained.

"I *am* a designer," Rachel countered with a grin. "He

gets grumpy because at some point he's going to have to find another partner to put up with him."

Pippa understood all too well the push and pull of siblings. She tapped the card. "I'll take a look."

"Whatever you decide," Craig interjected, "you'll need to wait twenty-four hours for everything to dry completely. We'll pick up the fan and dehumidifier tomorrow evening."

"Great. Thanks again."

She closed the door behind them as they left. Huddling into her sweatshirt, she realized the droning sound of the equipment was going to make it a long night. Why did people appreciate white noise? Again, she could escape to her brother's place, but she didn't want to send the message to whoever had done this that she couldn't hack it when things got tough.

The restored wall and clean carpets, free of every bit of glass and debris, filled her with a sense of peace. It was almost like moving in again. A blank slate full of potential. She pulled up Rachel's website and the social media idea board.

"Wow." The woman had good ideas, and although the beadboard pictures still struck too close to paneling for her taste, she saw the design merit. Distracted, she scrolled through several other idea boards on the page. Maybe she did want something more dynamic than paint after all.

She was hip deep in bamboo options, of varying colors, textures and layouts, when a text message from Kiely came through. Her twin and Riley would arrive at her place within five minutes, just as they'd planned. Pippa was glad she'd scheduled the cleaning crew when she had. Her siblings didn't need to worry about her, especially when the trouble had nothing to do with a CI case.

As she'd done with each of her previous visitors today, she felt the nerves building, and she waited until her sister and brother were right outside her door before she unlocked it. In the past she would've left the door unlocked or even slightly ajar. After the break-in that seemed foolish. More risk than necessary.

When Riley and Kiely entered, their gazes immediately went to the clean, bare wall and the drying equipment.

"He tagged the whole thing?"

"He did." Pippa tucked her hands into the long sleeves of her sweatshirt.

Riley turned, hot anger blazing in his eyes. Then his expression softened as he pulled her into a tight hug.

Kiely set the bag she was carrying on the floor and nudged them apart. She held up a boxy device and, with a look, asked for Pippa's permission to sweep the condo for listening devices.

Her stomach cramped as she gave a nod. Why hadn't she considered that earlier? She hoped she hadn't said anything during her chat with Elizabeth that would come back to bite her later. Riley chatted with her about the plans for the new wall until Kiely gave the all clear. "No bugs," she announced.

Pippa released a breath in a rush. "Thank goodness. Unless the police have found something more, the intruder somehow evaded the cameras around the building and in the hallways."

"Someone who knows security systems," Kiely mused.

"Still a pretty big suspect pool," Pippa said, thinking of the list she'd made. "We have one partial boot print near the back door, so I'm sure we'll narrow it down."

Riley deliberately moved toward her office. "Nothing was taken?"

"You know I'm careful," Pippa said.

"I need coffee." Kiely handed Pippa a bag from a nearby electronics store. "Go on and start with that."

Pippa looked into the bag and saw a new laptop. Taking the box out of the bag, she started to unpack the device. "How long do I have to wait to find out who you've turned me into?"

"Not you," Riley said. "We're not *Mission Impossible* with the masks here."

"Much to your dismay I'm sure," Pippa teased. "This is exciting." She plugged in the laptop and followed the prompts for the initial setup.

When Kiely had her coffee, the three of them gathered around the desk. At the point where the computer wanted personal information, Riley opened up an envelope. She was surprised to see what looked like a very real ID and a credit card. "Excellent work," she said, as she carefully entered the details for the persona CI had created for this fake Capital X loan application. "Did you make a passport too?"

"Not quite enough time to pull that off the right way," Riley said. "The loan application doesn't ask for that anyway. You need to remember her schedule. With the background we worked up, it would be out of character for her to do a loan application during business hours.

"We gave your alias a comprehensive employment history and banking records and one not-so-successful independent business, along with a shopping history on that credit card."

Pippa made mental notes as Riley talked, but it helped to know Kiely would have this all written out for her, as well. When she finished, Riley tucked the credit card into the envelope she would keep for reference. "The laptop was purchased with that card, and you should probably make one or two more purchases in person or online this afternoon."

"Maybe dinner," Kiely suggested. "Something special for two?"

Pippa did *not* appreciate the glint in her twin's eyes. Or the way her words brought back the inappropriate dream from this morning.

Riley, who had been relaxed in the chair beside her, sat up straight, his gaze locked onto Pippa. "What's she talking about?"

"Nothing," Pippa said.

"Nothing with serious potential." Kiely held up her hands when Pippa glared. "Okay, okay. Harmless teasing, sis. But that look on your face tells me I'm on the right track."

Pippa denied it. "You've jumped the track and crashed in a glorious blaze." There were times when having an excellent private investigator as a twin was a curse.

"One of you better start talking to me," their brother demanded.

The twins turned on him. "You do know we're adults?" Pippa queried.

"Yes, I noticed. For the record that only makes brothers worry more."

"That is the dumbest non-rule," Kiely protested.

"Too bad." He folded his arms and returned his attention to Pippa. "Is she talking about Iglesias?"

"She is," Pippa said immediately. A denial would only mean a more intense interrogation. "Ridiculous, really. We met last night for the first time. I'm sure he's seeing someone." A flicker in Riley's eyes alerted her to the misstep. She dragged her thoughts back into line. "We're on opposite sides of a critical case for my friend and my career." She continued ticking off each relevant point on her fingers. "And while I appreciated his help cleaning up—"

"He helped you clean up?" Kiely's eyebrows jumped up and down.

"I don't need his supervision or whatever Griffin asked him to do," she finished.

"Griffin disagrees on that," Riley said softly.

It was a challenge to argue with Riley whenever he did that quiet-voice strategy. "I do know Capital X is dangerous." She pointed to all of the precautions they were taking. "It's obvious we're doing everything the smart way."

"Pippa, I know this feels anonymous," Kiely said. "And it is. To a point. There shouldn't be any possible way to connect you to the application you'll put in tonight. But a little backup never hurt anyone."

"Is there some new detail you're not telling me?" she asked. "I'm not fragile, and you both know I won't back out."

"Of course you won't," Riley said. "That's why we're all so concerned about the break-in."

Her sister rested her hands on Pippa's knees. "I'm not sure you're concerned enough."

"Trust me, I was upset," Pippa said. She clamped down on the admission lodged in her throat. They didn't need to know how wary she was about answering her door. That would pass. "It was creepy to know someone had been in here long enough to trash the place and…"

Her voice trailed off as she stared at the fresh, clean wall. "And try to intimidate me," she finished, resisting the urge to rub the chill from her arms.

"You should come stay with us for a few days," Riley said. "At least until we get some movement on the loan application."

"No." She shook her head. "Thank you, but I need to stay put."

Riley swore.

"There's more to life than reputation, sis," Kiely said.

"I'm aware." Though she hadn't indulged in much of that life lately. "Beyond reputation, it's a matter of principle. I've never been afraid to take controversial cases."

"Right," Riley agreed. "But the cases you take on are rarely as high-profile as Wentworth. I think serial killers get more love than that woman."

"Pleasant or not, I won't leave an innocent woman in jail for a crime she didn't commit. This break-in won't put me off the case, no matter what the vandal intended. All of this protectiveness is appreciated but unnecessary."

Her brother and sister exchanged a look. "Is that code for get the hell out of your way?" Riley asked.

"It's probably more like code for I'm tired," she admitted with a smile. What was the use of having family if you didn't lean on them in problematic times? "I'm not trying to be obstinate. I'm trying to stay focused on what I can control."

"That's our Pippa," Riley said, hugging her again. "You're all right to keep working here today?"

"Pretty much. Some of my framed art was damaged, so I'll run that over to the frame shop for repairs." She tilted her head toward the drying equipment. "Looking forward to getting out for a bit. That fan is not my friend."

Riley was glaring at the wall again. "Sadie sent us pictures the police took last night."

"Somehow I doubt a common criminal also knows how to evade all the security precautions in and around the building," Kiely said.

Pippa agreed with her. "If we could get back to why we're really here? I'll log in at seven and fill out the application. Any trip wires I should be aware of?"

"We haven't found anything like that. Only that Capital X likely does a personal check on the applicants." Kylie walked her through the day-to-day patterns for Alison Carrington, an administrative assistant for a fake insurance company, per the alias they'd created.

"We're going to save lives," Pippa said as anticipation strummed through her bloodstream.

"We'll definitely save people the pain of broken bones," Riley agreed.

"Have you heard anything about Brody?"

Kiely frowned. "My last lead fizzled out. He's running scared. Until he makes a mistake or wants to be found, I'm afraid we're going to keep chasing our tails."

"I'll let you know if he sends me another text message," Pippa said. The idea of Brody out there alone, trying to stay one step ahead of violent enforcers, made her sad. In instances like this she took it for granted how lucky she was to have the support of her brothers and sisters.

"It won't be a problem once we shut down Capital X," Riley said.

"Count on me," Pippa said. "I need to get over to the frame shop for these repairs." Her siblings helped her carry the pieces down to her car, and they parted ways there after she promised to be cautious. She tuned the radio to a station with classical music. As she drove out of the parking lot, she noted the unmarked car across the street, and when she reached the frame shop, she sent Emmanuel a text message about her errands and expected return time. Assuming she didn't meet any traffic delays, she would have time to do some more digging into that new list of names before he arrived to watch her enter the loan application.

Overkill. Then again, Brody was in hiding and Griffin had another friend who'd been burned by Capital X. Enforcers had broken two of Brody's fingers. It was possible the woman playing the role of Alison could be hurt. Pippa could very well be at risk for retaliation too if Capital X discovered she'd duped them.

She had to focus on the positive, the potential to break open the loan shark operation so Brody could come home. The earlier excitement returned while she considered the big leap forward her efforts would make in a few hours. Nothing made her happier than doing the right thing and making a difference in the process.

Emmanuel pulled up, pleased to find an open parking space on the street in front of Pippa's condo. Hopefully he wouldn't need to spend the night out here again, but just in case, this gave him a great vantage point. He slipped his cell phone into his pocket and then reached for the grocery bag and the bakery box from the front seat. He'd offered to bring dinner, but she'd told him she had that under control, so he'd selected one of his favorite desserts.

With his car locked, he walked over and checked

in with the teams in the unmarked cars also on duty. Knowing Pippa's plan for the evening, he'd asked Lieutenant McKellar for a second unit on her place, a little surprised by the immediate agreement. Apparently it had been a quiet day. No one sketchy lurking around the building, and everyone who had gone inside as part of a service crew had a legitimate tie to their company. Maybe it was over-the-top, but his gut wouldn't let him back down.

In the building lobby, he pressed the call button, though he'd looked up the emergency access code provided to the police. Pippa buzzed him through the interior door, and he took the stairs instead of the elevator, wanting another casual look at how an intruder might still bypass every basic precaution in the building.

From the hallway in front of her door, he heard the drone of a fan and wondered how the cleanup and repairs had gone today. She hadn't mentioned any of that in her two texts. She hadn't responded directly to his first message. Probably smart, all things considered. He'd only received the two texts about running errands and dinner. Technically, she didn't owe him anything, and she had plenty of siblings in the immediate area, but it would've been nice to be kept in the loop anyway. Especially after he'd taken such a big chance solely on her hunch today.

That wasn't fair. It was his hunch, too, along with his persistent integrity that had forced him to search the evidence room.

His heart gave a kick in his chest when she opened the door. She was dressed simply in a white top and trim pants, with heels that put her in easy range of a kiss. If only this was a different kind of dinner. Her hair was down, and at the open collar of her shirt, a turquoise pendant in a silver setting drew his attention. The woman was giving him a fever.

He held up the bakery box between them. "Peace offering," he managed.

"What is it?" Her nose twitched as she accepted the box. She stepped back so he could walk in.

"I guess you'll have to wait until after dinner to find out," he teased, closing the door behind him and turning the dead bolt. To his astonishment she faked a little pout. It was dangerously sexy.

"Dinner is a simple stew," she said. "I hope you don't mind."

Something smelled delicious, and the equipment drying out the repaired wall pushed the aroma throughout her condo. "Wow," he said, taking in the expanse of clean wall. "They did a good job. And fast. You sure didn't waste much time."

"No one did," she said. "It was a long day, and the fan is getting on my nerves. I'm focusing on how delighted I am that the message is gone."

"I bet."

She stopped at the kitchen counter, her fingertips tracing the string tie on the box. "Don't tell me you're a white-noise type of person."

"Not a bit. Would you rather take this somewhere else?" His apartment was available. And far more disconnected from the Colton Investigations case than anywhere else in the city. No one would expect the new Wentworth lawyer to hang out with him.

She clearly wanted a peek at what he'd brought, but she deliberately averted her gaze. He admired that kind of discipline and couldn't help wondering what it would take to break it. In a good way of course.

Straightening her shoulders, she flicked a hand toward the stove. "Beef stew," she said. Her teeth sunk into her lower lip. "I'm having a really hard time not jumping all over you."

The admission caught him off guard, and he floundered for an answer, wondering what she expected. He wouldn't mind being jumped by Pippa.

"About the case," she clarified. "I know you couldn't tell me more via text earlier, but why should I be looking into any GRPD connections?"

He smothered the sudden disappointment that her thoughts hadn't matched up with his. This was the moment of truth. Sharing what he hadn't found in the evidence room could change everything. Correction: it *would* change everything. He'd wrestled with this moment all day. It wasn't exactly his job to tell her the evidence was gone. He had active cases that should trump her effort to undo solid police work. But treating her like the enemy wasn't working for him. If he'd ignored it, he wouldn't be able to look himself in the mirror. "There is no reason for what I'm about to say to become public knowledge. In fact, you can't tell anyone yet. Do you understand?"

"I know how to be discreet." She folded her arms over her chest. "And I can keep secrets locked down tight when it helps my client."

"This will help your client," he muttered. "I don't suppose you have a beer?"

"Once we're officially off duty," she said.

"I clocked out," he said. "Besides, aren't we officially having dinner?"

"Dinner before tackling a CI assignment," she reminded him.

"I happen to know Griffin has a beer, even when he's on an active investigation for CI."

"Fine." He must've passed some test. She went to the refrigerator and pulled out a beer. Before she handed it over, she said, "Tell me why you sent that message."

"Because the evidence box for your case is gone. Missing."

She was speechless and pretty adorable, her mouth hanging open in pure shock. He had a serious soft spot when it came to Pippa Colton.

"Who signed it out?"

He used the bottle opener she handed him and popped the top off the beer bottle. "No idea. That's the problem. Your name is actually the last one tied to the case, per the logs. I know you don't have it," he hurried to add when she started to protest. "I searched all over for the box and the contents. Nothing has been misfiled or shoved into the wrong box. Everyone who's been in and out of the evidence room since your visit is accounted for."

She sat down on the counter stool, her gaze drifting back to the wall that had been vandalized yesterday and was clean today, if drab and plain. "So how did the box go missing?" She turned to him, her eyes intent as she sorted through what he'd said. "I can see how the contents might be smuggled out, but the whole box?"

"Right?" He shook his head, feeling as if he'd let her down. Ridiculous, but true. "I can't see anyone outside the GRPD managing it."

She pursed her lips. "I'd have to agree."

He waited for her to shout at him that this proved

Anna Wentworth had been set up, but Pippa only sat there, her brow furrowed in contemplation. What was going through her mind? Did she suspect he was feeding her a line to impede her progress?

"That's it? You're not going to gloat or taunt me about the missing evidence box?" He'd expected…well, he didn't know what he'd expected. Definitely not easy acceptance.

"Did you take it?" she asked.

"Hell, no. I don't have anything to hide."

"Then why waste my breath shouting at you?" She shrugged. "Obviously, the disappearing evidence is a compelling problem. I'll work from what her defense team had during the trial and what I can glean from the notes I took before the box went missing. I will overturn that conviction."

And he would help her, whether she wanted him on board or not. He'd spent the majority of his day doing just that already. "What happened with your art?" he asked, changing the subject awkwardly. "I assume that was the errand you ran this afternoon. Was anything damaged beyond repair?"

"No, it will just take time to clean." She smiled up at him. "Thanks for asking. The framing shop thinks they can have the pieces cleaned and reframed and the glass replaced within a week. The cleaning crew told me I could repaint and redecorate as soon as everything dried out." She rubbed her temples. "Theory is, the fan will be gone by tomorrow night." She checked the clock. "You must be hungry."

She moved through her kitchen in the same way she did everything else, with an economy of movement that was streamlined and graceful and with a sense of purpose. Tonight she didn't seem to be braced for battle as she'd been when he'd shown up last night.

Filling two bowls with stew, she brought them over to the counter and then set a basket of thick slices of brown bread between them. She poured water for both of them and a glass of wine for herself.

The stew was a flavorful blend of savory beef, red potatoes, onion, carrots and celery. The aroma was amazing, and a spicy kick of heat surprised him. "This is delicious, thank you."

"My pleasure." She eyed him over her wine glass. "You sound surprised."

Another opportunity to prove his integrity. "I didn't expect you to cook. Not for me."

She pointed at him with her fork. "I'm going to play nice and not take any offense at that."

"Because I brought you something from the bakery?"

"Maybe a little," she confessed, amusement dancing in her green eyes. "Really, it's because my parents held us to a high standard of hospitality. On top of that, you brought me information that can change everything about how I work Anna's case." She took another bite of stew, chewing slowly.

Why did he find her every move appealing? He focused on the food, hearty and warm and comforting.

"I'm sure it's occurred to you that you've become a person of interest." She broke a piece of bread in two and dipped it into the sauce.

"It crossed my mind," he said. Unfortunately it was chased by the thought that he'd rather earn her interest on a personal level. Based on his role in the Wentworth conviction, that was likely just a pipe dream. "I had to be on your list even before I told you about the missing evidence box."

"Yes, but you were at the bottom of the list."

"Why?"

Being at the bottom of her list felt like a personal attack, though he knew she was speaking of the case. The chemistry he sensed between them was apparently one-sided, and it would be better if he could ignore that slow simmer in his bloodstream. He was eight years older than her, so maybe "seasoned detective" wasn't her type.

He'd seen formal pictures and candid snapshots of the Colton siblings during his visits to Griffin's place and the office located in their family home. It always seemed as if Pippa, a notorious workaholic, vacationed with equal focus and intensity by choosing hiking or sailing or otherwise off-the-beaten-path adventures with friends like Elizabeth Wentworth. "I felt too strongly about you," she said.

He smothered another flicker of that persistent attraction.

"In court, you were too sure of what you'd found," she was saying. "I didn't want to talk with you until I had a better handle on who you were as a detective and a man."

"You were going to ask Griffin about me," he said, seeing the truth in her eyes. "To find an angle."

"Yes." Her chin came up, unapologetic. "But then he declared that you were going to be my bodyguard, and I was too irritated with both of you."

"So when will the interrogation begin in earnest?" he asked, taking a second slice of bread. The stew was good enough that he wanted seconds, but his stomach was too jittery over what they might uncover as they discussed the Wentworth case.

"I'd really like to hear your thoughts on the evidence you found." She pushed her fork around her bowl and then set it aside. "I've read the report and listened to your testimony in court, and I'd like you to walk me through that whole mess again, but not tonight."

"What do you want from me tonight?" His body had an opinion and Griffin wanted him to stick close, but Emmanuel was more interested in her wants and opinions.

"Other than whatever you brought from the bakery, I'd like you to help me eliminate a few names from the long list of GRPD personnel tied to Anna's case."

He checked his watch. "We have a few minutes before you're scheduled to start that loan application, right?" He was pleased he kept his opinion on that to himself.

She nodded as she gathered up their dishes and rinsed them at the sink. He followed her, loading the items into the dishwasher. "Thanks."

He thought they'd move into her office, but she retrieved her laptop and a manila folder with notes from her case file. With everything in place, she changed seats so they were side-by-side. "After your text, I created this long list of names. Of course your name is here, too, but I don't believe you're a killer any more than I believe Anna Wentworth is."

"Thanks?" The low undercurrent in her tone put him on alert. "Are you thinking I'm protecting the *real* killer?"

She propped her chin on her fist and studied him. "Not intentionally."

"Are you always so hard to win over?"

"Probably." She fidgeted, tapping her pen against her knee. "I won't apologize for having high standards."

He smiled. "I'd never ask you to lower your expectations." Leaning forward, he scanned the list of names. "I will say I've learned through experience that good people are capable of doing bad things under the right circumstances."

"Anyone there have the right circumstances to frame Anna?"

"No one is leaping out at me," he said after a few minutes.

"Me either," she said with a gusty sigh.

It looked as though she'd listed everyone on the force. With good reason. The Hicks murder had been high profile from the first moment his body was found on the Wentworth estate. The case shook up the entire city, and no one involved was above scrutiny as they worked the evidence and interviews. He figured Sadie's name would be on that list if she'd been with the CSI that day.

"Is it chocolate?" she asked, her gaze on the bakery box again.

"Yes."

Another sigh that left him wondering how that soft breath would feel against his skin. Whoa. He yanked his thoughts back into line. Pulling out his cell phone, he took a picture of her list. "We have the same information on the computer at the station," he said. "But there, access to the files is also tracked."

"Which means possibly alerting someone to your search." He nodded, and she continued, "Off the record, does anyone on the list have a reputation for mishandling evidence or steamrolling suspects?"

"No one jumps out." He returned to the top of the list. "Let's clear out some of the easy ones. Not these two," he said, pointing at the names of the responding officers. Though they had answered several calls at the Wentworth mansion, that team always came back to the station more amused than bothered by Anna's non-sensical claims of thieving maids and scurrilous chefs.

"You're sure they don't hate her in secret?" Pippa asked. "Maybe we should check their social media for any latent despise-Anna tendencies."

Emmanuel shook his head. "Even if they did hate her, those two officers have other things going on in life. Little league, soccer practices. They aren't the kill-somebody-to-get-even type."

"I'll take your word." She pulled the list closer and crossed off those two names.

"Really?"

"Is there a reason I shouldn't?" she asked.

"No." Her acceptance felt as awkward as her resistance had last night. "I just… I don't understand you," he blurted it out.

"You don't need to." Her lips curled into a smile. "Last week, I did my best to pin down the last time Anna wore the brooch that was found under Hicks's body. Neither of those officers was near her bedroom suite in that time frame."

"So that was a test?" he asked, irritated.

"Not at all," she assured him. "I considered the outside chance of them having an accomplice within the mansion staff. Your confidence in their character is enough for me."

Pressure eclipsed the irritation. "Anna Wentworth

was the prime suspect from day one. Moment one," he amended. "Before the brooch was discovered."

"Being under a microscope didn't make you feel rushed?"

"Of course it did, but McRath and I worked the case beat by beat. We didn't jump to conclusions. We followed the evidence."

"You followed *planted* evidence."

Good grief. He hoped not, but he understood why she was devoted to that theory. "You have no evidence to support that theory. Look, no one likes your client, but she has serious influence in this town, not to mention the charitable donations. The prosecutor wouldn't have followed through with this case if he'd thought we half-assed any aspect of it."

"You're aware the prosecutor and Mr. Wentworth are friends."

"Everyone tied to the case was aware," Emmanuel confirmed. "The man was out of town with a rock-solid alibi," he reminded her. "You think the prosecutor was helping a friend get rid of his wife?"

Reaching up, she rubbed the back of her neck. It was all he could do not to jump in and help. "The prosecutor would have the means to manipulate things within the department." She shook her head, as if to clear it of the troubling thoughts. "I don't think Ed cared enough about Anna's flings to set her up for murder, but maybe I'm overlooking another reason."

"I doubt it," Emmanuel said. "Mr. Wentworth was solid in the interview. More embarrassed about a body turning up on the grounds once he learned it wasn't anyone he'd known. That sounds callous, but knowing the family, you get it, right?"

"I do. One of Ed's top priorities is protecting the reputation of the Wentworth name." She rolled her eyes. "For Elizabeth's future."

If Pippa succeeded in overturning this conviction, it would be all kinds of trouble for the prosecutor as well as the GRPD. Enough trouble that maybe the prosecutor hired someone to drive Pippa off the Wentworth case. Emmanuel couldn't put that doubt in her head, not when she had CI business to deal with.

Pippa's gaze returned to the paper in front of them. "Perception is a tricky thing," she said. "You arrived at a crime scene and saw things a certain way. When I look at the pictures, I see it all so differently. Who had reason to paint the picture you saw?"

"Let's take a different tack," he suggested. "Rather than consider who wanted to frame your client—"

"Because that's half the city," she interjected.

He cocked an eyebrow.

"Fine. It's ninety-eight percent of the city."

He liked the twitch at the corner of her rosy lips. "Who in the GRPD had any reason to get rid of Hicks? As soon as we found his intent to blackmail her, we knew Anna had means and motive. Combined with evidence at the scene..."

"Slam dunk," she finished for him. "I've been looking at this angle, too, though not within the GRPD." She open several windows on her laptop. "I need to get set up for the loan application, but go ahead and take a look at those articles. It's all from gossip sites and society pages. I'm going to compare his known dates and lovers. Let me know if any names have ties to GRPD or the prosecutor's office."

She went to her office while he tried not to groan

over Hicks's dating history. The man liked to party with the rich and slightly famous. He ran across one name and nearly swallowed his tongue. It couldn't be related, and yet it had to be connected.

"Here," he said, his throat suddenly tight. This had never come out before, and they'd interviewed everyone recently tied to Hicks. Or so Emmanuel thought.

"You found something?"

"Someone." He dragged the mouse and highlighted the name for her.

"Leigh McRath." Her eyebrows climbed toward her hairline. "Is she related to Detective Joe McRath?"

"His daughter." Emmanuel pinched the bridge of his nose. This looked bad, but it had to be a fluke. Joe couldn't be involved in this debacle. He was a decorated cop who took real pride in the work he did for the city. He was a mentor, an inspiration.

The sergeant pushed hard at times, but he closed cases and didn't cut corners. Years ago there had been rumors that he'd gone off the rails on a case involving the death of a little girl, but no disciplinary measures or formal complaints had resulted.

Joe couldn't have known about Leigh's ties to Hicks when they landed the case. If he had, he would've recused himself or spoken with the lieutenant about the distant connection to the victim.

"You never spoke with her?" Pippa asked. "I don't have any record of either you or Joe interviewing her."

"I didn't question her." He shook his head. "We did the divide-and-conquer thing on several peripheral connections." His stomach cramped, and he was glad he hadn't had more stew. "Joe took most of the prior relationships."

"On purpose?"

"No. No reason to think so at the time." What if Joe had taken the relationships to keep Leigh's name out of the investigation? He pushed back from the counter and swore low and long in Spanish. His mother would wash his mouth out with soap even now if she'd heard him. This was bad.

"Hey. Relax," she said, suddenly offering comfort. "It's a connection. One probably random link you didn't know to explore. Just because Hicks and Leigh dated doesn't mean she did anything wrong." Pippa nibbled on her lip again. "Maybe he just wanted to spare his daughter some embarrassment."

"You don't think a father would go to any lengths to protect his daughter and keep her out of jail?"

She opened her mouth to reply and snapped it shut again. "I'll grant you, that's a fair motive. But only *if* that's what happened. It gives me a new potential suspect, a new direction to check on, which is something I didn't have before."

No comfort in that for him. He had years of police service. Enough experience that he shouldn't have missed this piece of the puzzle. His career combined with his upbringing gave him a double dose of that protective instinct that made him a good cop.

Or so he'd thought. Had he been lazy that day at the scene, looking only at the evidence laid out for him? As a detective's daughter, Leigh might have a good idea of how to stage a crime scene if she'd tagged along with her dad and studied his cases.

"Clearly, you need to follow this thread," Pippa said. "What if it was Leigh? Look at the dates. They broke up six months before the murder. If she was brokenhearted, why wait six months and then frame Anna?" Pippa crossed her legs and drummed her pen on her knee. "As Joe's daughter, she might have easier access to a gun, but how would she have accessed Anna's jewelry?"

He didn't have those answers. A good detective would've asked those questions at the time, not weeks after the prime suspect was sentenced to life in prison. "Pippa, the evidence box is missing. No one else on your list has such a clear connection to Hicks or such a substantial motive.

"Leigh McRath has both. She has access if her father helped. Who knows what he might have done to keep the heat off his daughter?"

"Those are questions I can pursue," she said. "Thanks to you."

As if that made him feel any better. This was definitely a rock and a hard place kind of situation. When Joe caught wind of this, he'd turn on Emmanuel for helping Pippa. Missing evidence box or not, the entire GRPD was likely to turn on him for helping a lawyer working "against" them. He wanted to ask her to be careful, and yet he had no right.

"I won't throw you under the bus, Detective," she promised. "But first, it's time for me to infiltrate the Capital X system. I can't afford to be late on this."

Naturally, helping Brody was the only thing that would momentarily divert her attention from exonerating Wentworth. Through the years, Emmanuel had listened to Griffin vent about Brody. Everyone in the family agreed the kid meant well, but it often bothered Griffin that Brody usually looked for quick fixes to his troubles rather than putting in the tough hours to get where he wanted to go.

Days ago, Emmanuel thought overturning the conviction was a lark and the real threat to Pippa was moving close to Capital X. Now it felt as if both cases had grown teeth and claws and there was no clear path to safe ground.

For either of them.

Chapter 8

Pippa opened the new laptop and followed the directions provided by CI's resident tech expert, Ashanti Silver. She'd created a step-by-step list so Pippa could find her way to the Capital X site and loan application portal on the dark web.

Emmanuel was hovering, as promised. It wasn't easy to ignore him, and she wasn't even sure she wanted to try. The sizzle she felt when he was close was addictive. If she was reading the signals correctly, he felt something more than a passing cooperative interest.

Not that they could do a thing about it when she was neck deep in two cases, one of which he was far too entangled with.

"Wow, that's not what I expected at all," he said.

He was leaning close enough that she could smell the crisp scent of his cologne. He must have gone home at some point during the day, because the fragrance had been faint this morning and was much fresher now. She had no business being tempted or enticed by that smell.

"It looks as slick and clean as any other legitimate bank."

"Which is probably why they get away with what they're doing," she pointed out. She scrolled through the site, taking a look at products and account options. "If I didn't know how they operated, I'd think this was a great answer for a loan, especially to get a business off the ground."

"You're smart enough that you'd come to your senses when you saw the terms," he said.

His compliment warmed her. "True." She sat back, staring at the screen and giving herself some needed distance. From the man more than the assignment.

"Second thoughts?"

"A few," she admitted. And all of them were about him. She really hadn't expected to like Emmanuel after what he'd said in court, and she didn't know quite how to proceed since he'd shown himself to be a person of high integrity. "It's hard to imagine a person being so underinformed or so desperate that they'd agree to such exorbitant interest rates," she said.

"Not to mention the repayment schedule." Emmanuel stood up and pushed a hand through his wavy hair. She thought he could probably use a trim, then decided that was something Anna Wentworth would say. Pippa found him ridiculously attractive just as he was. The hairstyle wouldn't make any difference. She really needed to find a boyfriend or dive back in to the dating-app scene.

She shivered. During her last attempt, she'd lost patience with the whole messy system. She didn't mind casual hookups, but at this point in her life she was looking for something different. Something more substantial. The men those apps wanted to match her with didn't meet that criteria. Even when she changed her preferences, looking for someone a little older, she'd never been matched with anyone half as intriguing as Emmanuel.

Sliding away from her dangerous thoughts, she focused on the task at hand. There were big buttons on the loan screen for preset loan amounts. She chose the $25K button, the amount Kiely had determined her alias needed and would easily qualify for. Not that any of them believed Capital X turned down an opportunity to suck in a consumer.

Emmanuel was leaning close. "You don't have to watch every keystroke," she said, trying to be cool when she really didn't mind the warmth of him at her back.

"I'm curious you referred to this as an infiltration," he said.

"It feels that way," she admitted, her blood running hot with the excitement. Excitement over the role she would play in saving Brody, *not* over the man at her back. She couldn't possibly let those little flutters of attraction grow into something more. Even if he hadn't been Griffin's friend, they were on opposite sides of a case that was important to her heart.

"Why is the time so specific?" he asked.

"The timing fits with the background my sister and brother created for this person I'm pretending to be."

It was no shock when he reached over and flipped through the papers, quickly getting a read on the fake Alison Carrington. She was thoroughly distracted by his hands. A flat, long-healed scar wrapped under his right thumb, disappearing into his palm. During her single semester of art in undergrad, the professor had devoted a solid week on the mechanics of human hands. With a subject like Emmanuel, she might've aced that section.

Shifting her focus back to the application, she finished entering the personal information, including a social security number and driver's license. Then she added in the details about work history. If she screwed this up, Riley would never forgive her and they might never save Brody. She double-checked all of the basic information and then clicked the arrow to go to the next part of the application. Here she inputted information about her finances, including current debts and any collateral.

After that it was a page about the loan itself, confirming how much she was asking for and how she planned to use the money. She filled out those fields per the paperwork provided and clicked the button to continue.

"You sure about that address?" Emmanuel asked when it was time for her to review everything one last time before hitting Submit.

"This is the address they gave me," she replied. "Can't change it now. Why don't you approve?"

"I don't disapprove," he said. "It's just pretty darn close to this neighborhood."

"No one can connect me to Alison Carrington. That's the whole point of a new computer and the IP magic Ashanti cooked up."

"Right, right." He tucked his hands into his pockets and took a step back.

She appreciated his attempt to give her space, even if he wasn't much good at it.

She checked the box confirming she'd reviewed all of her materials and that it was all correct. As if Capital X would bother going after a loan applicant for a fraudulent application. Satisfied, she pressed Submit. They only got aggressive with clients who didn't pay them back in accordance with the absurd terms.

"Done?" he asked.

"Looks that way." She hesitated, since the loading wheel was still spinning. There. She pointed to the screen and the flag that said her application was successfully submitted.

The scowl on his face was evidence of his concern. "What next?"

She signed out of the program and shut down the new laptop registered to the Alison Carrington persona. "Time to relax," she said. "As much as possible anyway. According to the site, the approval process can take up to forty-eight hours for a decision."

She wasn't sure why butterflies were suddenly doing aerial stunts in her belly. It wasn't her credit or her person on the line. She had only used the materials provided by her sister and brother. They hadn't even told her who would be playing the role of Alison at the address she'd provided. Someone had to perform day-to-day tasks in case they were being observed, but Pippa's was still the face on the fake ID. There was no reason it should come to that, but Pippa accepted that she might have to step in and be familiar with the identity if there was an unforeseen emergency. She wasn't trying to be a slacker, but so far, all she'd been was a convenient pair of hands who'd completed a few online forms.

She carried the laptop and its charging cord to the office, where she knelt down near the floor safe. Having pulled back the rug, she entered the combination and tucked the equipment away. At Emmanuel's quizzical expression, she explained that she could check the email through an incognito window on her own device if necessary.

"I guess that's it." Pippa straightened the rug and dusted off her hands. What happened now? "At least we're making progress on one case." Even if her contribution was minimal.

It was nice to have that task done. No more wondering. Assuming the Carrington application would be approved, they would soon be drawing the ire of Capital X enforcers. Maybe even the same team who had broken Brody's fingers. Maybe she hadn't come up with the fake identification and background, but she was definitively helping. Thanks to Brody's ties to the family, Capital X would be smart to avoid the Coltons, but by taking on this alias, she was contributing for her siblings, Brody and everyone else Capital X would bilk if they weren't stopped.

"You do carry a strong sense about right and wrong," he said.

The look he gave her was pure appreciation, and she felt overheated in an instant. "Never tried to hide it. Besides, you've got plenty of the same traits."

"As character flaws go, I'll take it," he said.

"Same. Though I don't believe the pursuit of justice is a flaw." She turned to the wall, determined to ignore the noisy fan and dehumidifier. "What do you know about interior decorating?"

"Only what I can't forget when my sisters are chatting," he replied. "Why?"

"I might make this a feature wall instead of just repainting." If he wasn't going to leave, she had to find some common ground. She folded her arms and tried again to imagine floor-to-ceiling beadboard. "Beadboard or wallpaper or…"

"You're too modern for beadboard," he said absently, looking around the space.

She was inordinately pleased by that observation. "That was my thought. I'd invite you to sit down and toss around ideas, but—" She gestured to the fan. "And you probably want to get going."

"Only if you're kicking me out," he said. "We haven't opened that bakery box yet."

She'd almost forgotten about the treat during the thrill of making a stand online and the presence of the man who'd been thoughtful enough to bring over something special. "You can't possibly be worried about Capital X striking tonight."

"Let's just say I'm overly cautious about several things," he said.

"Does that include chocolate?"

"It's in the top five," he teased. "Can't go around indulging in mediocre chocolate."

She enjoyed the sparkle in his brown eyes, as if he might give way to honest laughter any minute. "Thanks for all you've done already," she said.

"You want to keep working on that list?"

"Not tonight." She was tired of thinking about the best approach to Anna's case. Trying to isolate someone within the GRPD without hurting careers and feelings would be a delicate proposition. "I need some time to let things mull in the back of my mind."

He didn't seem all that thrilled with her reply. "Let me know how to support you when you make a plan."

She tilted her head. "You mean that?"

"Of course."

"You continue to surprise me, Detective." One more new development in her life to mull over when she was alone. "Let's celebrate a job well done tonight."

Emmanuel followed her back to the counter that seemed to serve as her primary dining area. Pippa looked so damn proud of herself, as she should. She'd just laid a trap that could result in a significant leap forward on the CI investigation into Capital X.

The sassy glint in her eye and the tough set to her delicate jaw were an intriguing and irresistible combination. He didn't quite understand his infatuation or why she fired his blood this way. Technically, this was only their third interaction, yet he felt as if he'd known her for years. Sure, Griffin talked about his family, but this was a deep, certain awareness he couldn't shake.

Didn't want to shake.

She was younger, not an insurmountable difference when he thought about it, and he was aware, through his ties to her family, that she'd been through hard times just like he had. Yes, he'd come from a less privileged background, but the Coltons had been community-oriented parents, and their children understood the value of commitment and service.

Her optimism, especially as it related to her pursuit of overturning the Wentworth conviction, should have annoyed him. Pippa's blind faith in a convicted killer should have been a turnoff on its own. He was well aware that he wouldn't be going the extra mile for any other lawyer representing Wentworth. Yet here he stood, reluctant to leave her alone in her secure home, and it had nothing to do with his promise to her brother.

"What are you thinking about?" she asked.

Nothing he should be thinking. Her lips looked soft and kissable and his fingers twitched, eager to learn the feel of her hair. Though he tried to think of Griffin, he couldn't slam the door on his meandering thoughts. "I'm thinking I should stay the night," he said.

She pulled the tie loose from the white box. "That's ridiculous. I'm perfectly safe here. You have an unmarked car downstairs."

"Two," he clarified. It seemed important. "Front and back."

Coiling the length of string around her fingers, she said, "And no sign of anyone, right?"

"Not so far. That can change." He'd draped his jacket over the counter stool earlier and reached for it now, drawing the panic button from the pocket. "I brought this, too, but that doesn't change anything. I still want to stay."

"What is that?" she queried, eyeing the device.

"A panic button," he replied. "I've set it up so it sends an alert to my cell phone and the teams downstairs."

"That's...thoughtful," she finished.

He chuckled. "You think it's too much."

"Thoughtful and too much don't have to be mutually exclusive. You saw me update the electronic locks last night," she said. "The building is secure, and everyone is on alert now. What makes you think any Capital X enforcers would even try to get in here? I used an alias."

He wasn't as worried about the bogus loan operation right now. As she'd said, she used a pseudonym and masked the true IP address, though he believed the company could still find her. No, he was far more concerned about what the missing evidence box meant and the inexplicable red tape she couldn't cut through at the prison. Why couldn't she see she was painting multiple targets on her back? It made protecting her that much more difficult for everyone.

Which was exactly why Griffin had asked him to keep an eye on her. He decided to play the brother card. Family meant everything to the Colton siblings…and to him.

"Griffin insisted I stay close," he said.

"So you said last night." Her voice frosted over. "I'll remind you that he doesn't get to speak for me." She drummed her fingertips on the granite countertop in front of the bakery box. "I appreciate you answering the break-in call and helping so much. Thank you, in case I didn't say that last night."

He couldn't recall if she'd said it either, his mind on other things, primarily how to keep her safe from a distance. "If my partner and I hadn't caught that case clean, I would've come by as a courtesy."

"To Griffin."

Of course. He hadn't even met Pippa. Her tone was as crisp as the leaves falling from the maple trees lining her street. No sense massaging the facts. "Yes. As a courtesy to Griffin, I came by to check out the trouble and see if I could help."

"Or to see if you could worm your way into my world?"

There was a vulnerability in her voice he wasn't sure how to handle. "No. Not the way you're implying."

"Maybe you wanted to keep tabs on my progress during the Wentworth case."

"That's not how I operate," he said with all the calm he could. Maybe twenty-four hours ago he'd had different motives. More self-focused intentions. But not now, not after seeing that threat scrawled across her wall. "If the situation was reversed and I couldn't be sure my sister would be careful enough, I'd expect Griffin to uphold his promise. Even if my sister didn't like it."

"Careful enough?" She swore under her breath, folding her arms. "I don't like it. I don't need a babysitter or a watchdog or whatever you want to call yourself."

"It's a panic button. A precaution." Should he have expected her to give him any grace or cooperation? His testimony in court had pretty much nailed the Wentworth case shut. Clearly her friendship trumped the obvious—the *only*—conclusion the jury could have made. The defense had not provided an effective counterargument to all of the evidence he'd found.

Planted evidence. Her words echoed in his head. If she was right and someone in the GRPD had framed Anna, Pippa needed this panic button and *him* more than she realized. "You are taking strategic risks, and you deserve the best protection against any unpleasant consequences."

She wasn't swayed. "This is who I am. I can handle my consequences."

"Pippa, I understand. I'm not here to change you, or because your brother doubts your ability. Just call me the safety net. That little bit extra you ignore until you need it." He didn't care for the description, but it was accurate.

"I'd rather call Griffin and give him a piece of my mind."

"You can do that," he said. "Why not wait until after?"

"After what?"

He tipped up the lid of the bakery box. "After chocolate."

"Éclairs," she said, her tone full of all the reverence the pastries deserved.

He admired her unapologetic enthusiasm, and his mind detoured straight into a fantasy of Pippa demonstrating that kind of eagerness for a lover. For him.

Whoa. That was a big leap. He needed to dial it down. She might not be off-limits precisely, but the woman was prickly, and he suspected she wouldn't appreciate an ill-timed advance. No, Pippa would likely enjoy an all-out seduction with plenty of finesse.

What was wrong with him? He wasn't here to sort out what she did or didn't enjoy on an intimate level.

She bounced on her toes a little as she grabbed two plates from the cabinet.

"Forks?" he asked, sliding a napkin closer to her.

"Are you kidding? These are the best éclairs in the city. They deserve fingers." She wiggled hers, urging him to hurry.

He was doomed. She had no idea of her effect on him. He could quickly become addicted to this charming, playful side of her. It was a lovely counterpoint to her grit and drive. He enjoyed her serious intensity. It was one of the first things they had in common, a passion for justice and seeing that what was right prevailed.

"No forks," he agreed, placing an éclair on each plate.

"I'd suggest relaxing on the couch, but the fan is too loud."

"I'm fine right here." Her grateful smile hit him square in the chest.

"Would you like coffee?" she offered.

"Milk, if you have it."

"Done." She pointed a finger at him. "That kind of thinking gives me hope for you."

She poured them each a short glass of milk and they sat at the counter, neither of them willing to wait a minute longer to dive into the decadent éclairs.

The flavors of rich chocolate, perfect pastry and thick, sinfully smooth cream melted in his mouth, but the experience was enhanced by Pippa. Pure joy bloomed across her face at the first bite. Closing her eyes, she licked a dot of chocolate from her lip.

Emmanuel was hard in an instant, wondering how her unique flavor would make the éclair even better. He had to get his mind off sex before his reaction to her made it impossible. She would never let him stay if she noticed how stirred up he was.

He paused between bites. "So, Pippa Colton, a.k.a. Alison Carrington, you've set a trap for a notorious loan operation. What will you do next?"

"This." She took another bite of her éclair. "Better than any amusement park vacation," she said. "I might even have a second one."

"I'm glad I made the right choice," he said. He'd thought about calling Griffin for advice, but that had felt like cheating. Making the right call on instinct made this moment even sweeter.

"Did Griffin mention these éclairs are my kryptonite?"

"No," he said with pride. "All my idea."

"It was a good one." Her brow puckered over her pert nose. "How did you and Griffin meet?"

"Through a community event for the foster system years ago," Emmanuel said. "We hit it off and have been friends ever since."

She didn't ask any follow-up questions. Was she uninterested or just processing things while she enjoyed her dessert? When she finished her second éclair, he stacked her plate on top of his and carried both to the sink.

"You don't have to do that," she said.

"You weren't raised by my mother," he replied, laughing a little.

Pippa leaned back against the counter, and he felt her gaze like a touch as he rinsed the dishes and loaded them into her dishwasher. "I've had plenty of time to find the balance," he said. "Although most days you can still eat off my floor."

She laughed, and the merry sound along with the happy glow on her face rendered him speechless.

"Tell me something else about your mom," she said.

"Why?" He needed a few more minutes to gather his wits.

Her gaze lifted to the ceiling, and he catalogued every detail in that brief moment. Her wistful expression made him wonder about her past. He'd heard a few details about the difficulties between their parents from Griffin. The idyllic image the Coltons had projected while in public had not translated into a perfect home life. Apparently once close, the couple had drifted apart due to Graham's career and Kathleen's focus on raising their children and her charitable endeavors in the community.

"The way you talk about your family..." Her voice trailed off. "You make it sound as if your parents were happy."

"They *are* happy," he said. Closing the dishwasher, he waited on the other side of the kitchen, curious about the change in mood and topic.

"Sometimes I wonder what happens to people who don't have good examples to follow."

"In marriage?" he asked.

She met his gaze and one slender shoulder rose and fell. "In anything."

He knew she meant personal relationships. "I think, at a certain point, we have to make our own choices about what we want and how we'll get there."

"Right," she agreed. "That's being an adult. But do you think people without a solid example in one thing or another are doomed to struggle? Maybe it's a hurdle no one knows how to recognize," she said.

He was pretty sure psychiatrists knew how to recognize and fix those hurdles. "What about your friend Elizabeth?"

Pippa's eyebrows lifted. "What about her?"

"From the sound of it she's a kind person. She shows up in and around Grand Rapids helping out and doing good things. As far as I know, she's never once called the police to accuse anyone in her employ of any kind of crime."

"That was her mother's MO, the example she was raised to follow. Anna Wentworth shows up in the right places for the photo op, does good work in name only and often harasses her best employees without any true cause."

"You're of the opinion that we're more than what we've seen in life."

He closed the distance between them, drawn to her by a force he could no longer deny. Fast or not, he didn't want to hold himself back from something that had the potential for a life-altering shift. "I'm saying what you already know. Experience shapes us and informs us, but we can choose how to interpret those experiences, how we grow from them."

Slowly, giving her plenty of time to move or otherwise signal him away, he nudged a lock of her hair behind her ear. Hair soft as silk against his fingers; the shell of her ear warm to his touch. Those small discoveries heated his blood, not at all insignificant.

She held her ground, her eyes locked with his and his pulse kicked with anticipation.

"I've seen bad people come out of good families," he said. "And I've seen people do remarkably good things amid dreadful circumstances."

Emmanuel traced the pale skin on the inside of her wrist, pleased to feel her pulse pounding as hard as his.

"We have choices," she agreed. "I know that. We can choose to learn and grow." Her gaze dropped to their joined hands, and her fingertips trembled as she traced the shape of his hand.

Choose me. He couldn't resist her. Was there a chance she felt the same inexplicable draw to him? When she looked up at him again, he slowly bent his head toward her. He wanted her to have the time and space to say no to a kiss, even as he prayed like hell she wouldn't.

She met him, her lips brushing lightly across his. The

spark that sizzled out from his lips through his whole being was lightning in a bottle, a flash too powerful for the moment. The fleeting, brief contact left him craving more. Everything. All of her. He wanted to be her choice. Would happily beg for the honor.

Her fingers laced with his, but she didn't seem eager for another kiss. How would he exit gracefully now?

"Emmanuel," she whispered. Her hands came up to frame his face, her thumbs rasping against the grain of his short beard. Ever so gently she brought his mouth back to hers.

The sweetness of her was like a balm to that first jolt of electricity and power. Her lips were firm and sure. No surprise she knew what she wanted. Him. He nearly crowed in victory.

Gripping her hips, he boosted her to the countertop, standing between her knees. She giggled, and when her lips parted, his tongue stroked across hers. She tasted of the rich chocolate icing and the sweet cream filling of the éclair, and the taste that was hers alone.

It was a sugar rush of a completely new variety.

He tugged her to the edge of the granite surface, letting her feel what she did to him. This time there was no giggle, just a moan that nearly sent him over the edge. "Pippa," he murmured against her lips.

She wrapped her legs around his hips in response, holding him close. Close but not close enough. There were too many barriers keeping him from everything he wanted to learn about her.

Her lips and teeth scraped against his jaw and down his throat and he gripped her hips, fighting for control. "Pippa," he said again. Her name was the full extent of his vocabulary right now. Everything started and ended right here.

With her.

He speared a hand into her hair, angling for a deeper kiss. Her fingertips curled over his shoulders, then dragged down his chest until she tugged his shirt free of his jeans. Her hands slipped under the clothing, skimming his ribs and waist, around to his back.

"*Mmm*, you're so hot." She smiled against his lips. "I like it."

He was on fire for her without a doubt. He jerked when she touched a ticklish spot under his rib cage, and a peal of her bright laughter surrounded him.

"You're ticklish," she said, clearly delighted.

"Don't tell anyone."

Her eyes sparkled with pure mischief. "They'll never hear it from me," she vowed. "Just here?" Her fingers danced over the spot again.

He growled, sliding his hands under her skirt and gripping her thighs. She was burning up just like he was; he could feel it through the thin fabric of her pants. Feel the strength in her legs. "Pippa," he warned. His thumbs dipped low, following the curve of her inner thighs, teasing them both by staying well away from the most sensitive areas of her body.

Everything about her made him more aware, more sensitive to *her*. Every inch of her fascinated him. The entire fleet of police cars might come screeching to a halt outside her door, sirens blazing, and he wouldn't notice.

She wriggled under his touch, her hands working at the buttons of his shirt. "Off," she commanded, pushing at the panels. "Let me see you."

He grinned, skimming kisses along the shell of her ear. If she wanted to make demands, it would be his pleasure to fulfill her every wish. Standing tall, her knees still snug around his hips, he cast his button-down shirt to the floor and the undershirt followed.

Her eyelids were heavy, her lips flushed and plump from their kisses as she stared at him. They both watched her hands, small and fair against his deeper complexion, explore his torso.

He couldn't recall ever being quite this desperate to hear a woman's opinion of his body.

Her palms flattened over his pecs, smoothed across his shoulders and down his arms. With a firm grasp, she leaned closer and kissed his chest right over his heart. He couldn't bear it but didn't dare move as her tongue and mouth flicked a sigh-inducing path upward until at last they were kissing again, lips fused as tongues dueled.

He breathed her in, filled himself with her scents, orange in her hair, chocolate on her lips, and the arousal swirling thick in the air between them. His hands wandered over her delectable curves, from her breasts, to the dip of her waist, to her hips. Slowly, he dragged his touch back up until his thumbs were resting just below her nipples.

She was making soft, needy noises that tested his resolve. "Touch me." She rubbed her breasts against his hands.

"My pleasure." He teased her nipples, pinching lightly through the fine fabrics of her shirt and bra. With an arm around her waist, he bent her back a little, giving him better access as he kissed a path down around that gorgeous pendant and lower to her breasts.

He hesitated, unbuttoning her shirt slowly and keeping his kisses light. Her bra was sleek satin, but the glow was nothing compared to her skin. He could happily lose himself in her for the rest of his days.

"Emmanuel."

"Mmm?"

"Put your mouth on me before I die."

He cupped her breast and met her command, suckling hard on her nipple and then blowing lightly across the moistened peak. She held his head close, moving against his mouth, crying with pleasure when he used his teeth lightly.

The woman was a marvel of demands and responses. He dipped a hand lower, pressing his palm to the heat at her center over her pants. Her hips bucked, and he grinned against her breast, learning what she enjoyed.

"Stop," she whispered, her hands dropping from his head to his shoulders as she nudged him back so she could sit up.

He did, easing back as far as she would allow. She still held him with her legs. She was adorably disheveled, and whether or not they went any further with this, he was staying the night. In her bed, on the couch or on the floor in front of her door. He wasn't taking chances with her.

"You..." She paused, her throat working as she swallowed. "We, *um*...wc shouldn't do the rest of this out here."

Despite a critical lack of blood flow to his brain, he could think of several reasons why they should. "Okay?"

"Any of my siblings could walk in on us."

Us. He liked the sound of that. The rest of that, not so much. "Really? I told you not to share the code."

"Really?" she mimicked his tone. "Scolding me here and now?" She arched a golden-brown eyebrow. "You'd rather explain *this*," she circled her hand to indicate their state of undress, "to Riley or Griffin?"

"Well, no." Although she'd be worth the inevitable broken nose or bruised jaw. "Be clear," he said, stroking the length of her thighs, teasing them both. "Do you want me to take you to the bedroom and continue *this*?"

"Yes." That sparkle was back in her eyes. "And hurry."

His heart rate kicked into overdrive and desire flooded through him. They were on the same page. "You got it."

Chapter 9

Pippa couldn't suppress a shocked squeal as he plucked her right off the counter. She wrapped her arms around his neck and kissed him. His lips were a fantasy and she couldn't get enough of his taste. She might already have an irreversible dependency. Sliding her tongue over his, she pressed herself to him. Couldn't get close enough to his heat and strength.

She never lost control. Was never desperate. And where on earth had the courage to snap out demands come from? Until right now, her sexual experiences had all been very practical. Definitely satisfying, but practical. She'd never felt anything like the joyful abandon she felt tonight with Emmanuel.

He carried her out of the kitchen, but they'd made it only a few paces down the hall before he stopped to feast on her breasts again. Good grief, she was perched on the edge of an orgasm already. She'd prefer to be naked, with him buried deep inside, when the wave crashed over her.

"Wall is good," she decided.

"Next time," he said, continuing the journey into her bedroom.

Next time. The idea held tremendous appeal. Especially as he eased her to the floor, the backs of her knees bumping the bed. He shoved off her shirt and tossed it to the floor before he cupped her aching breasts once more.

They were leaving a trail of clothing anyone could follow. She started to giggle and stopped short when he removed her bra and covered her with his hot palms. "Oh, yes." His thumbs flicked over her hard nipples.

Reaching between them to work on his belt, she got it open and unbuttoned his jeans, carefully lowering the zipper. "Take those off."

He complied immediately, a sexy smirk on his mouth as he pulled a condom from his pocket and dropped it onto the nightstand. When he was naked, she just stared. Her skin felt too tight, too hot, and she craved his touch. Everywhere.

But first she wanted to kiss every inch of that glorious body. His fitness had been apparent from the start, but now, seeing every ripple and ridge, every firm plane, her mouth positively watered. She couldn't decide where to kiss him first.

"Pippa, you're killing me."

She looked up and saw the raw hunger, the blatant need, in his brown eyes. Tiptoeing, she gave him a searing kiss. "I don't know where to start," she whispered against his mouth. "You're so beautiful." She'd been spewing orders, and now she just wanted him to take over. Sliding her hand over his length, she delighted in his deep groan.

He covered her hand with his, let her stroke him a few times, then he knelt down to remove her pants. "Pippa." His breath teased the sensitive skin of her inner thigh, now bare to his view, exposed to his touch.

His next words were incoherent as blood pounded in her ears, and when his mouth met her center, her thoughts scattered. He tasted and teased her with his tongue and intimate kisses. He spoke in a flow of Spanish that made her feel like the sexiest woman, the most valuable treasure, on the planet.

Her legs trembled as he brought her to a shuddering climax and he caught her, held her close, so she couldn't escape the full rush of sensation. Tears welled in her eyes and she blinked them away, desperate to get herself under control. Easing back onto the bed, she barely had time to catch her breath before he was prowling over her, grabbing the condom he'd left on her nightstand.

"You are glorious," he murmured against her belly. "Amazing." His tongue circled her breasts. "A beautiful joy."

She couldn't muster a protest or find shelter from the emotions bombarding her. He'd stripped her bare, inside and out. Did she regret it? Too soon to know, especially when there was more to discover. All she could do was stare at his striking form as he rolled a condom over his jutting erection.

She took comfort in his kisses and touches, finding her way back to those playful and tantalizing moments in the kitchen until she was on the verge of another orgasm. Poised at her entrance, he pressed in just enough to make her crazy. To make her crave.

"More." She lifted her hips. He complied, but not enough, then withdrew. "Emmanuel," she pleaded, her hands gripping his lean, sculpted arms. "Please, Emmanuel."

He drove deep in one full stroke and her body soared, the physical demands and bliss blotting out everything but him. She clung to that pleasure, chased it as he did, looking for the touches and adjustments that made him growl and moan in pleasure.

When the next orgasm crashed over her, she was lost, then found as her gaze met his. A moment later he reached his release on a shuddering groan. They were both spent, but she didn't want to let him go, wishing she could hold him all night.

No. That couldn't be right. She didn't do the all-night thing. She wasn't the cling-and-cuddle type. So why did she nearly protest when he left to dispose of the condom?

She didn't have time to sort out the reactions spiking through her system before he was back and stretched out beside her, pulling the sheet over their cooling bodies.

Pippa was in shock, the bliss of moments ago shattered by the reality of what she'd done. There were consequences, and now she had to face them. But how? She didn't leap into physical encounters and to hell with the aftermath. Not like this. The worst part, aside from being speechless and breathless, was the intense desire for an encore.

Emmanuel had just gifted her with a series of orgasms that should have kept her satisfied for years. She was here, tucked up beside him, feeling greedy and wanting more. It would be comforting to think he had merely unlocked some previously unknown Pandora's box of passion. She knew better.

And it scared her.

"Wow," she whispered in the direction of the ceiling. "That was..."

He rolled to his side and propped his head on his fist, watching her with those deep brown eyes. He traced her lower lip, and she was afraid he would catch the tremor. There was a certain knowledge in his gaze that went beyond the physical. A deepening warmth that made her edgy and nervous.

This wasn't supposed to go down this way. She didn't fall into situations that left her ruffled or unsettled. She stayed in control. Always. He was waiting for her to finish, so she tried again. "That was..." She couldn't find the words that made sense without exposing this strange fear prodding her to run away and leave her own bed.

"Amazing," he finished for her. His smile was almost shy, and he seemed to be as much at a loss for words as she was. Maybe in another time and another place with another man that would have been comforting.

Emmanuel had come into her life as a definite enemy to the case. Tonight changed all of that. Irrevocably. But not publicly. Not yet. She could still deny any inappropriate connection to the detective who'd sealed Anna's fate. Her gaze drifted down his torso, and her hand followed before she could stop it. *Enemy* was such a strong word, a divisive word, not at all suitable after what they'd just shared. Honestly, he'd been winning her over since this morning when she'd found him grieving over an informant. Add in his guidance for her top case and determination to keep a promise made to her brother and she could so easily become a lost cause.

He eased her over, nuzzling her neck, murmuring nonsense about her beauty.

Finally, common sense kicked in, or maybe it was a jolt of self-preservation. Her hands on his firm shoulders, she pushed him away. "Yeah, okay. You should get going," she said.

"Pardon me?" His dark eyebrows disappeared under the wave of hair that fell across his forehead. "We agreed I'd stay the night."

Had they agreed? She couldn't remember, and that wasn't the point. "I've changed my mind. The panic button is enough."

His chin dropped. "Pippa, what—"

"You heard me." She scooted out of the bed and grabbed her robe, cinching the tie tight at her waist. "You heard me. Please go."

He sat up, the sheet falling low across his hips. "Pippa, talk to me."

She shook her head. How could he sit there in the middle of her bed, naked and unaffected?

"Talk to me," he urged. He indicated the pillows they'd just been resting on. "This was something special."

"Right. Sure." She stopped herself before she started wringing her hands. "Whatever it is or isn't, this is over," she said. "No sense rehashing every little detail." Though she already knew she'd do just that as soon as he walked out. The real thing had been infinitely better than her heated dreams last night.

"For tonight?"

She couldn't make herself say forever. Not when her body refused to accept this was a one-and-done thing. "Emmanuel, please leave." If he kept pressing, she might cry, and that would not be tolerated.

She didn't need a flood of foreign emotions right now, not with two major cases demanding her time. "This was fun. Amazing," she used his word. "It was an excellent experience." She folded her arms, her skin heating as his gaze cruised over her cleavage. "Clearly we were both in need of a physical outlet for our stress."

"This was more," he snapped, cutting her rambling short. "Why are you making it cheap?"

She didn't reply. Couldn't.

His next words were a string of Spanish, spewed so fast she had no idea if he was swearing or praying. Probably the former. Whether he was swearing at himself or at her, it didn't matter, as long as he left.

If he stayed, the temptation would be too big for her to resist. She held firm, held herself back from his enticing body as he gathered up his clothing, following the trail back to the kitchen. Good grief, the man was beautiful.

The neediest parts of her body begged her to reconsider, to take it all back and kiss him until his heat surrounded her again and gave her that rush of feeling so cherished.

Madness.

He was far too reasonable. Too easy to talk to. She was kicking him out of her bed and out of her home, and he didn't rage or rant. Of course not. Emmanuel Iglesias was suddenly everything calm and cool. A complete flip from the desire and passion not fifteen minutes past.

Emmanuel reminded himself this was her choice. If he wanted her to choose differently, to choose him, that was his problem. He'd honor her decisions. Didn't mean he wouldn't fight for more—for her—but this wasn't the time for that battle.

He was in the kitchen, tugging his shirt over his head, when her phone rang. It was there on the counter, impossible to miss the caller ID screen showing Elizabeth Wentworth's face.

Perfect.

Pippa rushed out of the bedroom to answer the phone while he slipped back in for his shoes and socks.

From what he could glean from Pippa's vague responses, Elizabeth was chattering on about something. Pippa paced up and down the hall; the tension of her kicking him out of her bed had faded into a friendly warmth for her friend. Whatever was going with Elizabeth, Pippa was all for it.

She nearly plowed into him at one point, and in her excitement over the call, she apparently forgot her anger. Pointing to the phone, she put it on speaker.

"Thanks for listening, Pippa. When I told her you were on the case, that I hired you, she smiled. Like, a *real* smile. Finally, it's sinking in that I'm in her corner."

Emmanuel managed not to roll his eyes.

"Well, you always have been. I'm glad something good has come of this mess." Pippa's tone was warm, but her eyes were cool as she watched him.

"Truly," Elizabeth gushed. "We haven't had conversations this open and sincere since before middle school."

It was hard to imagine Anna being an open and sincere mother at any stage of the parental process. Emmanuel knew a series of nannies had raised her daughter. But listening to the friends talk, he was forced to rethink his certainty about Anna's guilt in the Hicks murder.

The two people who knew the woman best were clearly aware of her inherent flaws.

"It's like she finally believes me," Elizabeth said. "I know you couldn't meet with her personally that day at the prison, but just knowing you tried to come out has given her some confidence. I've told her I believed in her innocence from the start, but I guess hiring you was the sign she needed to believe *me*."

"We are making progress on her case," Pippa promised.

He glared at her. That was a big stretch.

"Thank goodness. I'll let you go. I just wanted to tell you about the RevitaYou issue."

"I'll see what I can do from this end. That supplement is dangerous," Pippa said. "I'm so glad she's interested in being your mom again."

"Me too. It's more than refreshing." Elizabeth sniffed. "I'm such a baby. But..."

"I get it," Pippa assured her. "You deserve to have the best of your mom."

"You don't think it's the vitamins?"

Pippa laughed. "No. I think your mom is learning from a tough experience." She said goodbye and ended the call, and they both stared at her phone.

"What about RevitaYou?" he asked.

A lesser man might be offended that her attention had so wholly shifted away from him. He couldn't exactly call himself the bigger person here, but he wasn't offended. That tightness in his gut told him he'd rather have her attention, and he definitely wanted her body under his again. Or over. Being kicked out of her bed made his motions as jerky as his thoughts while he finished dressing.

"Apparently Anna has bribed someone in the prison system to deliver RevitaYou and other things to keep her comfortable and youthful during her incarceration."

"Of course she has." But if Anna had a cooperative network inside and she'd wanted to meet with Pippa, who had blocked that meeting?

"Elizabeth warned her. She's worried about the risks with the illnesses and deaths tied to the product," Pippa added, pacing again.

"Understandable. But if Wentworth won't listen, that's on her."

Pippa's nostrils flared as she whirled around to face him. "Manipulating a system doesn't make her a killer."

At last he had her attention. For the moment. "Did I say that?" He stared her down, waiting for her to argue. She didn't. "Remember to use the panic button," he said, with a little too much bite as he tapped the device. Her eyebrows arched in challenge, but he didn't back down. If she wanted to limit their conversation to the cases, it was fine with him.

"There are two unmarked cars on the street," he added. "One up front and one out back." And he would be close too. "Just in case Capital X figures out that application is bogus and originated with you."

"They won't." Her chin lifted. "Colton Investigations is better than that. Honestly, Griffin is your friend."

Yeah, and his friend would be pretty pissed off to learn Emmanuel had slept with the sister he was supposed to be protecting. "Pippa…" He just didn't know what else to say. "Forget it. We can talk tomorrow."

"Thanks for the panic button," she said. "Even though I know how to take care of myself."

Far safer to keep his mouth shut rather than be a jerk and remind her she'd let him take pretty good care of her in the past hour. No, he definitely was not the bigger man tonight.

Insulted, with no real cause, he stalked downstairs to his car. He'd known another night in the car was probable, and still it stung that she'd booted him out. He trusted the teams in the unmarked cars, but he couldn't leave her safety to others. He didn't want to pinch her independence, but that didn't mean he couldn't have her back.

Yes, Griffin was counting on him, but more than that, Emmanuel felt like he owed her. Especially after hearing Elizabeth and Pippa talk. He'd interviewed enough family members to know the difference between bluster and belief. He understood that believing wasn't always the right character assessment.

Elizabeth probably hadn't missed the signs of murderous tendencies. On the other hand, he'd let an unpleasant interaction color his view of the crime scene and the prime suspect. Anna wasn't a nice person, but thanks to the inconsistencies in the case, he was starting to think Pippa was right about the woman's innocence.

He looked up toward Pippa's window, half hoping he would see her watching for him. Of course, she wasn't there. Being there would imply he mattered to her. She had made it painfully clear he did not. What had she called it? A physical outlet.

And why was he so damn upset?

He dropped his head to the steering wheel and waited for his common sense and normal detachment to return. He wasn't the guy who got hung up on the girl. Especially not when the girl was a woman eight years his junior and had tossed a grenade into one of his closed cases.

He wasn't anyone's role model; he didn't want to be a hero. When it came to relationships, he wanted a woman willing to be warm and open. A woman to enjoy, who wasn't afraid to admit she wanted him back.

"Pipe dream," he said to the empty car.

Years ago, he'd proposed to a woman he thought fit those criteria, and he'd been burned. A reporter, she'd used his body and his connections to make a name for herself so she could move up to a bigger market. At least he discovered the truth before they were married. In his family, divorce wasn't an acceptable option. *For better or worse* was taken as a formal commitment.

It really sucked that the best sex he'd had in years would dredge up those old painful memories. Noticing that his battery was low on his phone, he plugged it in and turned on the car to charge it. The radio was tuned to an oldies station, and Elvis was singing a ballad about love. One of his mother's favorites. He switched off the radio and reclined his seat, closing his eyes and letting the hum of the engine lull him into a drowsy sleep.

Not much point in worrying about how Pippa affected him. When her brother found out, Emmanuel knew he was a dead man.

Pippa couldn't take the droning white noise anymore. She turned off the drying equipment and all the lights on her way back to her bedroom. She left her phone and the panic button on her nightstand while she got ready for bed. She stared at herself in the mirror over the sink, daydreaming about those sweet moments in Emmanuel's arms.

What had she been thinking? Too bad she couldn't blame the sugar high of the éclairs. She turned her back on her reflection, ashamed by the satisfied smile that kept flitting over her lips.

She had jumped Emmanuel as if he were the last slice of bacon on the platter on Christmas morning.

Oh, how the man could kiss. And do everything else with a master's touch, as well. That hadn't been good sex; it had been life altering. And she kicked the man out. What a fool. She walked out of the bathroom and stared at the rumpled bed. She should change the sheets, erase all traces of what they shared. Instead she caught herself hugging a pillow, breathing in his scent.

Why had she sent him packing?

Fear. A simple, if uncomfortable, admission. She was afraid of her feelings, afraid of losing herself and losing sight of her goals within the happy fog of a relationship. She'd watched her mom's goals and dreams get smothered by her dad's career. Her dad had subscribed to the theory that ambitious men deserved women who would support their goals. The rift and underlying unhappiness had left a lasting impression on her young heart. She loved both of her parents, and it was so sad to watch their marriage spiral out of control, to watch them fall out of love. She couldn't give that kind of support to Emmanuel without sacrificing herself, and she didn't expect him to adjust for her. It wasn't fair to either of them to pretend otherwise.

Pippa knew what she was capable of, knew how she dialed in on a case to the exclusion of all else. A man like Emmanuel wouldn't stick around for long when she had to cancel dates or change plans for the sake of a case.

Banishing all thoughts of "next time" from her mind, she straightened the bedding and traded her robe for her normal nightshirt. It wasn't nearly as warm as his skin or as comforting as having his arms around her.

He was a beautiful distraction, but she couldn't afford to become attached. Not to the man who had convicted Anna in the first place and definitely not to the man her brother had sent to keep tabs on her.

She battled back a blast of panic that Griffin would find out, but there was no way Emmanuel would volunteer any personal details of their evening. He didn't have a death wish, and deep down, aggravated or not, she knew he wouldn't want to embarrass her.

She appreciated his sense of fair play when he'd told her about the evidence box. If only it didn't feel as if she'd thanked him with sexual favors.

Eventually her sister would figure it out. That was going to be an awkward conversation, unless she could delay chatting with her sister for several days.

Considering how best to avoid her twin in the days ahead, she turned out the light and snuggled down into the bedding. Breathing in Emmanuel's scent, she closed her eyes and tried to sleep. She would have herself under control when she faced him again.

She wasn't sure of the time when a soft beep in the hallway brought her almost all the way out of a sweet dream of her body tangled with Emmanuel's. Ignoring the sound, she rolled to her side, trying to get back to the dream.

A squeak that sounded like the dry hinge at her front door brought her fully awake. She reached for the panic button on her nightstand while she listened for any confirmation that she might be in danger.

Maybe Emmanuel had let himself back in. Something to be mad about later. She was tempted to call out his name, but if someone was inside, it might be her sister Kiely. Sometimes her twin crashed in the second bedroom, so Pippa had given her a new code for the front door.

She must have dozed off waiting for another noise, because the next thing she knew, strong hands suddenly landed on her throat, cutting off her airway. The heavy body looming over her, a shadow in the dark room, made a low grunting sound as he choked her.

Gloves, not skin. She registered the different texture as she bucked and twisted away from the assault. Her hand gripped the panic button fob, fingers squeezing in a dazed hope that she'd pressed the right button and the signal was getting through.

She fought, twisting one way and kicking another, raking at the arms holding her. He wore some kind of coat and something over his face too. All she caught in her fingernails was fabric rather than skin. The man had her pinned down, and the bedding impeded her ability to escape.

Desperate, with bright sparks of light dancing at the edges of her vision, she planted her feet into the mattress and drove her hips up. The move loosened his grip, and she sucked in a short breath, but it wasn't nearly enough for her oxygen-depleted lungs.

She struggled against the inevitable while her lungs burned. Pain and panic filled her in equal measure under his crushing grip. She gave up on the key fob and managed to get an arm free of the bedding. Her hand landed on the stack of books on her nightstand, and she pummeled him with the nearest hardbound edition.

He grunted, then knocked the threat away, jerking her around as if he were wrestling with a small, crazed animal instead of a full-grown woman. The movement freed her legs and she kicked out wildly. Every time she threw him off a bit, she got a little more air. Another minute to live.

She heard a crash, followed by shouting and then the attacker was gone, off of her. Dragging in a ragged breath, she coughed and sputtered her way to the floor, crawling toward the safety of the bathroom. Behind her, she saw the shadows of two people fighting, one of them swearing in Spanish.

The room shook as the men slammed into a wall and then out of her bedroom and into the hallway. More voices were shouting now, but only one she recognized: Emmanuel. Disoriented and afraid, she huddled in the dark bathroom. Before she could remember she'd left her phone behind, she heard Emmanuel calling her name. Was it over? Her body quaked as she inched closer to the comforting sound of his voice. He hadn't gone home. He'd stayed close and come to her rescue, charging in to save her from that deadly, choking pressure. Was he all right?

Winded, his heart pounding in his ears, he couldn't tell if he was clear yet. He was getting too old for this crap. Rounding a corner, he paused, relieved that no one was on his tail. He removed the stocking cap and stuffed it into his coat pocket, exposing his graying hair. Yanking off the coat, he turned it inside out so the bright color showed, and concentrated on walking normally, despite the knee going stiff after wrestling with Iglesias.

The car he'd borrowed from his brother-in-law was still several blocks away. But at least now he wouldn't match the alert that was being broadcast for a perp in all black.

He took measured breaths, as more aches and pains lit up various points in his body. That little scrap of a lawyer had landed a couple of solid blows. He might have to call out tomorrow if the tenderness at his temple turned into a visible bruise. No way would he take a chance that Iglesias added up a defensive injury with the man in Colton's condo.

He'd been sure she was asleep, but her reactions had been too quick. And that panic button had been a mean surprise. Iglesias must have left that with her after the break-in. He'd given his daughter something similar when she'd gone to college. Just a little extra precaution in a dangerous world.

Stupid thoughtful detective. He knew his caring streak really should be fading, after all his years with the GRPD.

Iglesias was smitten, that was all, he decided. Hanging out and watching over the friend's little sister, it was natural. Hopefully he'd see through her before she burned him. The lawyer was surely as manipulative as her client. No decent person would help a conniving bitch like Wentworth.

He wouldn't be surprised if he peed blood for a day or two after that kick to his kidneys. Whoever taught Iglesias to fight dirty did a good job. Under other circumstances he might be impressed. Now, out of breath and afraid he was going to be scooped up any second, he hated the detective almost as much as he hated Hicks and Wentworth.

He'd heard the woman was tossing money around the prison, doing her best to pretend she was in charge. The guards would take the payoffs and consider it hazard pay for dealing with the Queen of Mean. No one inside got paid enough. He just hoped they took her money and didn't deliver on her silly demands.

When would she learn that the world didn't turn on her whim?

Insensitive people like Hicks and Wentworth deserved each other. He typically didn't judge others, but bullies? Never could stand one.

He pressed a hand to his aching side, wondering if Iglesias had cracked a rib. He hadn't seen that kind of skill and aggression coming from a smooth one like Iglesias. The man had been on him so fast he'd barely made it out the back door. Damn lucky he hadn't been exposed right then and there.

When he reached the car, he tossed the coat into the passenger seat, further distancing himself from the description Iglesias would be handing out. He wasn't hungry, but he needed more of an alibi, so he rolled into a drive-through for a burger, fries and a milkshake, not outside the norm.

Heading home, he contemplated the real trouble: the lawyer had survived.

He had to get her to drop this nonsense about finding the real killer. The jury's verdict had been good enough for everyone else—why not her? The sad daughter just had to accept that her mother wasn't a good person.

He'd give her forty-eight hours to come to her senses and drop the case. If she didn't, well, he'd think of something. Going back to her condo wasn't an option. Iglesias would surely up the security measures again. Hell, they'd probably add a dog to the patrol and put a bear trap on the back stairs.

He choked on a fry when he thought about what a scent dog might pick up. Had to ditch these clothes, the shoes, all of it.

Wentworth and her lawyer were costing him bigtime, making this entire mess worse.

He swore as he turned a corner, his back and shoulders already so damn sore. He couldn't go to his normal doctor, couldn't file the claim with his insurance through the department.

If he couldn't finish this, who could he trust to take over and make sure the Hicks case stayed closed and Wentworth never stepped out into the free world again?

That would take some thought, some finagling and more than a case of beer.

Before he invested another cent in this endeavor, he was going to dive deeper into the lawyer. If she wouldn't come to her senses for her own sake, maybe she'd make the smart choice to protect someone else.

Unlike Anna Wentworth and that sleazy David Hicks, the Colton family had a solid reputation in Grand Rapids, and everyone knew how tight they were, especially after their parents were killed.

There was an angle worth digging into.

"Pippa, honey?" She heard Emmanuel's voice, soft and close, just on the other side of the bathroom door. "Pippa, it's me. Can I come in?"

Instantly she felt calmer and took her first deep breath in too long. She tried to answer him, but her throat was too raw. He turned the doorknob and she squeaked in fear. On an oath, he slowly nudged the door open until he could come inside. "You're safe now," he said, crouching in front of her.

He had a split lip and a smear of blood on his cheek. Otherwise he looked just as he did when he'd left. He held his hand out to her and waited as if he didn't have anywhere else to be for the rest of his life.

Emmanuel. She put her hands in his palm, steadier just from that simple connection.

"That's my girl. Come on with me now."

Yes. His girl. She wanted to be his. Needed to be his. When she tried to stand, her legs quaked and wobbled, but he caught her around the waist and kept her upright.

Her bedroom was a series of tumultuous images as he guided her through and out to the hallway. She saw scuff marks on her walls, from the fight no doubt, and her back door was open too. Her condo was full of people, including the officers who'd been stationed outside and paramedics arriving with their bags and a transport chair.

She clung to Emmanuel's hand and shook her head. She didn't want to go to a hospital.

He pulled her into his arms and cuddled her close to his chest. "You're safe now. He's gone." He murmured more words in Spanish, too fast for her to understand.

"Wh-who," she stuttered. Trying to speak without pain was impossible. "Who was it?" she asked, wincing.

"Hush. Don't talk. Let the paramedics take a look."

She knew Emmanuel and the others had questions for her. She had questions of her own. But interviews had to wait until the paramedics were satisfied about her condition. They covered her bare legs with a blanket and gave her oxygen while they checked her vitals. Her blood pressure was up, as expected, but her lungs sounded clear.

"Do you want me to call Griffin or Kiely?" Emmanuel offered.

She shook her head. She wanted only him right now.

Emmanuel brought her tea laced with honey so she could answer a few preliminary questions about the assault. He drifted out of reach at one point, giving a statement or guiding the responding CSI to the crime scene. Thankfully, it wasn't her younger sister Sadie. She didn't want anyone else to see her while she felt so fragile. It occurred to her then that her bedroom was a crime scene, and tears rolled down her cheeks.

"Keep breathing," one paramedic said. "Easy and smooth."

She tried to comply, but it was easier when Emmanuel was close again, his hand stroking through her hair. When she refused a trip to the hospital, the paramedics left her with a cold pack and instructions, urging her to follow up with her doctor as soon as possible.

"You should go," Emmanuel said. "They can give you something for the pain."

"The cold pack is fine," she said with a croak.

"Please, don't talk." He escorted the CSI to the door, and finally it was just the two of them in the condo.

"Who was it?" she asked.

"*Shh.* I don't know," Emmanuel replied. "He wore a ski mask."

"And gloves." She turned the cold pack. "Did you catch him?"

"I couldn't get that mask off before he made it out the back door." His scowl was fierce, and it remained so even after he scrubbed at his face. "You sure you don't want a doctor?"

She shook her head. There was more he wasn't saying, but she didn't have the energy to press him for answers or theories.

Gently, he tipped back her chin and moved the ice pack to examine her throat. "The scene is processed," he said. "You can change clothes and take a shower if you want. I'll keep watch out here."

"Gloves," she repeated. "No prints."

"I'm begging you, Pippa. Please stop talking."

The worry on his face made it all so much worse. She had to talk to communicate, but when she flinched with pain, she saw it reflected in his eyes, so she kept her mouth shut. Her body felt stiff and sore as she headed down the hall. At her bedroom door, she halted, unsure if she could walk in alone.

Emmanuel was right on her heels, and she turned into his arms. His hands moved up and down her spine, comforting and gentle. "You saved me," she said, unable to hold it in any longer. She'd nearly become a statistic tonight. "Thank you."

"They took pictures and bagged most everything in your room," he explained. His cheeks colored. "Faster that way. I had to tell them I was here too."

It wasn't ideal, but it was better to volunteer the information than try to hide it and raise more questions. "How did the man get inside?"

Emmanuel grumbled something incoherent. "Somehow he sneaked past the unmarked cars and bypassed your electronic dead bolt with a key."

So she wasn't safe here anymore. Without the panic button she probably wouldn't be alive. The tremors of shock started in earnest, and Emmanuel picked her up and carried her back to the couch, wrapping her in a quilt. "I'll make more tea."

When he returned, she sipped the tea, letting the honey soothe her sore throat while he explained the events from his perspective. "I got the alert that the panic button went off," he began. "As I told the others, I charged up here to help. Your door was unlocked, not open. I followed the noises to the bedroom and knocked the man off of you. We went a few rounds on the floor and down the hallway. He was clearly aiming for the back door."

So the man knew the condo layout, if not her condo in particular.

"He seemed pretty familiar with the layout," Emmanuel confirmed her unspoken question. "In the back hall he knocked me into the fire extinguisher, and was down the steps before I recovered. I knew the other team was out there so I came back for you."

"Thank you," she whispered.

"There may be some follow-up questions by tomorrow."

This time she nodded, rather than worry him with the sound of her voice. When she looked at him, she wanted to cry all over again. Bracing against that, she stood up. "Shower."

This time she would make it all the way to her bathroom. She needed to wash away the memory of those horrible hands. It felt as if the attacker's breath through the ski mask had stained her skin. Stale breath and sweaty wool were not a good combination.

"Do you need help?" he offered.

She desperately wanted to say no, to be the independent woman she'd been before the assault. But at her bedroom door her feet froze again. The attack was too fresh. She turned toward the guest room. "I'll use the second bath." It had the supplies her twin sister preferred, but it would work for tonight.

"I'll get some clothes for you," he said.

She pointed at him. "Not leaving?"

"No."

The simple answer did more good for her than a longer explanation. "Thank you."

He pressed a finger to his lips. *"Shh."*

Everything was neat and tidy in the guest room and a stark contrast to the mess she knew was waiting in her bedroom. For right now, all she could manage was getting clean enough to feel safe in her skin. After that she'd figure out how to feel safe in her home.

When she stepped out of the shower, her hair dryer was on the counter along with a glass of water and a bottle of ibuprofen. Cozy flannel pants in a deep green plaid, a thermal shirt and thick socks were stacked neatly for her, as well. She didn't even care that he'd gone through her drawers to find the clothing.

"You okay?" he asked from the other side of the bedroom door.

The man was standing guard for her in the hallway. Her heart tripped and fell. He'd seen her naked hours ago, but he didn't presume that gave him the right to hover too close now. Still, he guaranteed she could feel safe. Were they back to the original detective and attorney status or were they walking at the fringes of friendship?

"Yes," she said. Although it hurt, she pitched her voice loud enough that he could hear. Was it vanity or fear that had her wondering how long it would take her voice to recover?

Dressed and ready for another cold pack, she opened the door all the way, grateful for his respect of her privacy. She stared up at him, knowing he didn't want her to speak, but needing to show him how much his kindness mattered.

She wound her arms around his waist and rested her head on his chest.

He let her hang on, his arms banding around her carefully, as if he was afraid she might break.

"You'll let me stay tonight? Inside," he clarified.

She nodded, her cheek rubbing against the warm, solid wall of his chest. She was so thankful she didn't have to be alone.

Chapter 10

Emmanuel understood Pippa's restlessness. She wasn't ready to rest, despite the pain and exhaustion plaguing her. He knew there were things she wanted to talk about, and there were things he needed to say. Once she'd relaxed a bit, he guided her back toward her living room.

"Do you want coffee?" she asked.

She didn't sound at all like herself. Her smooth, often prim voice was rough and damaged. "I'll make it," he said. "Do you want more tea?" She shook her head. "How about hot chocolate?"

He was relieved when she nodded her answer. Her throat needed time to rest, but she would want to hash through a few more details before she could settle.

When the coffee and hot chocolate were ready, they sank into opposite ends of her couch. She seemed steadier since her shower, but the signs of shock were still there. What he had to say wouldn't make it any better.

"I think I know who broke in tonight."

She raised her eyebrows, waiting with more patience than she'd ever shown before.

"Joe McRath." It didn't sound any better out loud than it did in his head. He was potentially accusing a decorated cop of doing the unthinkable. He wanted to catch the perp and he wanted to be wrong about the suspect. Maybe CSI would find evidence to lead them to a different conclusion. Catching his friend and mentor in an attempted murder was too bizarre to process.

Her brow flexed into a frown. "Saw his face?" she queried in her raspy voice.

"No." He sighed and leaned forward, bracing his elbows on his knees. "I've worked with him a long time. Trained with him, gone through various qualifications and exercises. The man under the hat and gloves and coat was built the same as Joe." Not enough for a confrontation or to take to the lieutenant. Just enough of a similarity that Emmanuel would have to take a closer look into why Joe might've done this.

"Not a Capital X attack?"

"No." He appreciated her brevity, though he had to hide the urge to cringe. Every word was a source of pain; he could see it in her eyes and the tension in her hands. He wished he'd insisted on a visit to the hospital.

He shook his head. "As you said, it would take some pretty speedy work to connect you and the alias loan application. They have no reason to suspect the application is a trap anyway. To hear Griffin tell it, the company has been operating outside of the law for years, and they're quite confident in their ability to keep it up."

"W Plenty of men are built like Joe."

He turned to catch her gaze. "Then call it instinct. Attacking you is minor compared to evidence tampering. It smells fishy, his daughter dating Hicks and Hicks dying at the home of his new lover, Anna. Joe has access to the evidence room, and I'm sure he has friends and ties to every prison in the state."

"To keep me away."

He nodded.

"But kill me and stage the scene?" Her gaze was skeptical.

Though he admired her willingness to be objective, Emmanuel was all but certain McRath had been under that ski mask. The sergeant had access to the building codes, and assuming he'd painted the threat on her wall, he would've had time to make a copy of the key for her front door that bypassed the electronic code.

"Who else?" he said. "He must have framed Wentworth. He knew about my dislike for the woman and complained frequently about her frivolous calls." He couldn't prove Joe was the culprit. Yet. "Nothing else adds up," he continued. "That evidence was laid out too neatly. You've said so yourself."

"A few times." She gave him a weary half smile.

Looking back, he could kick himself for following the breadcrumbs like an idiot newbie. And now all that perfectly planted evidence was gone.

Joe had access, and if he was guilty, he had motive to steal it out of the evidence room and threaten the lawyer determined to expose the real killer.

"Pippa, I'm going to dig deeper into McRath's connections to Wentworth and Hicks," he said. "He's been on the force long enough that she could have pissed him off a thousand times. Maybe it was just too much and he snapped."

Her eyes were still a little red from the attack and the subsequent lack of sleep. The stress was evident in the way her hand gripped the quilt over her lap. "She's difficult."

"More than difficult," he said. "Wentworth's calls tied up good police officers, wasting time. Not something Joe would appreciate."

The marks on Pippa's neck were already deepening, and tomorrow Emmanuel would have to answer to Griffin. He was here to protect her, from herself and any outside threat. So far, he was failing in grand style.

"Emmanuel." Her hand slid over his, and the coolness of it slayed him. She was always so warm and vibrant. "Did you hear me?"

"Sorry, I was lost in thought."

She tapped her own brow. "I noticed." The smile she gave him was a shadow of her typical self. He wanted to bolt out of here, or just hold her all night long. Neither seemed like an acceptable solution.

"Be careful," she said. "If we're off track, we could wreck his reputation. Won't send another innocent person to jail."

"I get it," he said, pushing to his feet. He paced behind the back of the couch. "I still have to take a closer look. No one else on that list has access, ties or motive." He couldn't believe he was saying these things. "He was my mentor, Pippa. I don't want to wreck a good man or a good friendship either."

"Motive," she said. Her voice cracked and she coughed, her eyes tearing up. "Never motive in this case."

"And who should've found that motive the first time around? Me."

He couldn't bear the pain clouding those beautiful green eyes. "You need to get some rest. Voice and body. Even if it's not deep sleep, you need to rest," he said when she started to protest.

She opened her mouth again, and he cut her off again. "Hush. If you lose your voice, you'll be more upset than you are now."

She glared at him.

"Finish your hot chocolate."

"Dictator," she whispered, once she'd polished off the warm drink.

He took the cup to the kitchen and came back for her. "Bedroom or couch?"

Her teeth sunk into her lower lip. "Couch."

"All right." He went to the guest room for pillows and a blanket and proceeded to tuck her in. "I'll take the chair." He kissed the worry that puckered her brow. "It beats the car," he joked.

When she was comfortable on the couch, he turned the lights down and settled into the chair, stretching out his legs. In the morning he would have another briefing with the officers who let the intruder through. And he would take another hard look for any evidence outside.

As much as he didn't want it to be Joe, he knew in his gut the sergeant was guilty. As Pippa said, he just had to figure out why, and then he could figure out the best path forward.

When Pippa woke again, early-morning sunlight was filtering through the front window. She wondered why she'd fallen asleep on the couch, and then all the chaos from last night came rushing back. Tears pricked the back of her eyes, but she would not start today as she ended yesterday. Sitting up, she rolled her stiff shoulders and gently stretched the battered muscles of her neck. Nothing a hot shower wouldn't fix.

Her cell phone was on the coffee table, but there was no sign of Emmanuel. The chair where he'd slept was empty, the pillow and blanket he'd used folded neatly in the seat. He'd probably gone home or even gone into the station early to get a jump on his new personal investigation.

His absence inexplicably irritated her, and she scolded herself for being out of sorts. She hadn't wanted a babysitter, and yet now that he was gone, she missed him. The man was entitled to live his life, regardless of the promise he'd made to her overprotective brother.

She checked her messages, mildly disappointed that he hadn't left her a text. Come to think of it, no one had reached out to her. The way information moved through the GRPD, Sadie must have heard about the attack. Pippa knew she could reach out, any of her siblings would happily give her a shoulder to cry on. But with everything going on, that comfort would surely turn protective and hiding wouldn't resolve this. Annoyed with her uncharacteristic neediness, she took a long, deep breath and slowly stretched her arms overhead. Getting to her feet, she padded to the half bath down the hall. She still wasn't ready to face her bedroom all by herself.

Had it been blissful ignorance or an ostrich mentality to believe things couldn't get worse after the break-in? That incident paled in comparison to last night's direct and violent attack. That man, whoever he'd been, was determined to silence her forever. To kill. She was alive thanks to Emmanuel's quick response. She should spend today celebrating being alive, rather than revisiting events that couldn't be changed.

Of course she felt violated and vulnerable, another stain on a home she loved. That was a basic human reaction to being attacked by a stranger in a familiar place. Once the wall was reset, she'd invite Kiely over and break out some champagne, reclaiming the space as hers. That was her approach to a setback: brazen it out and keep moving forward.

To hear her mom tell it, she'd been that way from the womb. While her twin sister might be more deliberate, once Pippa decided on a course of action, she ran with it. She had never seen the value in holding back.

This wouldn't be any different, no matter how hard her enemy came at her. Anna Wentworth was innocent, and she should not be in prison. If the process of freeing her caused Pippa some distress, so be it. This too would pass.

Ready to exit the bathroom, she heard footsteps in the hallway. Another intruder? Her heart raced and her fingers curled into fists. Damn, she didn't have her phone in here to call for help. She looked around the small space for anything she could turn into a weapon. As she tried to silently remove the heavy porcelain lid from the toilet tank, blood rushed through her ears, making it hard to distinguish the noises on the other side of the door.

At the knock on the door she had to stifle a scream, and the tank lid dropped back into place with a bang. Thankfully, it didn't break.

"Pippa? Are you okay in there?"

Not an intruder, Emmanuel. He hadn't left. She should've known better. Dropping her head against the door, she tried to catch her breath while her heart rate resumed a pace closer to normal.

"The shower's free," he said. "Sorry about that. Pippa?"

"I'm okay." Cursing her trembling hands, she unlocked the door and opened it. His smile smoothed the rough edges of her jangling nerves. "Good morning."

He winced at her voice. "Still hurts?"

She nodded. Somehow he looked as handsome as ever in yesterday's clothing. She just enjoyed the view with his damp hair curling at his collar and his beard neatly trimmed.

"I made a fresh pot of coffee, but I don't have time to do a full breakfast."

"No problem." She couldn't have eaten if she'd wanted to; her throat was so raw and tight it hurt to swallow more this morning than it had last night. Depending on how the coffee cooperated, she might try some soup later when her stomach woke up.

She followed him to the kitchen, where he clipped his badge to his belt and put the gun in its holster at his hip. "You're sure you're okay?"

Not at all, but she wouldn't be one more worry for him. "Go on," she insisted. "I need to go into the office today."

"All right." He dropped a quick kiss on her lips, the movement so easy and domestic it rattled her all over again. "Keep me in the loop about where you are today."

"You too."

"I promise." His sexy smile left her feeling feverish.

Normally she'd head straight to the shower, but she

didn't want to reveal the weakness that she wasn't ready to face her own bedroom. For now, she had the excuse of seeing him off. She perched on a counter stool and watched him make a cup of coffee in a stainless travel mug, a little baffled to discover having him in her space felt so right. Something else to analyze later.

When he was all set, he came around the counter and kissed her again. "Whatever you need, ask," he said. "There are two teams watching the building, and they have instructions to follow you today, so behave."

Obviously she was putting out a seriously strong victim vibe, and that wasn't at all who she was. It certainly wasn't the type of person she wanted to be. "I'll behave."

His phone hummed in his pocket. Checking the display, he groaned. "I forgot. My uncle will be here in about an hour to change the lock on your front door. I notified your siblings and assured them you were fine and had it under control. I'll check in on you throughout the day. Don't bother getting mad about any of it."

She laughed, but the sound was more of a rusty snort.

"Lock up behind me." He paused at the front door, indulging in one more kiss before he walked out.

Knowing he was waiting to hear the lock tumble, she flipped the dead bolt right away. Would it make any difference to the man with a copy of her key? Fear swamped her and her knees buckled. She slid to the floor, hoping she could drag herself up again when his uncle arrived.

She pushed her hair back from her face and tugged hard until her scalp stung. The discomfort cut through the fear and she stood up. It was either sell the condo or start reclaiming it as her own. Running was the coward's way. She would not let the person behind these attacks change her life.

She turned the fan and dehumidifier back on and then paused in the kitchen for a few careful sips of coffee. Next stop, the bedroom. She would never claim her steps were steady, but she made it to the doorway.

She expected to see remnants of the attack. The tangled sheets, the overturned lamp, the books from her nightstand she had used as weapons.

Tears dribbled down her cheek, but this time it was a wash of gratitude. Somewhere between tucking her in on the couch and making coffee this morning, Emmanuel had changed her sheets and made her bed, minus the duvet. He'd cleaned up the broken lamp and stacked her books in an orderly pile. Other than the missing lamp and duvet, everything was in its place. Her entire body relaxed; the sensation was almost as effective as having him here.

The man was a saint. She never thought to associate that term with the name Emmanuel Iglesias. From the moment she'd read the transcript of his testimony, he'd been her enemy. Now he was her partner in this convoluted pursuit of justice.

Her partner in more than that, if she was honest with herself.

Shoulders back, she marched through to her bathroom and turned on the water for a shower. Scrubbing clean again helped restore a sense of self and purpose. When she was dressed for the day in a cozy turtleneck that hid the bruises and makeup was deftly applied to blur the signs of her rough night, she took a cup of coffee into her office.

The original plan was for her to work from home

while she waited for the approval on the Capital X loan application. The break-in and attack had cost her enough time and confidence. Anna was counting on her to make real progress, and fast.

Every minute alone, despite the precautions, her agitation grew until it was an itch down to her bones. It was ridiculous to look over her shoulder in her home. She had to stay until the lock was repaired, but she couldn't work here all day. She'd just come back when the cleaning crew was ready to reclaim their equipment.

Technically she needed to open the computer only long enough to check the progress on the application and look for the approval email. Still alone, she opened her floor safe and withdrew the laptop. It booted within moments, and she confirmed there were no issues with her application. She just had to wait. She'd locked it away again when her phone rang.

Glancing at the caller ID, she saw it was Elizabeth. It was tempting to ignore the call and send her friend to voice mail, but that would only delay the inevitable. "Good morning, Elizabeth," she answered brightly to hide the rasp in her voice.

"I know I'm being a pain," Elizabeth said. "But is there any news?"

Since last night? Pippa stroked the soft fabric of her cashmere turtleneck, searching for patience. "Nothing definitive," she said, thinking of Emmanuel's theory. "It takes time, but as I said last night, we are making progress."

"Be honest, Pippa. Do you really think you can get her out?"

Pippa reminded herself that Elizabeth was a good friend. Her best friend, in fact. But she couldn't offer any guarantees. She had to stop and sip her coffee to soothe her throat. "Every step forward gets us a little closer." That much was true.

"Thank you." Elizabeth sighed. "I don't know what I'd do without you."

It gave her a boost to hear those words. "I do understand. You're worried, and I know this is urgent." Even more so now that Anna was taking RevitaYou.

"I'm going to see her again today," Elizabeth said. "At this rate, I might be better off buying a place near the prison."

"Don't go looking at real estate just yet," Pippa said.

"I don't trust the prison to tell me if she gets sick off that junk she's taking. She claims the supplement is offsetting the lousy food. You'd think prison would be a wake-up call, but she's as appearance focused as ever."

Despite everything, Pippa laughed. "When it comes to your mother, I wouldn't expect sweeping changes. She's far from typical, and you love her for it."

"True enough," Elizabeth said. "What's wrong with your voice?"

"Just allergies," she fibbed.

"Uck. I'm sorry my high from yesterday didn't last long."

Pippa searched for reassuring words. The police certainly hadn't been inclined to help her. Everyone on the jury was willing to think the worst of Anna. She wanted to meet with her client and ask the questions no one bothered to ask the first time around. "Has she talked at all about Hicks's connections? It's possible he confided in her about someone else wanting to hurt him."

"No," Elizabeth replied. "It's on my list of topics to tackle today. She is a little more approachable these days. Or maybe it seems that way because she can't dash off on her own agenda. Most days she seems genuinely happy to see me."

That was a different kind of progress all together and one long overdue in Pippa's opinion. Anna was never a touchy-feely kind of mother, though she was devoted to Elizabeth in her own way.

"I'll keep up the visits," Elizabeth said. "Maybe they're doing some group-therapy thing. It can't be the RevitaYou that's giving me a nicer version of mom lately."

Pippa chuckled. "I'm sure it's not."

"I'll let you get back to work. Take care of those allergies."

"Thanks. I'll keep you posted," Pippa promised as they ended the call.

In the silence that followed, Pippa's skin started to crawl. Thankfully, Emmanuel's uncle showed up. While he worked, she admitted defeat and packed a bag to go to the office as soon as he was finished. Better to make some progress there than stew over all the things she couldn't control here.

Once the new lock was in and working, and programmed, she paid for both new locks. Then she notified Emmanuel and let him tell the teams about her change in plans. She made it to the car without hyperventilating, and as she drove out of the lot, she decided that being in the car gave her a good reason to look over her shoulder.

On the short drive across town, she got a call from Kiely and answered using her voice commands.

Naturally the car didn't recognize her voice, and the call went to voice mail. Her sister called back immediately, and Pippa tried again—and failed again—to pick up. She listened to the voice mail as soon as it came through.

"Hey, Pippa. Just checking in on you. On *you*, not the case," Kiely clarified. "Griffin told us there was more trouble at your condo overnight. Call me back when you get this."

Pippa unwrapped a hard candy to soothe her throat, sucking on it for the duration of the drive. When she was parked in her space at the office, she called Kiely back.

"Pippa!" Kiely sounded relieved.

"Hi," she croaked.

"Oh, no. What happened?" Unlike Elizabeth, her sister picked up on the trouble in her voice immediately. Pippa reminded herself she was thankful for a big family. "If I told you I had a cold, would you believe me?"

"Not a chance. You're never sick," Kiely replied.

"Well, first of all, other than the voice and a few bruises, I'm perfectly okay," Pippa assured her. "There was another break-in, yes." Best to give Kiely the facts only. "We did not catch the intruder, and the GRPD has all the available evidence at their lab."

"We?" Kiely had that tone, the one Pippa knew she couldn't avoid. "Was someone staying over?"

"For a private investigator, you pick up on the wrong details," Pippa said. "And you're completely off track."

"Stop dodging the question."

"I said *we* as it refers to the protective detail Detective Iglesias assigned to watch the condo." It was only half a lie. A fib, really, and mostly for the sake of privacy.

"They did a lousy job if an intruder got past them," Kiely pointed out. "I'm coming over."

"Then turn around. I'm at the office." It was probably a good idea. "Come to the office anyway. The lock at my front door is completely new. There's no key option. And I have your new code."

She chose to wait at the car rather than face her sister in the office, where they might be overheard. Opening the app on her new door lock, she used the remote option to set a code for Kiely. The rest of her siblings would have to knock for a while.

Kiely parked and hurried to Pippa's car. Naturally her sister saw straight through the makeup and clothing as she climbed out from the driver's seat. "Pippa! What happened? You look like hell." She pulled Pippa in for a gentle hug.

"Thanks. I feel worse."

"Then go home," Kiely said. "Oh. I get that."

Pippa was grateful she didn't have to say a word for her twin to understand the higher stress of staying home. "The attack last night was direct. Emmanuel called it attempted murder when he gave his statement. No real damage to the condo, just me." She pulled down her turtleneck, showing the bruises on her throat. "At least I can talk today."

"If sandpaper could talk, maybe."

Pippa chuckled, then coughed. Just telling the watered-down version of the story face-to-face made her feel weak. She cleared her throat.

Kiely straightened her collar. "You need a security system."

"I had electronic locks in a secure building. I have better smart locks now. With a doorbell camera." Pippa didn't explain Emmanuel's role in the quick and expert lock service.

"Good." Kiely looked to the office, then at some

point behind Pippa's shoulder. It was all she could do to stand there and not panic. "You have to let the Wentworth case go," Kiely declared.

That was the last thing Pippa expected to hear. "You know I can't do that." Her throat burned, but she wouldn't let Kiely run roughshod over her life and career. "I won't drop a case or unpopular client just because things get dicey."

Kiely sighed heavily. "I know." She smiled. "Can't blame a sister for trying. At the very least you have to bring in some sort of personal protection."

"A bodyguard?" Pippa rolled her eyes. "Griffin already did that."

Kiely laughed. "The detective?"

Pippa nodded. "I should get inside and do some real work. Can we talk about this more later?"

"You're into him," Kiely stated. Then she beamed. "Tell me everything."

"Stop." Pippa wanted to smack that look off her sister's face. "This is not the time or place."

"Fine. But I will find out. From you or another reliable source." Kiely pulled her keys from her pocket. "Any word on the other case?"

"Still early, but you and Riley will be the first to know."

"Sounds good." She gave her another hug. "Call me if you need anything. And don't overdo it."

Pippa wanted to be snarky, but between her sore throat and her sister quickly dashing back to her car, the opportunity was missed. She hauled everything into the office and settled in behind her desk. She felt so much better here than at home.

In the privacy of her office, she pulled out the laptop for Alison Carrington and checked on the email account. No alerts from Capital X, only a customer service survey from the store where Kiely had purchased the laptop.

Satisfied she couldn't do more on that front, Pippa shut down the alias's laptop and stowed it back in her bag under her desk. Then she resumed her search for the real killer in the Hicks case. How close could she get to Leigh McRath without alerting the father? Pippa reviewed all of the personal details she had on Hicks. According to the prosecutor, Anna had been jealous of a different lover as well as threatened by his blackmail attempt.

No other lover was ever identified in the court proceedings, but the prosecutor only needed to create doubt. Hicks had a reputation as a player in high society, and that had been verified over and over again with a parade of witnesses that Anna had glowered at during the trial. Hicks's credit card history backed up an active and extravagant dating life. It seemed as if he blackmailed one lover to finance lavish dates and entertainment with another.

Definitely a slimeball, although handsome enough and connected enough to tempt Anna. She adored handsome men; moreover, she thrived on being the center of attention. Pippa wondered if anyone from his family would speak with her about his social life. It wasn't exactly a breach of protocol, and Emmanuel couldn't be the only one taking risks here.

She reached for the phone just as her older brother Griffin filled the office doorway. His expression was thunderous. "What in the hell are you doing here?"

"I beg your pardon." Thanks to the sore throat, she

couldn't work up a proper snippy tone. "This is a place of business," she said. "You're out of line."

He stepped inside and closed the door behind him. Rather than take a seat in a visitor's chair, he rounded to her side of the desk, crouching in front of her. The temper brewing in his eyes softened to concern. "Show me."

"You're not my boss or my doctor."

"Technically, I'm sort of your boss."

She latched on to the only excuse she could think of. "This is related to a situation that you are not the boss of."

"Pippa. Show me."

She wanted to argue, but her throat hurt. He'd get his way eventually. "It will only make you mad."

"I'm already mad." He rested his hands lightly on her knees. "Come on. I don't want to see you hurt."

"Then I definitely shouldn't show you."

"Stop talking like a lawyer." His lips twitched. "I mopped the floor with you in debate club."

"That was high school." He'd been two years ahead of her and far more experienced. "Only once."

"I need to know that you're okay."

"It's not enough that I'm sitting right here, the picture of health?"

"Your voice sounds like you're chewing gravel even when you're speaking softly."

Resisting wasn't going to get him out of her way, and she had work to do for Anna and Elizabeth. Choosing efficiency, she drew the turtleneck down so he could see the marks on her neck.

Griffin cursed. "I'm so sorry."

"Not your fault." She adjusted her sweater and stiffened her spine. "I appreciate your concern, but this has no bearing on you as a protective big brother or CI partner." She shooed him back to the other side of the desk. If this concerned-brother routine went on much longer, she might burst into tears, and that would be a disaster.

"Did you see a doctor?" Griffin asked.

"No need. The paramedics checked me over."

"Let's get you a protective detail."

"You already did that," she said. "And before you suggest it, I'm not walking around in bubble wrap, body armor, or with a full entourage of bulky men in dark suits and sunglasses. Detective Iglesias and his unmarked cars are enough."

Griffin's lips tilted at one corner. "What about stretchy velvet tracksuits and sunglasses? You can choose the color they wear."

"Get out of my office," she said, thoroughly exasperated. If he was cracking jokes, he was confident she'd survive.

"I thought Emmanuel could handle this," Griffin muttered.

"He did." She felt heat creeping into her cheeks.

Without Emmanuel she would not be sitting here today. She'd be in a hospital bed at the very least, more likely the morgue if the intruder had had his way. None of that was safe to say around her brother. She hadn't mentioned it, not even to Emmanuel, but she'd recognized the deadly intent in the man's breath, not just his grip.

"Emmanuel said you didn't get a description of the assailant." Griffin shoved his hands into his pockets.

Of course they'd talked in detail. "Emmanuel and the responding officers had better notes about his size and build. All I saw was the black ski mask, gloves and coat."

Griffin sank into a chair. "I heard. I came over hoping to get more to go on."

"Trust me, I'd love to give you more, but the man wasn't kind enough to attack me in daylight without a mask."

"Riley and I talked. It's best if you move back into the house until this blows over."

"No." She wanted to shout and yell at her brother for being an idiot. Out of respect for the resulting pain, she checked the urge. She smiled instead, an expression she knew her brother would recognize as false. "I'm an adult. My home and the new safety measures in place are sufficient." How could she explain that if she left, she'd only be more afraid to return? "And I'm staying on the Wentworth case until that innocent woman is out of jail."

He started to protest, but she cut him off. "Save your breath. Have you seen or heard from Brody?"

"Still in the wind," Griffin said, honoring the change of subject. "Let's all have dinner at the house. I'll get everybody together and—"

"No, thank you," she said. "I really can't cope with that. I'm tired," she confessed. "There are a few tasks I need to check off my list, then I'm going home, having soup and going to bed early."

Griffin opened his mouth and wisely snapped it shut. "All right. But you've got all of us at your back. Remember that."

He came around the desk again and helped her up so he could hug her. She didn't resist; in fact, she let herself lean just a little. "You are an excellent big brother," she said. "Bossy and overprotective, but excellent." Stepping away from him she added, "I'll let you know when the approval comes through from Capital X."

She could see how badly he wanted to say that didn't matter, but neither of them would believe it.

"I'll leave you to it." He paused at the door. "One last thing? Don't be afraid to ask for help."

"I promise."

With the office to herself again, she was just digging into her case file, making a plan, when Sadie stopped by, followed soon after by Riley. A veritable parade of siblings needing to see her with their own eyes.

In between, she fielded text message check-ins from Emmanuel. Somehow those didn't bother her. By the time she actually succeeded in dialing the number for Hicks's mother, she was almost grateful no one picked up. She left a voice message with her name and number anyway, assuring the woman she only wanted true justice for her son by making sure the right person was behind bars.

Only time would tell if that call had any impact or value for Anna.

In the meantime, she returned to the task of evaluating the victim's credit card records and banking history, matching the dates he'd been out with other women to the gossip columns in the local papers.

She couldn't call the man discreet, but he didn't seem prone to drawing undue attention when he was out at events or on casual dates. There were several pictures of Hicks with one particular woman around the holidays last year. But that was the closest she could come to finding anything that might qualify as a relationship. Nothing criminal in that. Unfortunately it gave her no leads.

Her stomach growled, and she remembered she hadn't eaten anything today. It was already past six. She checked her phone for any updates from Emmanuel, but he hadn't reached out since three, when he told her things were slow during his time on the tip line the GRPD had set up for information on the key players in the RevitaYou crisis.

Though they hadn't made any formal plans or declarations, she assumed he would show up at her place at some point this evening. Too weary to cook, she looked over the menu online of her favorite sandwich shop. She could pick up a meal for him and soup for herself and be ready to feed them both, or have extras for tomorrow.

Deciding to check one last time for any news on the loan application, she turned on the laptop and logged on with the alias's information. Once she opened the email, she saw the message from Capital X. Apparently they were moving through the approval process with lightning speed.

She opened the email, and her hand immediately touched her throat as she read through the information. They had approved Alison Carrington's loan request for $25,000 at a 30 percent interest rate. For the life of her, she didn't understand how people fell for such outrageous terms.

The schedule showed the first payment would be due in three days. Not a lot of time for an initial, legitimate investment to yield a return. A smart applicant would hold back the amount of the first payment from the original loan amount or risk getting in deeper.

All she had to do was click Accept. The money

would be transferred and the clock would start ticking. It wasn't even real. She was doing this to protect real applicants, people who didn't know better and felt as if they had no other solutions beyond the Capital X financial abuse.

She checked the box to accept the repayment schedule, and the screen changed. The next section was an acknowledgement that, in the event of a missed payment, Capital X had the right to adjust the interest rate, call in the entirety of the loan, and take any and all required action to recoup their investment.

A chill iced her skin. Understanding the Capital X tactics, she knew that any sincere applicant who accepted the terms was setting themselves up for broken bones at best. With Capital X so adept at eluding investigators and criminal lawsuits so far, Pippa could imagine what they would do if they figured out she had fooled them with an alias.

She reviewed all of the sections one more time, agreeing to the disastrous terms and accepting the loan. For Brody. For all the others who had been hurt or injured. CI would close down the Capital X operation permanently.

Another email came through within minutes so she could provide the routing number and specify where she wanted the deposit placed. In the case of this alias, the money would sit idly in an account, only to be used later as proof against Capital X.

Turning off the computer, she packed it back into the bag. She sent a group text message to Riley, Griffin and Kiely, with the full update and first payment due date. The reply came back in record time; the woman fulfilling the role as Alison Carrington was in place.

Somehow Riley and the GRPD had come to terms about using an undercover officer to impersonate the alias and give Capital X enforcers a physical target.

The woman was bait. Trained and willing, but still bait. Her job was to reel in the enforcers so the police had an opportunity to turn those brutes against the people calling the shots at Capital X.

She tidied her office, per her habit, putting everything in its place before she left. With a little luck the CI team could soon have actionable leads on Capital X and Brody could come out of hiding.

Chapter 11

When Emmanuel met Pippa at her condo that evening, they compared notes, and he learned his day hadn't been much more productive than hers. He hadn't had visits from siblings, but he'd bumped up against dead end after dead end trying to track the attacker's escape from her building. Such expert avoidance of traffic cams and the unmarked cars only fueled his theory that the intruder was indeed Joe McRath.

The sergeant had called out sick that day, all the more suspicious in Emmanuel's mind, though it made it easier for Emmanuel to return to the evidence room. No surprise the Wentworth case box was still missing. With the lieutenant's permission he had been reviewing the video footage of the evidence room, and he'd found discrepancies that warranted a closer look. On two occasions, Joe showed up on the video when he hadn't officially signed the log. It wasn't enough to take to the lieutenant, but he added it to the file he was building.

Over a sandwich piled high with thick slices of juicy roast beef for him and a bowl of vegetable soup for her, he shifted to simpler topics. The good news was the repaired wall was dry and the noisy equipment was gone. The quiet was clearly a relief to her, but he could tell she was sore and tired.

"I need to decide if I'll repaint or try something new."

"Go new," he suggested. "It can be a fresh start."

She tipped her head, considering. "I know feeling shaky is par for the course after what happened, so I don't want to rush that decision."

"It is a big wall," he teased. Personally, he thought doing something different was a good opportunity to put a division between the bad that had happened and moving forward.

Her amusement faded, and she pushed the remainder of soup around the bowl with her spoon. "I'm glad you're here." She took a deep breath and lifted her gaze to meet his. "I'm really glad you were close last night. Thank you," she finished, her voice cracking.

"You want me to stay over again?"

She nodded. "Please. If you want to."

"Whatever you need." He'd packed an overnight bag just in case. Reaching out, he covered her hand with his. "I really don't want to be anywhere else, sweetheart."

She bit her lip and her eyes misted, though she blinked before the tears could spill over. He decided his thought about the two of them could wait until a better time. Feeling vulnerable was unfamiliar territory for her, and he didn't want her confusing his feelings with the circumstances.

"The deli threw in a dozen cookies," she managed after a sniffle. "Chocolate chip."

"What do you say to cookies and milk and reruns?"

She smiled, that sparkle faint, but evident in her green eyes. "I'm in."

They demolished the cookies and milk and she snuggled next to him, quickly drifting off as they watched a series of mindless reruns on television. When she was sound asleep, he carried her to bed and stretched out beside her, pleased beyond reason when she curled into his body, holding him close.

He stared at the ceiling, thinking of the next move for both of them, creating a mental timeline for himself. Everyone would be counting down the hours to the missed Capital X payment. While Pippa had to stay away from all of that, Emmanuel planned to be close to the undercover officer when that deadline approached.

Until then, he had nothing but time to figure out how to get some kind of proof that Joe was involved with the attack last night, and the framing of Anna Wentworth months ago.

Pippa could practically hear the clock ticking toward the first payment deadline. All she had to do now was stay away from the Alison Carrington address, keep the laptop turned off and focus on the rest of her life.

If only it was as easy to do as it was to say.

It helped to have Emmanuel as close as a text message throughout the day, and she appreciated his presence keeping the nightmares at bay while she slept. As much as she valued her independence, he managed to give her support and care without stifling her. A strange and rare combination that she could get used to.

Would he want that, or was this closeness between them just a fluke of an ongoing investigation?

A final decision would have to wait. Elizabeth was still calling before and after every visit to the prison, and try as she might, Pippa wasn't making the strides necessary to pinpoint an event that led to murder.

An attorney for Hicks's mother had returned her calls, strongly suggesting she leave the family alone. She had to believe that closed door only put her closer to the right path.

Who had wanted that man dead, and why commit the crime on the Wentworth estate?

As much as Emmanuel believed McRath was involved and continued to pursue proof through his channels at the GRPD, Pippa wanted to find the real killer. Was it Leigh? Parents notoriously went to extremes to shelter their kids from consequences. Evidence tampering could be a felony. Would Joe risk his career and reputation to protect Leigh? If he had manipulated a case as publicized as the Hicks murder once before, it couldn't be his first. Everything had been set up too perfectly to frame Anna.

Her stomach churned. Did practice make perfect? Finding proof he'd mishandled previous cases would definitely bring the Wentworth case up for review. That helped, but still left the real killer unpunished.

Hicks had dumped Leigh McRath for Anna. Betrayal could cut deep, especially when compounded by a broken heart. But why would Leigh wait six months to act out? Crimes of passion usually merited an immediate reaction. Pippa couldn't see Joe having a motive for the murder. Most fathers would be relieved to learn that a man as slippery as Hicks was out of a daughter's life.

* * *

She didn't have enough to take to a judge or anyone else for a new trial. A press conference would be a flimsy publicity stunt at this point, and it could backfire in spectacular fashion. Trashing her reputation was one thing. Pippa didn't want Emmanuel getting twisted up in her pet project, especially if they were wrong. The whole point of this effort was to find the real killer, not drag another innocent person through the mud.

Her cell phone buzzed against the surface of her desk, and she smiled at the text message from Emmanuel. He was on his way and bringing food. Feeling better, she probably should have cooked, but that would have to wait for another night.

Listening for him, she opened the door before he could knock and was rewarded with the savory aromas of salsa and hot spices. The bag in his hand was from one of her favorite Mexican restaurants. Her mouth watered in anticipation of the meal and the man.

His smile was temptation and a handsome distraction from her swirling, go-nowhere case. She stepped back, and her stomach rumbled loud enough that he laughed in response as he walked inside.

"Didn't you eat at all today?" He strode directly to the kitchen.

How had he already figured out that she often forgot to eat? "I had a good breakfast." The breakfast they'd shared before he'd gone into the station.

He arched an eyebrow. "Pippa," he scolded lightly.

"I know, I know." She lifted her hair up to the top of her head, then let it fall. "I went into the office, then drove by the Wentworth estate. I would've eaten if I'd made it to the gym," she added, hearing the excuses. "My appetite is just—"

He cut her off with a kiss, and her appetite for food evaporated again. She pressed her body close, her fingers curling into his jacket, as she took the kiss deeper. For the past two days, he'd been treating her as if she was fragile, but she felt strong enough for anything right now.

"Take me to bed," she said.

"The food?"

"Can wait." She unbuttoned her blouse as she darted down the hallway. He was right behind her, catching her as she turned. His gaze skated over the lingering marks on her neck, then lower to her breasts. She shimmied out of her skirt and stood before him in only her bra and panties, stockings and heels. Only this man made her feel so bold.

"Hold it," he said, his voice rough with desire. "This is a fantasy I intend to enjoy."

She whispered his name, over and over, as they came together in a whirl of passion and tenderness that overwhelmed and empowered in turns.

Only him. Only him with her. Only them together, reclaiming her bed and restoring her confidence. She soared under every touch and reveled in every sigh. When at last they were sated, she knew her world had changed.

She was falling in love.

She should tell him. If the last days had proven anything, tomorrow wasn't a guarantee. But if telling him drove him away, the challenges in the days ahead might just drown her. She needed him like she'd never needed anyone else.

* * *

Hours later, after a long and steamy shower for two, Emmanuel and Pippa made it back to the kitchen. He reheated the food and she poured wine. It was so natural, so easy and comfortable that he nearly blurted out the only three words on his mind.

He was falling for her.

Impossible, but true. However it had come to pass, he couldn't deny it anymore. She'd slipped under all of his preconceived notions and shifted something deep inside him. He couldn't wait to see her at the end of the day, and whether they spent the evening debating suspects or watching cartoons, he'd never been so content.

Could he tell her? Should he?

Not yet. Hell, it had only been days. And a rough few days for both of them. Would she be this willing to have him around once the Capital X and Wentworth cases were done?

There was the crux of it. He didn't dwell on fear often, but he couldn't shake it this time. She wouldn't be safe while the person who killed Hicks walked free.

After two straight days of trouble, the person harassing her—had to be Joe—had gone quiet. Was he injured or just planning his next move to reduce the risk of another failure?

He had to find a way to flush out the killer.

Late the next morning, Pippa followed Leigh McRath to the juice bar with a pang of envy that the younger woman managed to look refreshed after leading the intense spin class. She'd signed up only as a way to get close to the woman without raising suspicions.

Pippa counted herself fit, but after this first spin class

she never wanted to repeat the experience. Her legs felt like jelly, and she couldn't wait to get home and shower off the sweat and soreness. "Thanks for agreeing to chat with me," she began while the person behind the counter prepared their order.

Leigh's chin came up. "Talking with you is the last thing I want to do," she stated.

"You want justice for David," Pippa reminded her gently.

Leigh's lower lip quivered. "I miss David so much." She pressed a dollar bill into the tip jar when her smoothie was delivered. "Why are you so sure that Wentworth bitch didn't kill him?"

Pippa managed not to wince. Most people referred to her client in those terms or some variation. With good reason. "Well, there are actually several reasons. Unfortunately, I'm not at liberty to discuss them in detail."

"I was in that courtroom," Leigh said, her voice low and hot. "Difficult as it was, I listened to all of the testimony."

And along with everyone else, Leigh had seen those arrogant and careless above-it-all gestures from the defendant.

"The motive has always bothered me," Pippa explained with far more patience than she felt. "I've known Mrs. Wentworth for many years. She's certainly capable of being cold, rude and, yes, mean, but I don't believe she murdered your friend."

"He was *more* than a friend," Leigh sputtered.

"Yes, he was," Pippa agreed. "That was obvious from my research into the case. It's exactly why I came to see you."

Leigh's surprise was obvious and genuine. Nearby,

she noticed Emmanuel walking past. Not close enough to be recognized by Leigh, but enough to remind her he was there. When he'd heard what she had planned, he refused to let her deal with it alone.

"They claimed he was blackmailing her," Leigh said. "He wasn't."

All of Pippa's preplanned questions dried up. Fact or fiction, she wondered as Leigh rambled on about everlasting love and all the plans she and David Hicks had been making.

"He didn't need her money," she insisted. "Well, fine. No one turns down easy cash, but he didn't *need* it."

"Regardless," Pippa interjected, "Anna wasn't afraid of his threat."

"Because he never threatened her," Leigh snapped. "You've got him all wrong."

Pippa refrained from mentioning the blackmail note that had been entered as evidence along with Hicks's previous patterns of bilking money from women. "I only meant Mr. and Mrs. Wentworth had an understanding about her extramarital affairs."

"Oh." Leigh blinked, her outrageous false eyelashes adding to the effect.

"Did you lend money to David when you were together?"

"Not a loan, an investment," Leigh said. "We had plans for a boutique fitness club until..." She pressed her lips together. "Until..."

Pippa had never understood how some women could cry so prettily.

"This is so difficult," Leigh managed, fanning her face. "I admit sometimes it annoyed me when David blatantly admired other women. But I was the one he came back to."

Pippa prodded Leigh a bit more until she had a couple of more names of women Hicks had "admired" while out with Leigh. Thanking her, Pippa took her smoothie and headed for the parking lot.

Emmanuel joined her as soon as she was out of sight of the juice bar. "You left her crying into her spinach smoothie."

"Kale," Pippa corrected, smothering a laugh. "She had kale and wheat berry, and I lost track after that. Her post-workout remedy is as much a mystery as the real killer."

He smiled as he held open her car door. "Did you get a lead?"

"Don't know yet. The names she mentioned didn't sound familiar."

"We'll figure it out."

She sat down behind the steering wheel and played with her keys. "Good thing we brought two cars," she said, zipping up her hoodie. She wasn't sure she'd stopped sweating yet. "That was one intense workout."

He grinned. "You're adorable when you pedal. Drink up. I'll follow you home."

Home. She smiled to herself through the entire drive. The man had a gift for making her heart feel lighter even when she was up against an insurmountable task. At first she'd thought his easy manner was a strategy as a detective. Now she knew it was just his way. These days, with everyone who recognized her shooting daggers at her or calling her names, it helped to know she had one person not named Colton or Wentworth on her side.

She turned into the driveway and pulled up at her assigned space behind her building and gawked at the mess that greeted her. Someone had dumped enough trash and kitchen scraps to fill her space, making it impossible for her to park. She drove on around to a guest space and walked back to take pictures and call it in.

Her legs were shaking, with anger rather than muscle overload now. Using her phone, she took several pictures. The odor alone made her post-spin-class-self smell like a daisy in a spring breeze. Just in case she thought this could be a coincidence, there was a sign in the center:

Leave the real trash in jail or else.

Or else what? Her condo had been invaded, twice, and now apparently the security was up to snuff, because her harasser had taken an easier shot at her today. Except it couldn't have been too easy to stage this without being spotted by someone. Still taking risks, still urging her to drop the Wentworth case.

She sent the pictures to Kiely for lack of a better immediate solution. What could be done? "I'm not stopping," she shouted, just in case the person who'd done this was watching and could hear her.

Emmanuel was striding over, having parked out front on the street as he normally did.

Seeing him, something deep inside snapped, and suddenly angry tears blurred her vision. She blinked furiously. She would *not* give her tormentor the satisfaction of knowing how much he'd upset her.

Lifting her chin and squaring her shoulders, she called building maintenance. This was just another roadblock in her way, nothing that would keep her from achieving her goal of proving Anna's innocence.

* * *

Emmanuel broke into a jog when he saw Pippa standing in front of the space where her car should be. The smell hit him before the full scene struck home. Another threat, executed while she was away from home. Joe or one of his many connections had been watching her closely.

How closely was what worried him.

He caught her just as she charged forward as if she was going to shred that nasty sign with her bare hands. "Leave it. Let me call it in."

"Don't," she snapped. She twisted out of his grasp, but she didn't try to wade back into the mess.

"Why not? It's vandalism."

She swallowed, then her chin came up. "Because I'm done."

"Done with Wentworth?"

"No." She shot him a look that told him he should know her better than that. "I'm done playing games. We both know there won't be any helpful evidence in that pile of trash."

"We do not know that," he said, calmly.

She arched an eyebrow and folded her arms over her chest, daring him to come up with a better explanation.

"Fine." He took a good look, analyzing the scene. It was a common plastic kitchen trash bag split along a seam. Based on the astounding lack of evidence found at the other instances of harassment, she was right. They wouldn't find so much as a single fingerprint or helpful fiber. More confirmation of his theory that it was someone in the department working to keep Wentworth behind bars. "There's a chance someone got sloppy."

She rolled her eyes.

"Either way, you can't stay here anymore," he said, braced for an outburst.

"I will *not* be chased from my home," she snapped, her voice low.

He was about to suggest a compromise when her phone rang. "Kiely," she said to him as she answered. "Hi. I'm fine, stop worrying." A pause as she listened. "No." Another pause. "Yes." She glared at him. "My sister wants to talk with you."

"Hi, Kiely," he said, taking the phone as Pippa stalked back to her car.

"She didn't call the police?"

"Technically, I *am* the police," he reminded her, moving around the scene. "There aren't any obvious tracks, but I planned to take pictures before anything else happens. My thought was to shove this all into another bag and have the lab take a look anyway."

"Agreed." Kiely sighed. "I'll call Sadie to swing by. I know why Pippa doesn't want to bother anyone in the department, but if the perp made a mistake, it could be the break we all need."

"Exactly my thought," Emmanuel said. "I'll take care of it."

"Great. Thanks, Detective. And the next time we have a Colton family dinner or CI meeting, Griffin wants you to join us."

Not about to give an answer without clearing it with Pippa, he wasn't sure what to say. "Thanks."

Kiely chuckled and wished him luck before she ended the call.

"Here." Emmanuel walked over to Pippa's car and returned her phone.

"She's insisting you do something to investigate isn't she?"

"Yes."

She muttered an oath in French, her preference.

"I know you're tired of all of this, so why take a chance that this time a critical error was made?" He could see her resistance to his logic, but he knew she'd come around. He held out his hand. "Come on, we'll go get a trash bag together."

She put her hand in his and they headed upstairs. It felt good to walk with her like this, as a team. As a couple.

"Building maintenance has extra bags," she said. "We can go in the back."

"All right." That would give him some time to think how they could best make a move that led to a resolution rather than more questions.

Chapter 12

The next morning Pippa was working at home again, too antsy for the office. The first payment to Capital X was officially overdue. She was trying to fit what Leigh had told her yesterday into the context of her notes from the official case file. Granted, her concentration was shot, knowing any minute now Capital X enforcers were likely to descend on the woman pretending to be Alison Carrington a few blocks away.

However her brother and the GRPD had coordinated the plan, Pippa couldn't get her mind off the risk to the undercover officer who had volunteered for this and the others who hoped to drop a net around the enforcers so they could unravel the operation.

Unlike Anna, Pippa had always valued the people who served the police department. It started with the example of her parents and the ways her siblings served the local police department and military justice, in the case of her other sister, Vikki. Spending this time with Emmanuel, falling for him, drove home the bigger risks of the people who chose to serve and protect the community. Pippa ran into the *proverbial* fire when necessary, but aside from these recent days, the direct physical danger was minimal. Would the woman working undercover be able to avoid serious injury?

Considering all the bones Capital X broke in the name of business, she wondered if they had a kickback arrangement with local orthopedic specialists. Not that she expected doctors to be that corrupt, but referrals were a thing in every industry now.

Another totally irrelevant thought that had no bearing on what she needed to accomplish today.

She had to focus on the things only she could do. Kiely would give her the play-by-play if Capital X made a move on the Alison Carrington alias. Pushing away from her desk, she went to the kitchen to prepare a cup of tea.

Maybe the soothing brew would settle her racing thoughts. Leaving the tea on the counter to steep, she returned to her desk and the pictures of the scene when Hicks's body had been found.

Every time she studied this file, she did it knowing Anna was innocent. But a jury convicted her on this same evidence. Why? They had to have thought the information backed Emmanuel's testimony.

The prosecutor presented a compelling case in court. A blood trail, the blackmail motive, even Anna's brooch at the scene. In the jury's shoes, with Anna's snobby reputation, that had probably been enough.

Anna had insisted on owning unique, often one-of-a-kind items, down to the smallest personal accessory. For years she'd seen it as a crime if someone else was spotted wearing the same outfit or jewelry design.

Like so many things, in Anna's view, David Hicks was technically disposable. Mr. Wentworth had put up with his wife's infidelity for years, most likely in an attempt to keep things stable for Elizabeth. Somehow staying married was less costly for the Wentworths than divorce. Factor in the negative publicity of a scandal affecting their charitable endeavors, and an objective person could find more motive for them to stay together.

Pippa knew marriages were tricky. By design the most intimate of partnerships, yet so often the most flawed. Maybe her view was skewed because of what had happened between her parents, but outsiders rarely got the full picture of another couple.

She turned the pictures of the crime scene around, studying them from all angles as Emmanuel would have done that day. The jewelry under the body bothered her almost as much as the idea of Anna doing the messy work of murder.

How long had the body been there before the coroner turned it over and found that brooch?

She checked the report and could only guess that Joe McRath might have had time to walk the house, find the brooch and plant it.

Anna was in a rarefied class all her own, but she wasn't stupid. Caught up in the moment or not, she wouldn't leave a piece like this behind. Her mind did not operate that way. Pippa closed her eyes and imagined Anna overlooking the moment when a prized piece went missing.

It just wasn't possible. Elizabeth's mother wasn't the

kind of woman to ignore that kind of sparkle. According to the time of death, it had been a sunny day. The sunlight would've caught in those stones, and based on the location of the body, if the brooch had fallen to the grass, Anna would have noticed.

If Emmanuel hadn't planted the brooch—and she knew he had not—it had to be McRath. The reports gave no indication of any other police officers entering the private suites in the Wentworth mansion until after the coroner cleared the body for transport. That was enough to get someone's attention, possibly enough attention to reopen the case.

Before she blurted it all out to a judge, or hinted at it in the media, she'd like to know why an honorable, decorated cop like Joe snapped. Whether or not McRath killed Hicks—and for the life of her she couldn't figure out why he would—only McRath had the opportunity to stage the scene so completely for his partner on that day, Emmanuel.

Would evidence tampering be enough to free Anna?

Could she prove it? Even Emmanuel, a seasoned detective, had not realized the murder scene was staged. And she would do anything to avoid the embarrassment of having him admit he'd been fooled. Her goal here was to free an innocent woman, Anna, not tarnish Emmanuel's reputation. With their recent personal involvement, if he changed his mind now about what he had seen then, his motives would be suspect. A detective working with a lawyer to free a convicted killer? She didn't want to think about the severe fallout that would rain down on him.

There had to be a way for her to draw out Joe.

* * *

Emmanuel walked into the coffee shop near the "Alison Carrington" apartment and placed his order. Though it seemed normal, there was nothing relaxed about this particular morning. Everyone was braced for an unprovoked attack. While he waited for his order, his thoughts wandered back to that first day when Pippa had brought coffee to him in his car.

He hadn't been at his best in that moment, having just learned of Ingrid's death by RevitaYou. She'd shown tremendous compassion and unforgettable hospitality. He might have started falling in love with her right then.

Coffee in hand, he left the shop and strolled on down the block. To anyone watching, he was another man distracted by his phone, although he was alert to any danger or disturbance. He knew where the GRPD spotters were located. He knew where Kiely and Riley were hiding.

Emmanuel's only role here was as extra support.

The female officer playing the part of Alison took a seat at an outdoor table with her coffee and a small takeout. Working undercover wasn't nearly as easy as it seemed on television. It could be equal parts boring and extreme. In this instance, Emmanuel was strung up tight as a bow.

Set on silent, his phone lit up with an incoming call from Griffin. "What are you doing out here this morning?" his friend asked.

"You can't expect me to sit this one out," he replied.

"I can expect you to keep an eye on my sister like we agreed," Griffin said. "She's not here, is she?"

"She's working from home. I just checked in with her."

"Why doesn't that make me feel better?"

Emmanuel assumed it was because Griffin had plenty of experience with the daring nature of his sisters. "If I wasn't out here, she would be," he said instead.

"What's going on with you two?" Griffin asked.

He'd known this conversation would happen, but the timing couldn't be worse. He walked along, circling the block. "I'm keeping an eye on her."

"Pretty close eye."

"Seriously? You just accused me of not being close enough."

Griffin might have laughed. "Stop before I need brain bleach. She's an adult. I'll shut up while we're working."

"Thanks for that." Anything to put an end to this uncomfortable chat.

"Just don't hurt her," Griffin snapped. "Pippa claims to be invincible, but she isn't."

Emmanuel wisely kept his mouth shut. His insights into Pippa were his own and likely wouldn't gel with her brother's perception. Not once had he believed her invincible. Too daring, maybe. And that was only because he'd fallen for her.

Which was ironic because her bold courage and determination had been the first things he'd found irresistible. Relationships were ridiculous. He didn't care for the way his feelings twisted him up when he needed to concentrate.

Before he could muster a suitable reply, he noticed the enforcers approaching their target. Neither man looked familiar to Emmanuel, but that didn't mean much. He ended the call, holding his position and watching the scene unfold.

The two men walked right up to her, almost as if

they'd been watching. The smaller of the two men pulled out a chair and sat down. He had deep-set eyes, a shaved head, and a swagger and build that implied he had plenty of fighting experience. The larger man stood there looking intimidating, his big hands clasped loosely in front of him. They didn't seem to care that they were drawing attention from other patrons of the coffee shop.

Then the big man reached for the woman playing Alison, yanking her up and out of her seat. She twisted out of his grasp and started to run, per the plan. Her job, once confirming the men were enforcers from Capital X, was to lead them to a less public area down the block for the takedown.

She didn't make it that far.

The bald man was too quick, catching her around the waist and pinning her to his side so she couldn't escape. The bulky man hemmed her in and they started to walk away.

Another customer stood up and blocked their path, offering her assistance. He was knocked aside by the bald man.

Other customers erupted, and both enforcers were suddenly more concerned with getting away from an angry mob than breaking bones for missed payments.

Hopes of a quiet takedown were dashed. Everyone in the area leaped into the chase, police and citizens alike. Cell phones were recording it all for later analysis on social media.

Emmanuel joined the chase when the bigger man ran across traffic to his side of the street. He called out, identifying himself and ordering the man to stop. He pulled his weapon but didn't dare fire with so many civilians between him and his target.

He saw the man peel off down an alley and shared that with another uniformed team in pursuit. When he caught up with them, they were calling in the report that they'd lost the larger enforcer.

"Do we have anything?" Emmanuel asked. "A name, a dropped wallet or phone?"

"None of the above," the officers replied.

"All right. Ask around for any security footage. We might get lucky with facial recognition. I'll get back and help smooth things over," he said. When he reached the coffee shop, he discovered customers and police had the bald man in custody. Police and customers alike were celebrating the cooperative effort to stop a bad guy.

Pleased, Emmanuel headed back to the station. He wouldn't be involved in questioning, which was probably for the best, considering all the other things he should be sorting out regarding Joe and the Hicks murder.

He hadn't found anything on Joe that his lieutenant would take seriously, and he was running out of places to look for useful proof. Ever since responding to the first break-in call at her condo, it felt like two steps forward, one back, and then a brick wall at every turn.

Just like in the Wentworth case, the department was under serious pressure to make progress to resolve the threat of the poisonous RevitaYou vitamins and find the people behind its development. Riley Colton had pulled serious strings for this cooperative investigation into the deadly product and the loan operation that had bilked hopeful investors.

Joining a few others in the observation room, Emmanuel got chills watching the henchman stonewall

Lieutenant McKellar and Detective Gomez. They wanted the name of the devious person at the top of the Capital X food chain, profiting from deception and death, but the bald man refused to cooperate. The brute in the interrogation room provided only his name, Gunther Johnson, as answer to every question.

McKellar, using a card from the man's wallet, finally got him to admit he'd gone to the coffee shop on behalf of Capital X, but he refused to say who'd sent him. A few minutes more of McKellar threatening far more serious charges and Johnson shared more.

"Look, I'm just an enforcer," he insisted. "I bust a few bones for good pay. Really good pay. Targets are a whole lot easier than organized fights. No crime in that."

Detective Gomez shared a look with McKellar. "Beating up people actually *is* a crime, Mr. Johnson."

"Well, so is missing a scheduled payment." Johnson shifted in his chair. "You can't get money for nothing."

Gomez stared at him and McKellar asked, "What do you know about the payments?"

"Nothing. I go out and encourage people to make their payments on time. You may not like what I do, but it's honest work."

This guy was priceless. Either this guy just didn't get it or, more likely, didn't care.

"Who pays you?" McKellar asked.

Johnson shrugged. "I do my job and cash shows up. Not like they withhold for benefits and retirement."

"So you just work broken bone to broken bone," Gomez said. "No retainer?"

Johnson puffed up with pride. "Trust me, it's steady

pay. Plenty of people think they can blow off their debts. Capital X doesn't tolerate it."

"How many fingers have you broken this week?" asked McKellar. "This month?"

"Hell, I don't keep track. I go where I'm told, do what's needed. Most of the time after we visit someone, they pay their debt and everybody's happy."

"I imagine the people with medical bills aren't happy," Lopez said.

Johnson snorted. "They can always get another loan."

McKellar didn't bother hiding his disgust. "And you don't know anyone at Capital X by name other than your fellow enforcer."

"That's right."

"What happens if you go out, break a few bones and the customer still doesn't pay up?" Gomez asked. "Your boss come after you?"

"Course not. You think I'm trash, but I got value. I broke some fingers on a skinny kid with big dreams. He went underground without paying up. I'm actually getting a bonus to look for that Brody Higgins when I'm not on other jobs."

Emmanuel rocked back on his heels. Pippa and her siblings would be thrilled by that admission. Delighted that the police had the man who'd broken up their foster brother. He sent her a quick text update.

Johnson didn't seem to realize what he just confessed. Gomez kept him talking about some other less pleasant meetings. But he wouldn't budge about knowing anyone by name at Capital X.

"Even if I knew names, I'm no snitch," Johnson said. "If I'm out here breaking bones for missed payments, what do you think they'd do to me if I talked?" He sat back in the chair, lifting his wrists so that the cuffs banged against the tabletop. "You caught me trying to rough up someone. Big deal. That lady gave her word and reneged on the deal. That's all I'm saying. I want my lawyer."

Emmanuel started back to his desk when he was waved down by Officer Simmons. "Detective Iglesias, I have a caller on the RevitaYou tip line I think you need to hear."

"Lead the way." Emmanuel followed him across the bullpen.

"The caller claims to have spotted the Toxic Scientist," Simmons explained.

Emmanuel's instincts prickled as he picked up the phone. "This is Detective Iglesias, how may I help you?"

"Yes. The police wanted us watching for that man who poisoned the vitamins. I'm looking at him right now. The Toxic Scientist," the caller said in an overexcited rush, referring to the media's nickname for Landon Street, the scientist who came up with the RevitaYou formula. "You should hurry if you want to catch him."

"Where are you?" Emmanuel asked.

"I'm at the Grateful Bread."

That bakery was only two blocks from the station. Emmanuel wrote out the name, and Simmons started organizing personnel to respond.

"Well, I'm across the street," the caller said. "But I'm looking right at him. He's wearing a light blue baseball cap and dark sunglasses, but it's definitely the Toxic Scientist."

"Your name?" Emmanuel thought the caller was female, but it was hard to be sure. The line went dead. "Hello? Hello?" He looked at Simmons and shared the description. "Let's move," Emmanuel said. "I want two officers with me on foot and roll backup from all directions to cut him off."

"We're ready."

Emmanuel and the others hurried out of the station toward the bakery. It would be a red-letter day if they managed to nab both a Capital X enforcer and Landon Street, scientific genius behind the deadly RevitaYou vitamins.

This was a huge break. With everyone searching, Emmanuel couldn't believe Street was still in Grand Rapids. What kind of fool would stick around when everyone was looking for the man behind that lethal compound?

Emmanuel approached the bakery as casually as possible. He even checked his phone as if this was a normal sugar run. It wasn't unheard of for the officers to make frequent runs down here, so their arrival shouldn't surprise anyone. Again, that made it an odd place for Street to show up after going completely off the grid.

They systematically combed the area, and no one spotted him. He was in the wind again. Damn it. No one matching the description was inside or outside the bakery. They fanned out to cover more area, but still nothing. While the others searched, Emmanuel went inside to question the staff, speaking first to the slip of a girl at the register and then her manager.

The cashier remembered waiting on a man wearing a light blue hat. "It was weird," she said. "His glasses were super dark, but he wouldn't take them off." She shrugged. "People are funny. I thought maybe he was blind."

"All right," Emmanuel said, amused. "Do you remember what he ordered?"

The cashier recited the order of a tall black coffee and a bear claw.

"Cash or credit card?"

"Cash," she said with a big smile. "He tipped two dollars."

Emmanuel showed her a picture of Street. "Was this him?"

She squinted at the photo on his phone. "Maybe?"

The manager invited Emmanuel to the back room to check the security cameras. The grainy video feed wasn't much help. The man who might have been Street kept his head down and his sunglasses on, just as the cashier said.

He did, however, take his coffee and bear claw to one of the tables outside where other cameras might have caught him after he left the bakery.

Emmanuel thanked the manager, placed an order for two dozen doughnuts and checked in with the teams searching while it was filled. The caller had said they were across the street when they spotted the Toxic Scientist. He walked that way, keeping in mind where Street had been sitting when the tipster called in. He imagined a man in a hat and sunglasses at this distance wouldn't be very distinctive. Whoever had called in the tip must have known Street to make such a confident identification. Resigned, he called the searching teams back and went to pick up the doughnuts for the station.

He walked in, an instant hero just for delivering the sugar rush.

While Emmanuel refilled his coffee, Joe McRath

came in and, with a big smile, chose an apple fritter. "Thanks, Iglesias."

"No problem," he said, managing not to choke on the words.

With Joe around, Emmanuel immersed himself in the Landon Street file, writing up the tip and the response, even though it had failed. While he worked, another name caught his attention. Flynn Cruz-Street was a half brother stationed at the US Army base nearby. He wondered if the brother had made the ID and urged another customer or passerby to call it in.

He could see that. It was a way to help without quite turning on family. Everyone wanted to ask Street what he knew about RevitaYou and why he kept working on a flawed product.

When he thought of sharing this news with Pippa, he realized she hadn't replied to his earlier text about Johnson. As much as he wanted to talk, reaching out again was more about the temptation than the work on his desk.

She'd been cool this morning, determined this would be the day she found a pertinent clue. He admired her determination to exonerate Anna, and he could relate to that single-minded focus. What he didn't understand was her suddenly pushing him away. She needed his help, and honestly he needed to help her. But she'd dug in her heels, insisting he had done enough.

That kind of talk made him wary. She was a woman used to going her own way, and frankly he didn't like the chances she was willing to take for her cause of the moment.

Striving for discipline and logic, he picked up the phone and called another of the Colton sisters. Victoria Colton was a paralegal in the JAG office on the same base as Flynn. It would be easier for her to follow up with the half brother about Street's possible location and reason for visiting a bakery right under the GRPD's nose.

Pippa wasn't making any progress on her discreet inquiries about how much evidence was needed to trip a review of the case.

Taking a break, she noticed a text alert from Emmanuel. She read through his brief message that they had the Capital X enforcer who had broken Brody's fingers in custody. She breathed a sigh of relief that something was starting to break in their favor. She sent him a quick reply to thank him.

It was temping to keep the conversation going, but she needed to get back on task and she wanted to keep her work and his as separate as possible.

Her phone rang and she cringed at Elizabeth's number on the caller ID. If she hadn't had it memorized before, she certainly would now. Pippa understood Elizabeth's concern. No matter what Elizabeth said, Anna refused to stop taking RevitaYou. The increasing instances of illness and death didn't matter to Anna.

"Hello, Elizabeth. How are things today?"

"You have to do something," Elizabeth wailed. "She was awful today. I think she's getting sick. Tell me you've made progress."

She knew her friend was looking for hope. "I'm working every angle as fast as I can," she said. It was the same thing she'd said on every call yesterday and the day before.

"Pippa, I know I'm being unreasonable and asking

too much. These deaths…" Her voice broke. "I know Mom won't quit taking this junk until she's out of prison. Please don't let her die in there."

She was doing all she could and failing her best friend. She didn't know how to help either one of them. The brooch was the key; she knew it. She just had to tie McRath to putting it there and everything would unravel in Anna's favor.

"This is a nightmare," Elizabeth said, not for the first time.

Desperate to calm her friend, Pippa looked at the case spread out before her on the desk. "I'm planning another interview," she said, deciding on the fly. Confronting McRath directly was her only option. "Before you get your hopes up, it might not even happen. If I can work it out—"

"You can, Pippa. You can do anything."

No pressure. "Thanks for the vote of confidence," she said. "I need you to be realistic. If, and this is a big if, I can get the interview, it may turn everything around for your mom."

"Anything that moves the needle. Please," Elizabeth begged. "It would be a tragedy for her to die in prison just because she's too vain to be a normal prisoner."

Pippa heard the humor in her friend's voice, but she couldn't quite muster a laugh. If Anna died in prison, the case would slip away. No one would pursue the truth. And none of that would compare to the loss Elizabeth and Ed would bear.

She shook off the worst-case scenario. Anna was still alive and mostly well. Pippa would find a way to see the right person locked up behind bars for the Hicks murder. Wrapping up the call with Elizabeth, she turned back to the photos on her desk.

The brooch was the key. Who would've seen McRath in the mansion? She made a list of household staff, wondering if any of them would speak to her or if they were happier without Anna's demands day in and day out.

She went to send Emmanuel a text message, asking for a few minutes of his time, and noticed he'd texted her about having one enforcer in custody. Good news on any front buoyed her spirits.

His reply to her request for a meeting came back so quickly that she wondered if he'd been watching for any contact from her.

They met at a food truck famous for its creative tacos and burritos near the station, and it was all she could do not to hold his hand or give him a kiss. But that kind of display would be noticed this close to the police station. For the first time, she regretted that they couldn't be seen as a couple in public. Not while she was leading the charge to overturn a conviction he'd investigated.

At the window, they ordered, but when he tried to pay, the woman wouldn't take his money. He argued, but it was clear he wouldn't win without holding up the line behind them.

"I can't stand it when she does that," Emmanuel said when they'd found a spot to sit down with their food.

"Why won't she take your money?" Pippa asked.

An older woman with weathered skin and bright dark eyes brought out paper baskets overflowing with tacos for her, a burrito for Emmanuel and crisp tortilla chips to share. She beamed at Emmanuel, and her gaze slid meaningfully toward Pippa. "Introduce me to your friend," she said with a gleam in her eye.

Emmanuel did the honors. “Pippa Colton, this is Maria Alvarez. Maria, Pippa is an attorney and a friend.”

“A pleasure to meet you, Pippa,” Maria said. The older woman squeezed Pippa’s hands between hers. “We do not take his money because he saved us.”

“Years ago, Maria,” he said, exasperated. “You can’t feed me forever.”

“I can and I will,” she countered. “You’re a good boy.” She patted his cheek before she returned to the truck.

She waited, but he dug into his burrito, his mouth too full to talk. “Come on, you know you want to tell me about it,” she pressed.

“I really don’t. Just eat.”

That was no hardship. “This is amazing,” she said. She knew he’d share the story eventually. She could see it in the way his eyes crinkled.

“It’s not a big deal,” he said when he dipped a chip into homemade salsa. “One of my easier cases.”

“How easy?”

“They were robbed and the truck was vandalized. I solved the case, and they stayed in business. Of course if they keep feeding me for free, how long it stays that way is up for debate. But the food is so good I can’t stay away.”

Pippa laughed. “So the culprit must’ve been some-one in the family?”

“You are smart.” He nodded. “One of her grandsons got caught up in the wrong crowd and tried to make it look random.”

“What gave him away?” she asked.

"Part of the vandalism was graffiti, and the kid's a pretty good artist," he explained.

"You recognized his work."

Emmanuel nodded. "We ended up charging the kid who slashed the tire, and another who stole a set of expensive knives. But they both got probation, along with the grandson. All three of them put in the elbow grease to get the truck back up and going. Last I heard, the kid who was so fascinated with the knives is in cooking school and doing well."

She couldn't suppress her smile. "You really are a talented detective and a good cop."

"Don't tell me you just figured that out?" he asked, his grin full of pride. "None of the discipline was my idea. I would have thrown the book at the two rowdy friends. Maria, though, she's all about second chances."

They finished eating, chatting about kids and neighborhoods and memories, but that only kept Elizabeth at the front of her mind.

"Pippa, you didn't come by for tacos." Emmanuel crumpled his napkin and dropped it into his empty basket.

She hated to ruin such a nice break. What she had in mind was sure to take the smile off his handsome face. "Elizabeth called again," she began. His smile disappeared just as predicted. "I need to make tangible progress for Anna."

"I understand that," he said.

"You do?"

"I may not like the woman, but she shouldn't be doing the time if she isn't the killer."

They were well past ifs in Pippa's opinion. It was pointless to drag this out when they were both busy, and she wasn't here to ask permission. "I'm going to set up a meeting with Sergeant McRath."

He paled. "You what?" He shook his head. "No way."

"I'm not dumb enough to accuse him of murder," she said defensively, keeping her voice too low to be overheard.

"Well, do share your plan." Emmanuel folded his arms over his chest.

"I'll approach him as the lead detective and ask if he'll help me review the initial persons of interest in the case."

"Uh-huh." His nostrils flared. "You take that route and you're playing with fire. He'll see through that so fast. It's too dangerous."

"To reiterate, I won't accuse him of anything."

"He won't see it that way." Emmanuel tucked in close to her. "If he is responsible for any wrongdoing then or more recently, he'll be on the defensive. It's too dangerous," he said again.

"Need I remind you we have a lead on Capital X only because I was willing to do the dangerous thing?"

"Yeah, and that's working out so well."

She bristled. She didn't expect him to roll over and cooperate, but she also didn't expect this much resistance.

"How many times can you do the dangerous thing without consequences?" he demanded. "You're an attorney. Stay in your lane."

She wanted to yell at him, but it would draw too much attention. "Fine. I'll stay in my lane. As an attorney, tenacious comes with the territory. And risk, as well." She had to stop; she was too close to making a scene that would wreck everything. "When I set up the meeting, I'll let you know."

He cut her off with a shake of his head. "There is no chance I'm letting you do this alone. Not after the attacks and harassment."

"Stay in your lane," she suggested.

He rolled his eyes and shifted to block her view. All she could see was him. "You *are* my lane."

Though her heart broke into a happy dance, she folded her arms and stared him down. This was about her case.

"I can't talk you out of it?" he asked.

She shook her head.

"Will you wait long enough for me to arrange backup?"

She'd learned to read his expressions, and though he tried to hide it, she felt like she had an inside track now. "If I don't wait, what happens?"

He blanched again, and then color slowly crept into his face. He was angry, and it surprised her that she mattered so much. They were friends, on some level, and lovers. For now. Thinking beyond the present moment was foolish. She couldn't let blurry thoughts of a future push her off course now.

"I'll have you followed," he vowed. "If necessary, I'll take personal time and follow you myself," he said.

His deliberate tone unnerved her. Thrilled her. "As long as I'm not blamed for the crime spree that follows if you are off duty trailing me."

"Then we're going to go talk with Lieutenant McKellar and do this the right way."

"What do you mean?"

"We're both convinced McRath is guilty."

"Hold on," she said. "I'm convinced he railroaded Anna. It would be nice to know why. Nicer if he'd come clean."

Emmanuel snorted. "Because that's what all good criminals do."

Now she did smack him lightly in the shoulder, but it counted and it made her point. "I won't accuse him of murder without proof. The Hicks case went that way once already."

"Fair enough. Give me a second."

After sending a text to his lieutenant as fair warning, Emmanuel led her into the station. "Let me do the talking," he said at McKellar's office door.

"By all means," she agreed. "Though this might go better if I had something to show my reasoning."

She had a point, but he wasn't taking chances. There was no way he was letting her put herself out there as a target. Although she didn't agree with his assessment, that was exactly what she was proposing.

It was one thing to use a fake ID and a laptop that couldn't easily be traced to her. A meeting with McRath was akin to being front and center on a shooting range. Especially if he was the man who'd trashed her condo and tried to strangle her. A detective like McRath would chew her up and spit her out before he admitted any wrongdoing.

Why couldn't she see what that kind of risk did to him? Why couldn't he tell her?

Probably because telling her now wouldn't make any difference on this particular issue. When Pippa made up her mind, he didn't think anything could knock her off track.

The lieutenant glowered as Emmanuel ushered Pippa into the office. Fortunately Joe had left for the day, so that was one hurdle they could avoid for the moment. Emmanuel started the introductions, but McKellar cut him off.

"I know who she is," he barked. "You have five minutes, out of courtesy to your sister, Sadie."

"Thank you."

She started to speak, but Emmanuel spoke over her. "We have reason to believe Anna Wentworth is innocent."

McKellar gave a derisive snort. "Well, allow me to clear my schedule. I'm not in the mood for Mystery Theater right now."

"You said five minutes," Emmanuel reminded him.

"Use it wisely," McKellar warned.

Emmanuel quickly reminded him about the missing evidence box and informed him it was still gone. He listed the trouble Pippa had endured from the red tape at the prison to the garbage in her parking space. "In every instance, McRath had means and access."

"Any proof? Eye witness, surveillance, anything?" He didn't give them a chance to answer. "Even if you're right, what do you want me to do? Other than free your client," he said with a glare for Pippa.

"Not you, sir. Me," she said. "I would like to set up a meeting with McRath to discuss the case."

"To accuse him of what?"

"I suspect he tampered with evidence, particularly the brooch found under the body," she said. "But I have no intention of making any accusations. My approach would be as an attorney convinced my client is innocent and interviewing the lead detective simply to gain insight and information."

"Back it up," McKellar said, wagging a finger. "The brooch?"

"Yes, sir. Based on my review of the case files, Sergeant McRath is the only person at the scene who went into the house, particularly Anna's suite. He is the only person who had time to remove the item and plant it under the body."

"Good grief, you believe that." McKellar rubbed his temples. "If you approach a decorated detective, he'll see it as a personal attack, an attempt to undo his hard work."

"Detective Iglesias has warned me of the same thing."

"You haven't given me a reason to agree to this interview."

"Lieutenant, I've known Anna Wentworth for most of my life. As a friend of the family, I can give you a host of reasons why she didn't kill Hicks, but the most compelling is her passion for her jewelry. There is no way she would've left that piece behind."

"And you?" McKellar turned on him. "Why are you suddenly so cooperative with the enemy of your hard work?"

He winced at the choice of words, but answered quickly. "If an innocent woman is in jail because I misread the scene, that's a mistake that needs to be rectified." He took a deep breath. "I have documentation of Joe's presence in the evidence room between Pippa's review of the Wentworth case and the day I discovered the case was missing. In addition, I suspect Joe was the man who attacked Pippa in her bed a few nights ago."

McKellar swore. "I was told there wasn't any conclusive evidence of the intruder's identity."

"I've trained with him for too many years not to know how he moves in a fight," Emmanuel said. He hated to implicate a partner and friend. A mentor he'd admired and learned from. "I wanted to come to you with more, especially a motive, but Pippa is concerned that Anna is at risk in prison."

The lieutenant swore again.

"My primary goal is to wrangle a confession that he tampered with evidence," Pippa said. "That should help me overturn the conviction."

"And if he does, I'm up against, it and the entire department will be overrun as we review every case he ever handled."

"I'm not minimizing what this could do," she said. "But an innocent woman is in prison for a crime she did not commit. Love or hate Anna Wentworth, she's not a killer."

McKellar rocked back in his chair. It didn't escape Emmanuel's notice that they had been granted an extra five minutes. "How is Wentworth at risk?"

"She's managed to start taking RevitaYou," Emmanuel said.

"How in the hell?" McKellar waved his hand. "Never mind. Prison reform isn't my priority today. You," he pinned Pippa with a hard look. "You cannot do this without backup."

"Yes, sir."

Emmanuel was a little jealous that she acquiesced to the lieutenant so easily.

"On top of that," McKellar continued. "I'll lead the backup team. If one of my detectives confesses to any kind of crime, I want to hear it firsthand. You'll wear a wire, provided by my technicians. Go set your meeting," he said.

"And if he chooses somewhere private," Emmanuel asked.

"Then he's a fool," the lieutenant replied. "He'll want somewhere public if we're lucky. Somewhere remote if we're really lucky."

Seeing she was about to ask more questions, Emmanuel stood. "Thank you for your time, Lieutenant." He let Pippa add her thanks, and then he hustled her out of the office and straight out of the building. His heart was pounding. "Success," he said at her ear.

She stopped at the bottom of the steps. "You expected him to shoot me down."

He sighed; there was no easy way to do this, not with her. "No. I expected him to do the right thing."

"And he did," she said.

"Looks that way." He wanted to kiss her more than he wanted his next breath. "You need to get home." Wanting her to get there safely, he walked her to her car. "Sorry if I got a little tense about this."

"I understand." She flipped her car keys around her finger. "We can't leave an innocent woman in prison."

"No, we can't." He shoved his hand into his pocket, for fear that he would handcuff her and hide her away until he could get McRath on his terms. "I just want you safe."

"I don't want you taking chances either," she said. "But this is necessary."

She was right—they had exhausted all other options. "Together we'll get through it."

"I like the sound of that," she said.

He wished he didn't care so much. His life was simpler before she'd turned him inside out. Now she was rooted deep in his soul. It was uncomfortable. He always thought falling in love was supposed to be a beautiful, nurturing thing. He should just tell her. He would, when he knew how to give her the words without her believing it was a way to manipulate her.

He didn't want the truest feelings he'd ever had to be mixed up in a case he'd already botched. "Drive safe," he said. "I won't be far behind you."

She smiled, giving his hand a warm squeeze. In the past he might have appreciated her reluctance to confirm their physical relationship. Now that discretion cast a glaring light, making everything between them feel all wrong.

"I want to kiss you," he said when she settled behind the wheel of her car.

"I want that too." A sassy grin transformed her face from serious attorney to sexy girlfriend. "I'll keep you posted."

He knew she would. Pippa was a woman of her word.

"How does Italian sound for dinner?" she asked.

"Sounds great. I'll pick it up when I'm done here."

"Oh." She toyed with her keys again. "I thought I would cook."

"Seriously? Can't wait." That gave him something wonderful to look forward to. If she wanted to cook for him, chances were good she wasn't about to dump him for being overprotective. "Let me bring dessert."

"Éclairs?"

"We'll see."

Returning to his desk wasn't easy when he wanted to follow her and shield her from every threat, seen or unseen. That wasn't how things got done in his world.

She was strong and smart, and he trusted her even if he didn't trust her enemies.

Throwing himself into the last few things on his to-do list, he picked up the phone to return a call from FBI agent Cooper Winston. "Give me some good news," he said when Winston answered. "Have you heard anything more on Wes Matthews?"

Brody had told them that Matthews had been the banker taking cash transfers from the RevitaYou investors. But the man had seemingly disappeared into thin air, like the Toxic Scientist, and all law enforcement agencies were trying to track him down.

"No such luck," Winston said. "I was letting you know he hasn't turned up in or around Grand Rapids. For that matter, he hasn't been spotted anywhere in Michigan. We did get a couple of reported sightings in the Caribbean. I have local law enforcement down there checking out those tips."

"Offshore banking must be good work if you can get it," Emmanuel said.

"No kidding," Winston agreed. "Don't worry. We're not letting this one fall through the cracks."

"Then we're all on the same page." Emmanuel updated his case notes after the call. He figured it would take a real team effort to reel in all of the moving pieces in the sprawling RevitaYou scam.

Finally he was leaving the station, and he sent a text to Pippa to let her know. He got a quick reply, which put a smile on his face. He stopped at the restaurant and picked up the tiramisu he'd ordered to round out the Italian meal she had planned to make. And after dinner, he could hardly wait to stay over again.

That served his purposes on two levels, loving her and protecting her.

He was only a few blocks from her condo when his cell phone rang, and the connection in his car announced the district attorney's phone number. Would this day never end? He answered with the hands-free option. "Detective Iglesias."

"You at a point where you can talk?" the DA asked.

"It's just you and me on this end."

"I just got the word that Gunther Johnson is willing to make a deal."

"No kidding?" That was phenomenal news. And a huge break for the case. "What's he demanding?" Emmanuel asked.

"He'll give a sworn statement about the name of the Capital X kingpin in exchange for a new identity and specific privileges that include a personal television and a down pillow."

Emmanuel was impressed. He'd underestimated Johnson. "He's thought it through. A new name means no one can call him a snitch in prison. That's one way to stay alive."

"Can't fault his logic," the DA agreed. "I guarantee, when this information gets out, it will set Grand Rapids on its ear."

Emmanuel couldn't wait to hear, but he couldn't ask. If the district attorney wasn't sharing details, it was because he didn't have it in writing yet. "Thanks for the call." He couldn't wait to tell Pippa that there was good news and positive momentum on the Capital X case.

Parking in front of her building, it was second nature to look around, scanning the area for any threat. So far all clear, which made him wonder if she'd set the meeting yet. At her door, he entered his code and walked in, announcing himself.

The rich scent of tomato sauce and spicy sausage brought his appetite to the fore.

Pippa came out of the kitchen and slipped into his arms, greeting him with a kiss that set his blood humming. It reminded him of his parents returning to each other at the end of a day and, in that one moment, forgetting everything but each other.

"I could get used to this," he teased, his free hand gliding over her waist.

"Careful." She smiled. "Dinner on the table every night when you walk in isn't something you can count on from me."

"Well, to be fair, having me home at the same time every night isn't something you should count on either." But he wanted to come home to her, whatever time, and walk into the heat of her kisses and the quiet peace of a place they shared.

He really should tell her how he felt.

Instead, he settled in to enjoy the wonder of a normal night with an amazing woman. If she got a confession out of Joe, she might not need Emmanuel around for protection anymore. As much as he wanted to close this case, to get the right person behind bars for the death of Hicks, he felt a twinge deep in his chest. What if the closed case meant the end of his time with Pippa?

Chapter 13

Joc couldn't get close to her. He'd kept his car to the ground, but so far no opportunities had materialized for him to take out Pippa Colton and put this case to bed for good.

Not likc when he'd been trailing Hicks.

Greed had made that slimeball easy picking. Or maybe it was a matter of focus. Admittedly, Joe had tunnel vision after the jerk dumped his little girl, breaking her heart, for a new moneybags lover.

A career on the force had taught him some cases resonated and when it came to family, they all pushed the envelope once in a while to see justice done. In his mind, if you took the right action, discreetly, the world was a better place. Wasn't that the true goal?

The rumors at the GRPD were enough to convince him that Colton had sunk her teeth into something that could wreck everything. She wasn't letting go. Far as he could tell, she hadn't connected him to the gun or how Hicks had arrived at the Wentworth rose garden, but he figured at this point it was better to act first and wonder no more.

She'd visited with Leigh. Thankfully, his daughter was an excellent witness and provided him with a clear rundown of the conversation. She'd described Colton as friendly. Said she'd left disappointed after Leigh couldn't point her to anyone who might've hassled Hicks while he and Leigh had been dating.

He still didn't see what Leigh had found so endearing about that loser, but his baby girl had been in love, certain they were going to live happily ever after and build a franchise of fitness centers for the young and beautiful.

Instead, Hicks shifted his attention to other women, women with more money to spend on him, and left Joe's daughter wondering what she'd done wrong.

On the evening of Pippa's meeting with McRath, Emmanuel struggled to contain himself as they wired her so they could listen in. A war over her safety raged inside him. Revealing his concerns would only make matters worse, so he locked it down. She needed him to be confident in her and in the plan.

The rest of the backup team was already taking their positions, hours ahead of the expected meeting time. Emmanuel kept swallowing the advice he wanted to give. She knew what she was doing, and she knew the Wentworth case as well as he did.

Fortunately Lieutenant McKellar took the lead, reviewing the location and all possible approaches with her. He even insisted on reviewing two escape routes, all factors she would have resisted if Emmanuel had tried to make suggestions.

"Heritage Park is a favorite of mine, Lieutenant. I know it inside and out," she assured him. "I'll be fine."

"Joe knows it too," the lieutenant reminded her. "He chose it for a reason. If he is dirty, he will be on his guard and ready to do anything to save his ass."

To Emmanuel's relief, she was taking the advice well. They did a sound check and then let her head out in her personal vehicle when they had confirmation everyone was in place.

He and the lieutenant would be the last ones to reach the park. That made Emmanuel more nervous, but there was no way McRath would make a premature move on Pippa. She was too well-known in the community, her family too connected to take that kind of chance.

"If this goes sideways," he said to McKellar once they were alone, "I'll never forgive myself. Or you."

"Iglesias, if you're not good with this, you have to stay behind. I'm not risking two officers today."

"I'm good," Emmanuel lied. If McRath touched a hair on her head, he wouldn't hesitate to intervene and protect her.

"Thank you for meeting with me tonight," Pippa said when McRath finally joined her at the designated place within the park. "I do appreciate your time."

The older man grunted. "I admit these conversations aren't my favorite. Why are you even looking twice at Wentworth? She's a nightmare. Always has been."

"She has a daughter, Elizabeth, who's my friend,"

Pippa replied. After hours of debate, she thought appealing to him as a father was her best strategy.

"Stirring the pot for friendship?" he asked, incredulous. "Better uses of your time."

She'd known this wouldn't be easy, or straightforward. "I don't think so. Although my friend is hurting." She paused. "Hypothetically, without the overwhelming evidence against Mrs. Wentworth, who did you like for the crime?"

McRath shook his head, the light teasing his graying hair. "You lawyers play with hypotheticals. I play with reality. All of the evidence pointed to Mrs. Wentworth. She did the crime, and now she's doing the time."

"I just can't agree with you."

His lip curled in caustic judgement. "You know the prison system is full of innocent people, right?" He shook his head, gazing out over the park. "I got better things to do than cater to your feelings for a friend."

If she could find the right angle to open him up, he'd have plenty of time to contemplate his hypotheticals in prison. "I guess I just find it all too convenient," she began, trying another tack. "Hicks had run through several women. I know there has to be someone else involved, someone else who wanted him dead."

"Really?" His gaze narrowed, and she smothered the urge to run. She'd seen those mean eyes through the holes of a ski mask not too long ago. "Like who?"

"Well, that's why I'm here. Several women were angry with him and felt cheated. Do you think the killer might've been a different woman?" McGrath was a problem solver. He might well be a murderer, too, but that was just a bad way to solve a problem.

When he didn't respond, she rambled on. "I noticed

you questioned Elizabeth. She normally tells me everything, but I can't help wondering if she was involved with Hicks?"

"All I learned about Hicks is that he charmed women into costly mistakes." McRath pushed to his feet, and even in the fading light she could tell she'd hit a hot button. "I am sick and tired of your kind digging into closed cases. My partner and I did good work, and you are wasting my time. Stealing that girl's money. All you damn attorneys want is a sound bite. A way to move up the political ladder. You make the job impossible for those of us out here taking calls and talking to witnesses and putting criminals behind bars to keep the city safe.

"The Wentworth case is done. *Over.* The bitch is in jail where she belongs."

Pippa didn't know what she'd expected, but it wasn't this vitriol and sheer hatred. "Detective McRath, I don't mean any disrespect. I only want justice. I know you don't want an innocent woman wasting away in jail. And she is innocent. I'm sure of it."

"That woman is *not* innocent," he barked. "She was sleeping around on her husband and barely knew the names of her staff. They worked with her every day, and she didn't bother to *learn their names*. Do you have any idea how many times she called the police with false complaints? Murderer or not, prison will do that woman and this city a world of good."

Were they catching all of this? "Joe, you can't mean that."

McRath pulled a gun, and it was all she could do not to scream. Only knowing she'd hurt someone's ears kept her quiet.

"Oh, I mean it."

"What are you doing?"

"I respected your father," McRath said. "But you, not so much. I'm sick of the whole damn mess. I'm sick of the lies and the deals and the cheats like Wentworth. You think you've got me?"

"No, Joe," she said quietly. "I have no idea what you're talking about."

"Bull. Get up," he ordered.

"Why don't you sit down and we'll finish our conversation."

"I'm done with you and everyone like you. Get up!"

She stood, intending to edge away and put the bench between them. It wasn't much cover, but it might buy her a few seconds.

"This way." He gestured with the gun. "Run and I'll kill your lover instead. I can't believe Iglesias fell for you. What a sap."

She froze, locked in a nightmare of losing Emmanuel. Her hands were cold as ice and her knees wanted to buckle. She needed him in her life to lean on, to love. Needed to be there for him at the end of the day, as his safe haven. Her fears about her feelings for him paled against the prospect of a future without him. She couldn't let Joe steal the beautiful opportunity to share her life with him.

"Come on, girl." He waved the gun. "You're going to pay for not letting this rest." He pushed the gun into her stomach, walking her backward toward the trees.

"Joe." She sucked in a breath as he grabbed her, spun her around. She couldn't resist too much. If he saw the wire, or dislodged it and broke the connection, it was over, and her efforts would be for nothing. "Whatever's on your mind, the gun isn't necessary."

"It is. You'll pay the same way that lying cheat Hicks paid. I put a bullet in his black, shriveled heart." His hand was clammy and bruising on the back of her neck. "Hicks hurt my daughter. Stole her money and then tried to blackmail his wealthy lover. The world is better off without him. You didn't heed my warnings, so it's time to stop you too."

If he got her into those trees, it was over. She wasn't that much older than his daughter, and she tried one last appeal to his fatherly nature. "You don't have to do this, Joe. I'm not going to say anything. I'll leave it alone. I'll stop."

His laugh was bitter and sharp. "I can't trust you to keep quiet. There's only one solution."

He was going to kill her. She could see it stamped in the unyielding lines of his face. She wouldn't be his first kill, and if they didn't stop him now, she probably wouldn't be his last. Emmanuel and the lieutenant must be hearing every word. Where were they? Her head was spinning and her composure in tatters. That had to be enough of a confession. Enough to clear Anna.

"Joe, put down the gun," she said. "Think about this."

"I don't have to put down a gun to think. That's the difference between you and me. I can think on my feet. I can react in the blink of an eye and make a decision and know it's the right one. You lawyers have to analyze and look for precedents."

"Put the weapon down!" Emmanuel's shout ripped through the evening.

McRath swiveled to fire, and she shoved him hard, hoping to throw off his aim. Gunfire erupted all around her, along with shouts for McRath to stand down.

McGrath hid behind her, using her as a shield between himself and the officers closing in. One of the officers called her name, urging her to duck down out of the line of fire. She was blocking the only clear shot.

It was like a scene from a classic Western movie, but she wasn't about to faint or swoon. Dropping to all fours, she charged McGrath, knocking him out of his hiding place. He twisted around and aimed the gun at her, but the next shot flattened him.

Officers swarmed McRath, and she heard someone pronounce him dead as she was led back to the lighted path. Emmanuel rushed over, and her knees buckled. He caught her, holding her close. She wrapped her arms around his waist and simply held on.

His heart pounded under her ear, his hand smoothing over her hair. He was whole. Safe. McRath would never hurt him.

"Pippa, you scared the life out of me."

She'd scared the life out of herself. Nothing was guaranteed and she was done holding back. "I love you, Emmanuel." She tipped her head up to study his face. "I'm in love with you. I should've said so long before now."

He didn't answer right away, kissing her instead. His lips fluttered over her hair, her eyelids, her nose and mouth.

When he paused, his warm gaze melted away the last of the chilling encounter. "I love you too, Pippa. I didn't think I'd ever want to say those words again."

"It's a big step." And nothing in her life had ever felt quite so right.

"A good one," he agreed.

She wanted him to take her home, take her to bed and forget the rest of the world. Hard to do in the glare of the emergency lights. She'd come out here to wrest a confession out of McRath that they could use to save Anna and she wasn't sure if they'd succeeded.

"Emmanuel." She caught his face between her hands, his short whiskers rasping against her palms. "Did we get the confession?"

"Yes. You were brilliant." He kissed her again. "Now don't ever do anything this foolish again."

But it wasn't censure in his voice as much as affection. Respect. And yes, love.

"Never without backup," she promised. She understood his reactions. She'd experienced a sharp and desperate fear when McRath had fired in Emmanuel's direction. "Do you think it's enough to free Anna?"

"Absolutely," he replied. "The lieutenant will send the information up the line as soon as we get back to the station." He drew her back as an ambulance rolled up.

"Thank you," she said. There were more words, better suited to a private moment. This wasn't the right time for her personal declarations. They both had work to do. "I'll call Elizabeth," she said.

His thumb grazed the skin just above her collarbone. "Elizabeth can wait until after the ER," he said.

"I don't need the ER," she protested as paramedics approached her. But she couldn't stop trembling, even when Emmanuel was close.

"For me?" When she met his gaze, his eyes were warm and full of all that love and emotion she wanted to believe in. "Please."

She supposed she might be in shock. A violent killer had nearly added her to his body count. With a nod, she let him lead her to the paramedics and didn't protest as they loaded her for a trip to Grand Rapids Central.

* * *

Emmanuel had to follow protocol and handle the entire operation by the book. Man, he wanted to rush. Focused, he helped McKellar clean up the dead body at their feet. No way to keep this out of the papers; the department was going to take a hit.

The lieutenant pushed a hand through his hair and muttered an oath. "They'll reopen every single one of his cases."

"I know," Emmanuel said. "For what it's worth, I know I did my job the right way."

"Still going to be sticky."

Knowing his lieutenant was correct, Emmanuel kept quiet. There would be some uncomfortable days ahead, but they would get through it.

"Hell of a woman," McKellar said.

Emmanuel couldn't argue with that. And he couldn't wait to share the praise with her as soon as possible.

"Go on to the hospital," McKellar said. "That's where your head's at."

With a quick thank you, Emmanuel bolted from the scene. He called Riley on the way to the hospital and filled him in on the sting operation and what a hero Pippa was. It didn't surprise him that Pippa hadn't made that call yet. More than likely she was still on the phone with Elizabeth.

"She's okay," he assured her brother. "They sent her to the hospital just as a precaution."

"Then why do you sound panicked?" Riley asked.

"It's been a wild night," Emmanuel said. He wasn't about to tell her brother just how dicey things had been out here. He wasn't sure he could even discuss it coherently yet.

"Thanks for your help," Riley said. "I'll pass on the word, and we'll be over to the hospital right away."

"About that." Emmanuel hesitated to make the request, but Pippa deserved his courage. "She probably won't be happy if you all descend on her tonight."

"We're family."

"Right. I get it. I'm just saying." He wanted a few minutes to tell her everything he should've said before she was face-to-face with a killer. "You know Pippa," he said. "If everyone's there—"

"She'll get belligerent," Riley finished for him. "Yeah, we can keep our distance until tomorrow. Let me know if her situation changes."

"You know I will."

"Thanks. I really do owe you. Between this and the Capital X case, we're all on edge. It helps knowing you've been watching her."

More than watching, but those were words a brother wouldn't take well. He was done pretending this was temporary, or convenient or simply a favor for a friend. "I'm sure Pippa will fill you in about Wentworth's release. One more thing while I have you on the phone." He paused to gather his courage. "I want to marry your sister." Blurting it out might not have been the right approach, but he was pulling up to the hospital and running out of time. "I can't ask your father, so I'm asking you."

"Does she want to marry you?" Riley queried.

"That's the big question," he admitted on a half laugh. "I think so," he said. "It may take some time for her to come around."

"Must have been some night in the park," Riley said. "If you're looking for my blessing, you have it."

"And your silence?" Emmanuel asked. "I don't want her to feel rushed."

"Wow. You really do know her." Riley chuckled. "Good luck, man."

The difficult part over, Emmanuel jogged into the ER. Thanks to his rapport with the staff, they allowed him back to see Pippa. They had her hooked up to an EKG, and his heart skipped.

"What's all this?" he asked, trying for casual and missing by a mile.

She shook her head. "They tell me it's a precaution. My vitals were a little ragged. It's been a rough night."

He was doubly glad now that he'd warned her family to stay away. He caught her hand in both of his, stroking some warmth and color back into her soft skin. "I called Riley and told him you were fine. That there was no reason to storm the hospital."

That earned a chuckle, and he felt like a knight in shining armor.

"Thank you," she said, raising his hand to her lips. "You know I love them. I just don't need anyone hovering right now."

"You want me to go?" The last thing he wanted was to cling so tightly that he smothered her and drove her away. "Tell me what you need."

"I expected you to go to the station," she began, her voice as shy as he'd ever heard it.

"That's all under control."

"I wanted to call Elizabeth and then…"

He felt as if his whole life hung in the balance of that one pause.

"Then if it's not too much trouble, I… I want you to

hold me. All night." She looked down at their joined hands. "I sleep better when you hold me."

"Done," he said, touching his lips to her forehead. He knew what that soft-spoken request cost her. Pippa wasn't a woman given to asking for help. She coveted her independence, and he was honored and floored that she had turned to him.

Holding her all night might be enough to convince him she was fine after all.

Chapter 14

Pippa was so thankful. Emmanuel had held her all night long that first night and in all the nights that followed. As much as the condo had been hers, it felt more like home when he was there. Her safe haven, a little personal space carved out of a large boisterous family and a demanding career, was better with him in it.

Having shared space with someone from the womb, those were thoughts she'd never anticipated. Naturally the Capital X investigation was ongoing, though her role was momentarily diminished. Her brothers and sisters had checked in after her encounter with McRath. They knew better than to scold her, though it was clear to her that they wanted to.

Although Emmanuel and the lieutenant offered, Pippa never listened to the tape of McRath's confession. It wasn't a moment she wanted to relive.

She'd spoken with Elizabeth every day until at last the system scheduled Anna's release.

Pippa and Elizabeth waited outside the gate. Restless, Elizabeth couldn't stop wringing her hands. "She vowed to be a kinder person," she said.

Pippa tried not to roll her eyes, but she had to avoid making eye contact with Emmanuel. "I'm sure she means it." She touched her friend's shoulder. "I hope she can break those old patterns. You deserve the best mom she can be."

Elizabeth gave her a big hug. "Thank you for believing me. Thank you for helping her."

An alarm sounded, and a light flashed over the door where Anna was expected to exit. Flanked by two prison guards, she walked out into the sunlight, wearing the same suit she'd worn in court when the guilty verdict had been read. She looked like a slightly softer, faded version of the woman she'd been before this ordeal.

Pippa stood back as Anna and Elizabeth were reunited, her hand seeking Emmanuel's comforting touch. She'd been wary that he wanted to be here, but he had just as much right, and frankly she still needed the support.

Once Anna released her daughter, her eyes locked onto Emmanuel. This would be the test. Would she revert to that arrogant, pushy, entitled woman?

"Detective Iglesias? I didn't expect to see you. Is there a problem?" she asked with a delicate tremor in her voice.

Emmanuel didn't move, but Pippa felt the tension humming through his body. "I wanted to be here to apologize personally. You can expect an official apology from the Grand Rapids Police Department, and I'm sure your attorney is working on reparations."

Pippa almost chuckled.

"Elizabeth tells me you were instrumental in uncovering the truth," Anna said. "Thank you."

Pippa exchanged a dumbfounded look with Elizabeth. Maybe Anna really could make this improvement permanent. As mother and daughter drove off, she turned to Emmanuel and caught him grinning.

"You thought I was going to read her the riot act," he said.

"Maybe a little," she admitted. "You didn't even ask for an apology for your mom."

"I thought about it, but what's the point? She's been through an ordeal very few people can imagine. And honestly she owes my mom the apology, not me."

"Maybe that will happen. Someday."

"Whatever she does, I'm the real winner," he said, opening the car door for her.

"How so?"

He shut the door and rounded the car to the driver's side. When he got in, he leaned over and caught her chin in his hand, giving her a heated kiss. "Without Wentworth or McRath, I wouldn't be here with you right now."

"Making out in front of a prison," she said, smiling against his lips. "So romantic."

On a soft laugh he started the car and pulled away. "I'll show you some romance," he promised.

"I'll hold you to it."

She was particularly fond of cozy dinners and waking up in his arms. This man had changed her. Although they were both still working demanding hours, she had a reason to take time for herself. For him.

A woman couldn't work 24-7 and call it a balanced life. Wherever they went from here, she would be better for her time with him. The trouble was she didn't want to let go and fall into old habits. If Anna could change, maybe she could too.

It was time to tell him she loved him.

Emmanuel drove back to Grand Rapids, enjoying the randomness of their conversation now that the Wentworth case was over and done.

The trees were vibrant with changing color, and he didn't miss the correlation between the changing seasons outside and the changes Pippa had made inside him.

He had a ring in his pocket and a plan in mind as he turned back to Heritage Park.

"What are we doing here?" she asked.

For a split second he doubted his decision. Maybe this wasn't the best place, but she'd mentioned it was one of her favorite places in the city. She'd reclaimed the condo after McRath's destruction. Now they could reclaim this place too.

"I thought we could take a walk. Stretch our legs after the drive." He took her hand. "You said this was your favorite place in Grand Rapids."

Her gaze narrowed as she studied the landscape through the windshield.

"It's a beautiful day," he prompted. Reaching over, he gave her hand a squeeze. "If I made a mistake, we can go."

"No." She took a deep breath. "It's like riding a bike, right? When you fall, you need to get right back on."

"Something like that," he allowed. The ring in his pocket felt like a lead weight and a helium balloon all at once. It was as if the diamond wanted to be out, and all things weighing on his heart were tiptoeing around the facts.

With her hand in his they walked on a path well away from where she had confronted McRath. "You're a true hero," he began. "I want you to be able to enjoy this park again."

"I will. One difficult night can't erase all of the good memories." She gave him a smile, then turned her attention to the trees. "I've always loved the changing leaves."

"Me too," he said. "It's nicer sharing these changes with you." He had to stop dawdling and just say what was on his heart. "Pippa, I love you."

She stopped in the middle of the path. "What?"

He felt a thousand times better sharing the words. "I'm in love with you." He found a bench and sat down, drawing her next to him. Holding her hand, he continued, "My parents set a high bar in the way they cared for each other and for us. As far back as I can remember, I've thought I want a piece of that. That stability and trust. That beautiful partnership that exists between lovers.

"I've always wanted that and never found it. I gave up on it," he confessed. "I threw myself into my work, thinking that would be enough. It was. Until you."

"Emmanuel," she whispered as a tear rolled down her cheek.

His heart took flight, that she would trust him with

her tears. "I love the way you focus, that glint in your eye when you're mad, how you drop everything and run when your family needs you. I want to be your family. I want to be the person who drops everything for you."

"But I don't want that for you," she said.

His heart stuttered, and he was glad he was sitting down.

"I love you too much for that." She kissed him. "Yes, you heard me. I love you too. But I don't need rescuing." Her gaze drifted across the park. "At least not very often."

"On those rare occasions when you do, I want to be the person you call."

"Oh, Emmanuel." She kissed him again. "I don't know when I fell. I think I fall a little more every day. Thank you."

Thank you? This wasn't going at all as he had hoped. They'd veered way off the script he had in his head. He fished into his pocket and pulled out the ring. Her eyes went wide and her lips parted.

"Pippa, I'm butchering this, obviously. Please make me the happiest man and say you will be my partner, my lover, my wife. I don't want you to change who you are, and I'm hoping you will apply all of that amazing courage to our future. I can't guarantee the road will be smooth—"

"Yes!" she exclaimed.

"Yes? Really?" He felt like a kid rather than the man she needed.

She held out her hand, her fingers shaking with excitement.

The ring looked perfect on her slender finger, and the autumn light made the diamond glow. But it was her kiss that told him everything he needed to know about happiness and hope in their future.

Together.

* * * * *

Don't miss the previous installments in the Colton 911: Grand Rapids series:

Colton 911: Family Defender *by Tara Taylor Quinn*
Colton 911: Suspect Under Siege *by Jane Godman*

Available now from Harlequin Romantic Suspense

And look out for Book 4
Colton 911: Agent by Her Side
by Deborah Fletcher Mello

Available in October 2020!

#2107 COLTON 911: AGENT BY HER SIDE
Colton 911: Grand Rapids
by Deborah Fletcher Mello

FBI agent Cooper Winston is determined to take down a deadly pyramid scheme and PI Kiely Colton has the information to make that happen. She's not going to let him push her out of the search, but when danger flares, they're forced to rely on each other and face the attraction they both fear.

#2108 COLTON STORM WARNING
The Coltons of Kansas • by Justine Davis

The last thing security expert Ty Colton wants is to play bodyguard for a spoiled heiress. But just as he begins to discover that there's more to Ashley Hart than meets the eye, the threats against her are acted on—and the very weather itself tries to tear them apart.

#2109 FAMILY IN THE CROSSHAIRS
Sons of Stillwater • by Jane Godman

Dr. Leon Sinclair is trying to rebuild his life when Dr. Flora Monroe arrives in town and threatens his job...and his peace of mind. But Flora and her twins are in danger and Leon must face the demons of his past in order to keep them safe.

#2110 GUARDING HIS MIDNIGHT WITNESS
Honor Bound • by Anna J. Stewart

The last time he lost a witness, Detective Jack McTavish nearly lost his job. Now, protecting Greta Renault, an artist who witnessed a murder, is his top priority. As he's forced to choose between believing her and saving his career, Jack's decision could make the difference between life and death.
